NIGHT OF THE PANTHER

————

OTHER TONY LOWELL MYSTERIES BY E. C. AYRES

Eye of the Gator

Hour of the Manatee

NIGHT OF THE PANTHER

E. C. Ayres

ST. MARTIN'S PRESS ❧ NEW YORK

F
Ayres

PUBLISHED BY THOMAS DUNNE BOOKS
An imprint of St. Martin's Press

Library of Congress Cataloging-in-Publication Data

Ayres, E. C.
    Night of the panther / E. C. Ayres. —1st ed.
        p.   cm.
    "A Thomas Dunne book."
    ISBN 0–312–15607–3
    I. Title.
PS3551.Y72N5   1997
813'.54—dc21   96–53625

First edition: May 1997

10 9 8 7 6 5 4 3 2 1

110942

NIGHT OF THE PANTHER

1

CORKSCREW SWAMP, FLORIDA
FRIDAY EVENING, 6:00 P.M.

It's a funny thing, loneliness. It eats away at your spirits like unseen cancer of the soul, until there is nothing left but tattered, fading hopes. And then those, too, are gone. That's how Marge sometimes felt, when darkness closed in on the swamp on nights like this. It had been too long, she knew. Not since her beau Tom Gardiakos had been killed that night on Dixie Highway had she even looked at a man. Oh, they looked at her all right. Leered more like. Came with the territory. That and the isolation. But it did get to her at times. The loneliness. Tonight was one of those times.

The weather was changing. Marge could feel the coming chill deep in her marrow as she packed the weekend supplies into the back of her pickup, even though it was still warm that evening. In spite of the government shutdown that winter weekend, in spite of the threats she had been getting as of late, state Wildlife Officer Marge Pappas felt she had a job to do. She had even taken the extraordinary steps of informing her boss, Deputy Superintendent Dave Connors, of her intentions.

"Go home, Marge, for chrissake," he'd urged her. "You're not gonna get back pay in this state. Let it be a few days, go to the beach or somethin'." This being winter, nobody went to the beach except the snowbirds who didn't know any better. He was just being facetious. Marge wasn't amused. She was straighter than a Caloosa Indian fishing arrow, as Dave liked to tease her. And somewhat devoid of a sense of humor.

"The animals need watchin', Dave," she insisted.

Dave Connors figured they could make it through the weekend, all fifty-two of them, or however many were left. True, he'd had to admit one day to the press, they were getting hit along Alligator Alley and I-75 at an alarming rate, although the new pass-through tunnels seemed to be working. Even so, "it's just one weekend, Marge," he insisted. "Give it a rest."

Marge had a secret she shared only with her young acquaintance Billy Patterson, whose father ran the disreputable combination tavern, meeting place, and convenience store up on the Caloosahatchee River, at Patterson's Landing. She had serious misgivings about the teenager, but he'd proven trustworthy. At least so far. It had been Billy who'd found them, actually, nestled into a limestone cave on a tiny hummock of virgin forest near Lake Trafford, nearly surrounded by a half mile of snake- and gator-infested wetlands.

Marge could barely repress her excitement as Billy told her how he'd hardly gotten out of his canoe, when the panther mother had come home. But he'd stayed around long enough to see the kits. Marge had gone out later in hip boots and found the place. She'd been enthralled. A whole new family! She'd counted three. One was sick, but the others seemed well, and by the footprint (she hadn't seen the mother yet) the mother was large.

Marge was especially worried about poachers, this weekend. They had been proliferating in troubling numbers in the preserve as of late. She had caught two red-handed a week before in Big Cypress Swamp: sheepish local businessmen whom she actually knew, taking out two big gators. They insisted they'd been hunting redtail deer, unrestricted, when the gators "attacked," but she knew perfectly well they'd been after something more exotic and elusive. No pushover, she had ticketed them with a severe rebuke. If she caught them or anyone else this weekend, they wouldn't get off with just a fine. She hadn't told Dave everything that was on her mind. About the letter, for instance. Or the sets of tire tracks in the protected area of Corkscrew Swamp, which was her beat and had been for the last nine years.

She decided not to bother Dave about her concerns, just now. He had enough to worry about. But she remained adamant about working. "I'm goin', Dave," she insisted.

As usual, Dave backed down. "Just be careful out there," he admonished her. She turned, brushed back her short black curls, flashed him a cheery smile, and drove off in her truck.

It was sundown by the time Marge got her field camp operational, at her little cabin on Punta Creek not far from the state campground. The swamp smelled of peat and cedar. The air was alive with the calls of winter birds: Canadian geese, cranes, songbirds, and native fowl such as the anhinga with its haunted evening cry, as though in fearful protest against the coming of darkness. Silence crept in as night fell, and Marge hummed to herself as she stoked her camp stove and began rinsing her pans and dishes in the cold trickle from the small hand pump in the kitchen area. She had a small portable radio she sometimes played, to ward off loneliness. She didn't like to play it a lot, just once in a while. Like now, when she felt the chill coming on. Other times, she felt like it interfered too much with her connection to the woods, and the wild creatures that were her responsibility out there. Tonight she was playing that country station from Naples. Humming softly to herself along with Lyle Lovett's latest, she almost didn't hear the whine of gears at first, out in the scrub. Then she heard it, and turned off the radio. She went outside, careful not to let the screen door slam, and listened. But whoever or whatever was out there, fell silent.

"Hello?" she called. "Somebody out there?" No answer. With a little shiver, she went back inside, to finish cleaning up. Carefully, she cleaned the grease from her dinner of chicken-fried steak and beans. She used sand to absorb the fat, which she would then dispose of in the saw grass beneath the knees of cypress and salt palmettos. There it would be recycled as a short-order feast for the "crawlin' critters," as she called them, that shared her little corner of paradise.

Taking her Coleman camp lantern, Marge went outside once more to dump the fat, then rinsed her hands in the creek. Swiping at the mosquitoes that swarmed around her head, she turned to retreat to her cabin when she heard the whining noise again. She recognized the sound of tires, probably stuck in the mud from the last rainfall. Damn fools, she thought to herself. Then she saw the light. It was just a momentary gleam, some distance across the creek on the north side. Marge stopped, and considered whether or not to dim her lantern. She decided against it. If there was someone out there they would know of her presence by now. The lantern was like a beacon in the forest.

She listened, and could just make out the telltale sound of boots in the swamp, the sucking noise they made as they pulled out of the wet sand and black mud. The light went out. She stopped, uncertain, listening intently. The footsteps resumed. They were moving her way!

Marge hesitated, her pulse quickening. Then she heard the low gutteral laugh of a voice she recognized. A voice that chilled her the way no weather change ever would. Along with the cold grip of fear that her sudden knowledge brought

4

was the even more terrifying knowledge of why they had come. Heart pounding like warning tom-toms deep in her chest, Marge turned to run for the safety of her cabin and the standard issue 9-mm Browning pistol she'd left sitting on the table. But she had hesitated a moment too long, and found herself face to face with her enemy, who stepped out of the darkness directly in her path. Now she knew how the deer must have felt when the panthers came for them. But there was one difference: Marge Pappas would not go down without a fight.

2

Lena Bedrosian was doing something that Friday night almost unheard-of in her circles: making love with her husband. They had been planning the occasion for days, actually, which admittedly took some of the excitement of spontaneity out of it. First they had to hire a sitter for the kids: no small feat these days, and expensive to boot. They'd managed to pull it off without a hitch, thanks to an unlucky neighborhood girl named Kara who didn't have a date that night. Breaking out the still-unrestored old Mustang, they'd gone for dinner at the Old Spanish Inn down on Route 19—wonderful for paella—then taken in a movie at the Manatee City Mall. They'd had a minor quarrel over dinner as to what movie to see, had settled on a compromise neither of them had liked, and hadn't spoken the rest of the way home.

It was Michael, actually, who'd managed to break the ice: mostly by plying his overworked police detective wife with the chocolates he'd been hoarding for the occasion in his sock drawer (one place neither the kids nor Lena would ever think to look), and that blatant down-home old-fashioned remedy: booze. The booze, actually, which Lena had succumbed to only because she literally "needed a drink" after the week she'd had, was a six-pack of Red Dog beer, Michael's current favorite. He'd managed to appease her after the first beer, cajole her after the second, and lure her to bed after the third. Then she'd fallen promptly to sleep, and it had been only with the greatest of effort and difficulty (interrupted twice by small inquiring children), that he'd managed to arouse her—literally—with some very special oral ministrations.

"Mmmmmmmm," she'd finally murmured, coming awake. That's when the phone rang.

Michael stopped in midministration, trying to restrain his annoyance and maintain his enthusiasm for the task at hand at the same time. "Let it ring," he'd protested.

"I can't," she'd gasped, and reached clumsily for the receiver, almost tumbling them both out of bed.

"What is it?" she'd demanded, now pretty annoyed herself. This wasn't a treat she got very often either.

"Lena, this is state Game and Freshwater Fish Superintendent Dave Connors, down in Collier County. I'm really sorry to bother you at this hour," he went on, while she attempted to stifle a snort of sarcasm. "But I'm calling about your cousin Marge Pappas."

Lena was immediately on her guard, her husband sensed it, and stopped what he was doing. "Don't stop," she whispered, but the moment was gone. "What about Marge?" she demanded of Connors, her annoyance renewed.

"I'm afraid it's bad," Connors told her.

Lena's heart stopped, for a quick moment. Marge Pappas was not just family. She was Lena's best, and oldest friend. They had grown up together in Tarpon Springs, both daughters of fishermen, both lovers of nature, and the woods, and the mysteries of the Gulf and their homeland of west coast Florida. They had gone to Girl Scouts together. In fact that was

8

where both of them had gotten the idea of a career in government. Law enforcement came later, but the seeds had been planted back then.

Lena remembered her most recent conversation with Marge. How Marge had seemed preoccupied somehow, distracted. She had wanted to talk about more than just the latest movies, Lena remembered. She'd mentioned something about threats. But it had been old Nicholas Pappas's birthday, and the occasion had not presented itself. They'd promised each other to meet for lunch sometime soon, maybe at Arcadia, or even Sarasota. But even now, she sensed that lunch was never going to happen.

"What happened?" she breathed, finally, her heart pounding so hard she was afraid it might burst.

"Honey, what is it?" whispered Michael, sliding up beside her as Lena swung her feet over the side of the bed and sat up. She waved him off without answering.

"I think you'd better get down here," Connors told her.

It took her almost two hours to reach the site, deep in a vast area of Big Cypress Swamp that straddled four counties—Lee, Collier, Hendry, and Hondo.

Deputy Superintendant Connors had taken it upon himself to arrange a state Department of Law Enforcement chopper up to Manatee City to pick up Lena, over the objections of local law enforcement—especially Sheriff Riker down in Naples, who knew (and disliked) Lena Bedrosian ever since she spurned a drunken advance by him at a Gulf Coast Policeman's Benevolent Association Thanksgiving party a few years back.

Lena had grimly thrown on her work clothes—in this case heavy tan cotton slacks and a dark navy pullover underneath her dark blue lined satin Manatee City Police jacket—grabbed a cup of leftover coffee that Michael reheated for her in the microwave, stirred in some sugar and 2 percent milk, then wolfed down a bagel and the fat-free cream cheese she detested but ate anyway. She was ready and waiting at police HQ when the DLE Bell Ranger helicopter arrived thirty minutes later. As she scrambled on board, Pilot Ed Shanklin told her she'd be met at the state campground near Corkscrew Swamp. It was a quick flight south to the Caloosahatchee River. But then it would be a half-hour trek into the forest, in the darkness, to where Marge had been found. Dead.

Fighting back tears of pain and rage as the cold night wind whipped past, Lena Bedrosian stared out at the darkness as the helo beat its way south. Marge Pappas dead. It didn't seem possible, or sensible, or fair. Cousin Marge was like a pack horse—strong, capable, trustworthy, and reliable as the sunrise. Whoever, or whatever had done her (and neither Connors nor Shanklin had said just yet) would pay dearly. This she vowed to herself bitterly, as they banked and dropped into the sheer vast dark expanse of the southwest Florida wilderness toward an apocalyptic spread of powerful floodlights, savagely illuminating the scrub flatlands below.

3

Part-time private investigator Tony Lowell was ecstatic. After years of painstaking and often frustrating effort his longtime nearly impossible dream was about to be realized. His prized forty-four foot wooden schooner, *Andromeda*, was ready for its "maiden" voyage (if, as he'd joked with his friend Perry Garwood, virginity can be recovered). "Relaunching" might be more appropriate. He'd originally salvaged the venerable old Herrshoff after a rare but devastating hurricane had ravaged the Gulf Coast ten years before, and left the abandoned hulk in its wake: literally on Tony Lowell's back doorstep. Lovingly, laboriously, he'd taken it on as his own, with gargantuan effort winched it ashore, hoisted it with rented equipment onto a handmade cradle, and begun the mammoth task of hand restoration.

His motivation, back then, had been simple: He'd always wanted a first-class sailing vessel, and could hardly hope to afford one except to build it himself. Also, in his own mind, in his state of semiretirement from a once-commanding career as a press photographer (and as he'd put it to his friend Perry) he rarely had anything better to do.

Perry wouldn't help much, usually, except to pass a beer can, or hold a tool with a look of amused perplexity while Tony labored away. But he was more than ready to assist with the launching. Especially since champagne was involved. Or so he presumed, and had therefore brought his own: a full magnum of Dom Pérignon.

His spirit of the event, however, had its limits. "Seems like a terrible waste to break something like this," he'd muttered, as the two of them prepared the christening.

"That's why I was planning on a plastic bottle of 7Up," said Lowell. "Cheaper, less wasteful, besides which," he added, "it won't mar the finish."

"Then we have no choice," Perry sighed, feigning sorrow, "but to drink this sucker." At which point the two of them postponed the launching, sat down on the newly varnished mahogany side rails, and polished off the magnum. Since there was no one lurking about wearing tuxedos, they didn't bother with glasses.

"Sure is a beaut!" declared Perry, hoisting the magnum to toast the soaring brightwork spars above their heads.

"Indeed she is," agreed Lowell, modestly. "Let's hope she floats!"

That gave Perry pause. "She might not float?"

"Well, she probably will," Lowell assured him. "Except with wooden boats, the planks shrink when they dry out, and it's hard to seal them. Hopefully she'll float. But, you never know."

Perry was outraged. "Lowell, you are one crazy SOB," he shouted. "You work all these years to finish something like this, and it might not even float?"

"Well, it'll *probably* float," said Lowell.

" 'Probably'? " Perry shook his head in sorrowful disbelief. "Man, you are worse than Sisyphus," he lamented.

12

"Anyway," said Lowell, finishing off the last of the champagne, and carefully tossing the bottle into his waterside trash receptacle (a cardboard box), "there's only one way to find out."

Actually, the schooner wasn't really finished. What it was, was *mostly* finished. The hull, spars, sails, decks, and superstructure were bright and spanking new, as beautiful a boat as had ever sailed the seven seas. Belowdecks was another matter. Lowell had finished the bulkheads and structural work. The main compartments, cabinets, and cabins were all functional (except the self-contained forward head, which leaked around the through-hull valve), but only roughed in. Likewise the plumbing and electrical work. The finish work lay before him: endless hours, weeks, months, and probably years of fine finished carpentry: building the little cubbies, laying in the paneling, the edging and woodwork, cabinetry, the galley, the electrical outlets and fixtures, navigational switches and relays, completing the plumbing and heads, the lighting, all of that still remained to be done. But getting the boat afloat was a good beginning.

They were ready to launch before noon, Perry easing the big winch out while Tony guided a towline from the water in a borrowed Boston whaler with an eighty-horse outboard. Sufficient, he figured, for the job. He didn't even need to pull very hard, which was a relief since he hated putting so much stress on the transom. After a moment of high tension gravity took over. With a suddenness that startled both of them, the schooner broke loose from its cradle and slid magnificently down its heavily greased skids and into the water, towing a now-prone and loudly yelling Perry Garwood in its wake.

Perry scrambled to his feet, unmindful that he had a face covered with sand, brushed off his faded denim shorts, and let loose with a rebel yell that would scatter flocks all the way to Bradenton.

Lowell brushed his long sandy hair from his eyes and just sat on the water awhile admiring his creation, a huge tipsy grin on his well-weathered face. A breeze was coming in from the south, and the temperature was a mild seventy-four degrees. The sky was puffy clouds and deep azure blue. Lowell was beside himself. "Hey!" he shouted. "Let's go sailing!"

"I thought you'd never ask." Perry grinned back, and didn't even bother waiting for Lowell to bring in the whaler. He dove into the clear amber water, unmindful of the chill, swam to the schooner, and clambered aboard. He was waiting on the top deck sitting with arms and legs crossed like an Indian (which he happened to be) by the time Lowell tied up the whaler, and after a brief hesitation followed suit and dove in.

"Jeezus! I can't believe I did that!" he stammered, teeth chattering as Perry hauled him over the side. "We're gonna freeze our buns off."

"Nah," said Perry, airily. "We'll dry out in no time. How do you drive this thing?"

"Y-you handle the foresails and I'll take the main. Hold the rudder and bring her to full into the wind, so I can loosen the sheets," Lowell instructed him.

Perry nodded, sagely. "Which one is the foresail?" he asked.

Here we go again, thought Lowell, remembering Lena.

That's when the phone rang, up in the house.

"Hey, man, just ignore it," Perry suggested, seeing as how they were already fifty feet from shore and drifting.

"I probably don't have much choice," agreed Lowell. He felt a twinge of reluctance though. Sensing, somehow, that it was important. He hoped it wasn't Ariel, stuck in another snowdrift or something, up in Syracuse (she was in her senior year now, and had actually managed to survive up there to Tony and her mother and grandfather's amazement).

As it turned out, the sail was a short-lived one. The fine sailing yacht *Andromeda* had a problem: the very one Tony had most feared and expected. It did indeed have a leak. Not that all wooden boats didn't leak a little bit. This one, unfortu-

14

nately, leaked more than a little. It leaked a lot. Right along the main seam between the centerboard housing and the keel. Lowell barely managed to bring the schooner about—half-rigged, not a quarter-mile into the bay—and maneuver it into his own little inlet when it went down. Luckily, it went down only about twenty feet from the mean high-water mark, which was more like fifty feet out at the moment, it being high tide. Even more luckily, the water in the estuaries of Manatee Bay were shallow. The boat didn't have far to sink. It just sort of squatted down on the sandy inlet bottom like a giant indolent water buffalo, and refused to move.

Lowell hung his head, wiped his blue-gray-green eyes with the back of his hand, and tried not to think of all the time and effort, all the years of hopes and dreams and labor, now sitting on the bottom of the bay. He wouldn't give up, of course. This was just a temporary setback. Albeit a painful one.

Perry was sympathetic. "Tough break, man. What're you gonna do?" he inquired, as they waded ashore.

"Nothing," sighed Lowell, reaching the bank, and picking up the nearest hauling line. "Just tie her down, and let her think it over a bit."

Perry decided not to ask what about.

"The planks needed to soak, anyway," explained Lowell, with a shrug of resignation. "Now they'll soak."

Lowell went about rigging a heavy-duty bilge, with a powerline from shore. The pump ran on either a battery or the generator, which wasn't needed or practical so close to shore. "I figure the pump will bring it up, once the planks expand," he predicted, hopefully.

"If you say so," said Perry, actually relieved in a way. He hadn't really looked forward to the sail all that much, seeing as how he didn't know a hawser from a hose. No sooner than he'd attempted to hoist his first sail, he'd begun to get the idea that this was starting to look a lot like work.

"Let's get a sandwich," suggested Perry. Lowell couldn't

think of a single reason not to. They headed for the house.

"Still got any clean sides left on your Beatles collection?" Perry asked, hoping to distract his friend from his misfortune.

"Beatles?" Lowell scratched his head. "Beats me. I haven't actually listened to any Beatles in years."

"Let's check 'em out," Perry suggested.

They'd just reached the porch, when the phone rang again. The house was unlocked. Lowell led the way in the kitchen door, edged his way past some wrapping from the canvas he'd ordered for the sails some weeks ago, and was unable to pick up the receiver in the studio before the answering machine kicked in. Lowell snatched the receiver and shouted it down. "I'm here, just wait a minute," he yelled. He'd been expecting a call from an old friend. More than a friend, actually: his longtime one-time love interest Caitlin Schoenkopf. They'd been talking as of late, mostly about their daughter, Ariel, but somehow the conversations were beginning to work their way around to the possibility of their getting back together again.

"Even if we were to do something crazy like that, hypothetically speaking, of course," Lowell had finally pointed out, "the admiral would never go for it, are you kidding?" The admiral was Caitlin's ever-controlling father. Even so, Lowell was sensing what he was beginning to think might be inevitable.

"What does he have to do with it?" she demanded. "We're adults."

"Hypothetically speaking, of course."

"Ha ha."

"It's just that you do still live under his roof, and he still runs the fleet," he pointed out.

That was a sore point with Caitlin. She insisted she was no Daddy's girl, but some people, it seemed, were pretty hard to convince. Such as Tony Lowell.

"Anyway, I'm more concerned what Ariel might think," she'd then said.

"Yeah, right," responded Lowell, dryly. "It could really mess up a modern kid's head, the idea of her parents actually getting together."

They'd both laughed and chatted a bit more. Then concluded, once again, to leave well enough alone.

The phone call wasn't from Caitlin. It was another old friend. Sort of: Lena Bedrosian.

"Lowell? Where were you? I've been trying to reach you for hours!"

"Well excuse me for living," retorted Lowell. "I didn't realize I was supposed to report in to you every hour. Nobody told me Big Brother had finally taken over."

"Lowell, I'm not in the mood, please don't aggravate me." She sounded tired.

"Why, what's wrong?" He asked.

"Something bad. You remember my cousin, Marge Pappas? I think I introduced you that one time, at that Law Enforcement seminar thing I think it was, in Bradenton that time?"

Lowell remembered Marge Pappas only too well. More than Lena knew. It hadn't been at the Law Enforcement thing in Bradenton. It had been at the Wildlife Management thing in Sarasota, that time he'd gone out of concern for the manatees. He and Marge had wound up in bed that night. And had managed to part as friends in the morning, once getting over the surprise of finding themselves in each other's company. The Wildlife Management thing had been pretty wild, and had involved, as Lowell now remembered, a great deal of beer.

"So how is Marge?" he asked. He sensed his mistake at once. Lena had said "something bad." Lena wasn't much prone to hyperbole.

"She's dead, Lowell!" He felt the pain and rage in her voice. For the first time since he'd known her, Lena Bedrosian's armor cracked.

"Aw, hell," said Lowell, jolted at the news. "I'm sorry, Lena. Where are you?"

She mended the seam at once, returning to her brusque, businesslike manner.

"I'm down in Collier County, near a place called Corkscrew Swamp." She was trying to maintain control, but was barely hanging on.

"I'm sorry, I don't know it. Where is it?"

"North of Big Cypress, near Lake Trafford. She was the Wildlife Officer down here, do you remember?"

It was coming back to him. Marge was just like Lena, in so many ways. He knew they were close, as well as kin. Again, for perhaps the first time ever, he felt a strong empathy for his longtime rival and colleague, Detective Lieutenant Lena Bedrosian of the Manatee City Police Department. Also of the human race.

She was trying desperately not to cry, he could tell. Like a good cop, she was trying to take it like a man. But she wasn't a man, she'd admit under pressure. She was a woman. And a mother. And a wife. This had to be hard.

Suddenly sober, Lowell had some feelings of his own, but was more adept at suppressing them. Or ignoring them.

"I'm really sorry," he managed to say. "What happened?"

For once, he wasn't fishing for something, and she understood his concern was genuine. She sniffed a little, and regained her composure. "I don't know yet. But I smell politics. They're not letting me take the case."

"Isn't that a different jurisdiction?"

"It isn't just that."

The authorities would probably have other reasons for keeping Lena off the case, he realized. It was too personal for her, too close to home for her to be objective.

"They're claiming it was an accident. You know what really pisses me off though?" she said, almost a non sequitur.

18

She must be close to the edge, he thought. "No, what?"

"Jeffries. My boss. He's the one who took me off. Told me to take administrative leave. Son of a bitch! He expects me to sit at home and knit, I suppose, when my best friend and first cousin got found in a ditch down here with half her head blown off!"

"But they say it was an accident?"

"She had a gunshot wound in the back of the head, Lowell," she stated flatly. "You tell me." That's when she lost it. Lowell stayed with her, using tones and words of comfort and encouragement he'd almost forgotten he knew. She calmed down after a while, and the old hardness he knew returned to her voice. "Lowell," she went on, "Marge called me about a week ago. She'd been getting threats."

He thought about that. "I'll tell you what," he suggested. "Let me go down there first thing in the morning and nose around. I'll let you know what I find out."

"You can't go now?"

Lowell sighed. "I usually throw myself prone before your every request, Bedrosian. But it'll take me three hours to get down there, and it'll be late in the afternoon. I'd rather start out fresh in the morning."

"Fine, no doubt anybody possibly inclined to destroy evidence will have the courtesy to wait on your convenience," she snapped.

He knew she was stress-impaired just now, and didn't push it. "All right, you win. I'll go down this afternoon."

She sounded relieved. "Thanks, Lowell. I'll be home by tonight. Call me as soon as you get there."

"No problem."

Lowell hung up and looked at Perry. He felt a sudden chill, as though someone had dumped a bucket of ice water over his head. Maybe it was just because he was still wet from the cold waters of the bay. Perry, also wet, seemed perfectly comfortable as he sipped his beer, impassively sorting through the stack of vinyls.

"Here's one," announced Perry. *"Revolver."*

"Perry," Lowell finally said. "You doing anything this weekend?"

4

SATURDAY AFTERNOON, 2:00 P.M.

At her home on the suburban edge of Manatee City, Lena
Bedrosian had been on the phone making frantic calls to
everyone she could think of. She had already gotten three
warnings to back off, and didn't like it. Especially since her
own family had taken the hit this time.

"They're trying to muzzle me, Arlen!" she'd angrily complained to the captain that morning down at HQ, who—like
Tony Lowell—had promised to keep her informed. She'd told
him about the threats Marge had gotten. He said he'd look into
it, but agreed she'd have to lay low.

"You're just too close to it to be objective, Lena," Arlen had
tried to cajole her, with that calming way he had. He was another family man. He figured he could reach her on those
terms. "If it was my family. I'd step aside, too, otherwise I'd
probably do something I regretted later." He knew what she
was thinking. Retribution could be a career killer, for a cop.

"And what would that be?" she demanded, unappeased.

"Forget it, Lena," he advised her. "I've already gotten word this thing goes all the way up to Tallahassee. You're nipping at the heels of the heavyweights."

"What heavyweights?" she demanded. "Arlen, are you telling me this thing is *political?*" Of all the words she knew that one was probably the dirtiest.

"Sorry, Lena," he told her. "I just can't say." His voice softened. "Look, I know what you're going through. You just take it easy. We're doing all we can."

Lena wasn't appeased. "You just make sure the killer is caught, and brought to justice, Arlen. That's all I have to say. I don't care if the whole damn legislature did it. I wish it was, in a way. They all should be put away anyway."

"Listen, I feel the same way you do, Lena." God knows, he thought. The Florida state government, like any state government, was rotten to, and at, the core. White-collar crime and criminals flourished in Tallahassee—as in all state capitals—with impunity. Special interests ruled, lobbyists were crown princes, and big money did all the talking. But the murder of a small-time game warden? For what? It didn't make sense.

It didn't make sense to Lena, either. "You just get 'em, Arlen, damn it!" she shouted, and hung up.

Tallahassee, she thought, in dismay. She wondered who she knew up there. The following week was going to be slow in the state capital, what with this latest government shutdown. Only a few committees were meeting: behind-closed-doors sessions on various interests. Maybe she could slip into town on the q.t. and look around. That was when she finally got through to Lowell.

Luann Perla was working extra long hours. A career lobbyist from Jacksonville, Luann represented several important Florida industries including the Florida Builder's Association, the Professional Golf Association (which promoted golf course expansion and construction) and the Caloosahatchee Hunt

22

and Gun Club of South Florida. It was the latter group that had her primary focus of attention this week. Senator Kranhower was being lobbied hard to change his vote regarding the new Collier County land acquisition. Kranhower had boasted more than once that he couldn't be bought. Luann knew better than to try. Gentle persuasion, in the vivacious Southern tradition, was more her style. True, she was no beauty. No spring chicken either. But she had manners, and savvy, and money to burn. Her eyes were hard and steely—the product of years of toughening negotiations and demanding church work. Her famous pincushion hairdo had earned her the behind-the-back nickname Porcupine. Her porcine appearance hadn't helped dispel that image, and she'd learned to live with it, although she had warned more than one colleague and legislative aide "just don't even try calling me Porky." The legislators themselves wouldn't dare. They valued their contributions too much. But more than one Young Turk had been booted for such indiscretion. Yes, Luann could live with her critics just as the rest of Florida would live with the consequences of the special deals she'd rammed through, again and again, in the back rooms of Tallahassee.

On this particular Saturday morning she'd gotten up early, anxious to get out of her cramped hotel room at the Hyatt, and took a taxi over to the capitol. She had a breakfast meeting scheduled with Senator Kranhower, his legal counsel Buddy Burke, and one key legislator, Bob Hathcock. There was also a guy from the NRA. The latter addition had caught her by surprise. Which was rare, because not much that happened in Tallahassee surprised Luann Perla any more.

The meeting was to be held in Senator Kranhower's spacious office, with coffee and croissants catered from one of the popular capitol area four-star restaurants, courtesy of the Gun Club. Senator Jack Kranhower was Chairman of the Joint Natural Resources Committee, which governed and funded all state lands and waterways: some ten million acres in all. The

23

senator himself seemed to be distracted, concerned about some more personal issue. He was reputed to be open-minded, though, which Luann and the others considered hopeful. As they were ushered in, she wondered what the NRA guy was doing there. She knew Bill Naylor well enough from their long years together patrolling the halls of state, and didn't care for him. He was a typical humorless single-issue zealot. People like him had been proliferating in the capitol of late, much to the annoyance of the professional lobbyists like Luann, who considered themselves above advocacy.

The senator's aide was a young woman, whose name was ignored by everyone except Luann. She had long ago learned the value of remembering names and faces. The young aide's name was Amber. She was dark, sharp-eyed, and seemed to take a keen interest in the proceedings—more so than the senator himself, Luann noticed. And she seemed really upset about something.

"So," said Senator Kranhower, entering with his typical brusqueness, as though he found the business at hand distasteful (which he did). "What've you got?"

With a nod from the staff, Luann took over the meeting. "Senator," she began. "We understand you enjoy a good hunt now and then, am I right?"

The meeting was actually about a small amendment Luann's client wanted to tack onto a minor piece of legislation still in committee that had escaped practically everyone's notice in the media, much to her glee. That one little piece of legislation would open up any state land "not currently in use," to "open or closed bidding" for "recreational development or other development beneficial to the public." In the fine print, the amendment stated that, if any of those millions of acres of remaining state forest land were not specifically designated as "State Park" land, or specifically leased such as to mining or ranching concerns (another sweetheart deal she's worked on as an apprentice, years ago), then it was open for commercial lease and development, so long as said development was "beneficial to the public." Naturally, "beneficial" was open to interpretation—one of the key points to be discussed this morning. Her client was actually Representative Hathcock's own club, in Hondo County. But, judging by the presence of Bill Naylor, someone else had managed to hang their hat on her bill, as well.

Everyone at the table except Senator Kranhower was in agreement that "beneficial" meant "for the public enjoyment." "What the hell do you mean by that?" demanded Kranhower. "Some folks I know of might think that meant you could lob hand grenades," he scoffed.

"I could support that," remarked Bill Naylor, nodding eagerly. Burke coughed, and stared into his coffee. The legislator, Bob Hathcock, seemed agitated about something. Kranhower looked at the NRA lobbyist, wondering how he'd gotten into the meeting in the first place. The man is serious, he realized. "I'm sure you would, Bill," he remarked, smoothly. "Am I to assume that your constituents are also promoting this hunt club?"

"I don't represent the hunt club, Senator," Naylor replied, tapping the table with his fingers. "I represent the Hondo County Militia, and the National Rifle Association."

Luann looked at Naylor sharply, and realized that she wasn't nearly as in control of the meeting as she had thought. Furious as she was (and she let Naylor know it with one blistering look) it was essential to keep the ball rolling. Maybe she and Naylor could negotiate something later on. Better share the pie than no pie. But trying to slip something by her like that, at the last minute. The gall infuriated her. Time for damage control, she realized. Maybe even turn this new development to her advantage. "This isn't just a hunt club, sir," she said, quickly. "This is an all-purpose public facility we're proposing."

Naylor slapped his palm on the table, unable to control his glee. He threw her a smile that promised more, later, and took the baton at full sprint. "I couldn't have said it better myself, Senator. My people are also interested in serving the public in our district."

"Wait a minute," growled Kranhower. "Which is it? Hunting, or militias?"

"Both!" shouted Perla and Naylor, at the same time. They were practically slapping each other on the back, by this time.

"You intend to have hunters out there?" snapped Kranhower. "And bivouacs both? What about canoeists and picnickers?"

Luann was only momentarily at a loss, and looked around the room. Hathcock looked at her, hopefully.

"We only need it weekends," cut in Bill Naylor, earnestly. "That leaves five whole days for other folks."

"Big of you," remarked Kranhower. "Weekends just happen to be when most families and working people are out there. Your guys yell 'incoming' before they open fire?"

"Easy, Jack," whispered Buddy Burke. "Those boys down there send a lot of contributions our way, come election year. They're entitled to their fair share of outdoor recreational facilities." Buddy was a thin, nervous city-bred lawyer whose idea of outdoor recreation was drinks in a beach cabana.

"As protectors of the Constitution," continued Naylor, "we're just trying to look after the public good. We need to expand our training areas to the south and east. But I'm sure there's room on the adjacent property for the hunt club." So that's it, thought Luann. She was annoyed and pleased at the same time. Naylor should have consulted with her, before the meeting. But on the other hand, bringing in the NRA and Representative Hathcock gave her some powerful allies. Too powerful, she figured, for Senator Kranhower to ignore.

"So, what do you think?" she asked the senator. Kranhower shrugged dourly, and shook his head. The loony tunes really have taken over, is what he thought.

The other "minor" issue on the table had to do with the

26

meaning of the word *public*. Again, the committee members had decided that *public* was also a discretionary term, which could include, say, a private hunt club, or a "people's militia," or in this case, both. *Public*, in other words, meant anyone willing to install the necessary "improvements." Like fences. At state expense, of course. *Improvements* was another one of those favored buzzwords Luann had managed to slip in there, which had inspired more winking than the Pillsbury Dough Boy.

Again, the senator balked. "This is nothing but a backdoor handout of state lands!" he complained. The others looked indignant. They'd been warned by Luann herself (and no one knew better) that once aware of the actual intent of the bill, the senator was going to be difficult if not impossible to hurdle. He usually didn't read the bills. The problem was that this time, for some damn reason, he had.

Actually, the entire wording of the amendment had been personally written by Luann, in consultation with Hathcock, faxed over to her lawyer for quick review, then to the legislative committee, all in the last thirty-six hours. Representative Hathcock, despite his personal interest, had sponsored the piece, and Senator Braun had agreed to cosponsor in the senate, attaching it to the budget financing bill.

All that had been needed was the usual rubber stamp approval of the powerful Joint Committee chairman. Senator Jack Kranhower. And this time, at least for the moment, it was apparent to everyone that they weren't going to get it.

Luann was not worried yet. She had more than one fish to fry. If a public official couldn't be persuaded by reasonable discussion, there were always other ways. Everyone in Tallahassee had their weak spot. All she had to do was find Jack Kranhower's, and probe it a bit. She looked at the young woman who had come in with him. His legislative assistant. She had a feeling that this young woman might be an important link to her goals. And a glance at Naylor told her he felt the same way. She wondered what else Naylor knew. And what else the young woman knew. She decided to find out.

When the group had all left, the senator took a deep breath. He hated meetings like that. He wondered why Bob Hathcock had been there. He needed to talk to Hathcock about this damn government shutdown. All over a budget impasse. Hathcock was holding the legislature hostage over what had looked to him like a routine budget proposal. Was there something he was missing here? And why hadn't Hathcock said two words at that meeting? He glanced at his watch. He had another one in ten minutes with the Budget Committee, of which he was also a member.

"Amber," he told his slim, attractive dark-haired young female assistant. "Hold the fort. I'll be back as soon as I can."

"I will," she said, with a smile that he knew concealed a lot of personal pain, just now.

As soon as the senator was gone, the girl surreptitiously lifted the phone and made a call to Manatee County. A familiar voice answered.

"Lena? This is Amber. Amber Pappas, I think you've been trying to reach me." She lowered her voice, with a nervous glance around the empty office. "There's somethin' goin' on up here, I think you oughta know about."

Lena hung up the phone, thoughtfully. Her second cousin Amber had taken Marge's death very hard, but had insisted on staying at work. "It's just too important," she'd tearfully explained. "Marge would understand." Amber had a tendency toward hyperbole, which might be an asset in state government, but not in police work. It was hard to tell when she should be taken seriously or not. When Lena and the Pappas girls were growing up together, Amber, the youngest, was al-

28

ways the first to run home screaming about coral snakes, or swamp gators, when they were out playing hide-and-seek or Nancy Drew along the Anclote River. Usually it was just a floating stick, or some garbage from the sponge boats. But sometimes, every once in a while, Amber would be right. Like the time she announced that a tornado was coming, and it was a perfect Florida day. Then out of the blue, whoosh! Cousin Hector's double-wide suddenly had no roof. "I heard it on the radio," she'd said modestly, skipping off as though nothing at all had happened. She was a strange one, that Amber. But she had also been the beauty of the family, as well as the youngest, and Lena had to admit to herself that while Amber might have gotten cut extra slack from the doting men of the family, she had therefore gotten none at all from the women.

In any case, Amber had done fine: majored in poly sci at Florida State, and gone straight into politics first as an intern, then soon afterward, legislative assistant to the most powerful man in the state senate: Senator Kranhower.

Lena paced the house, hating being home, hating the fact that she hated it. Her husband, Michael, had given her a wide berth. Unfortunately, the girls treated it like a holiday, and were on her the moment they got off the school bus, with gleeful demands for attention, games, special treats, and all those things Lena never had time for under normal circumstances. She could hardly begrudge them their joy at her unexpected presence. She just wished they wouldn't overdo it so. She had to admit to herself that she wasn't used to all this parenting. She also had to admit to herself, somewhat ruefully, that she found it easier coping with snarling criminals than whining children. Why couldn't it ever be easy?

"I'm home, honey!" called Michael, coming in from the garage with shopping bags under each arm, two girls in tow, and a small wailing boy trailing behind. Mikey Junior was three now, and in terms of demands was more than a match for his two older sisters, Jackie and Sarah. Jackie was at an age when she wanted no part of whining little brothers.

"Will you stop?" she demanded, rolling her eyes. Sarah, however, at seven, was into her prepuberty motherhood phase, and happily took over, hoisting up the little guy like he was the latest Ken doll and weighed nothing, and calming him with a remarkable tolerance that Lena realized she herself could have never summoned.

"Michael!" Lena practically flew into her surprised husband's arms. He dropped the bags on the nearest countertop, narrowly averting a catastrophe of flying pretzel sticks, and held her a moment. "I'm going out of my mind!" she confessed. "I feel so powerless, just sitting around here."

"Have you tried the talk shows?"

She nearly spat. "How can I listen to a bunch of morons," she exclaimed, "when I have Marge on my mind?"

"You mean you're not interested in the confessions of reformed alcoholic puppy molesters?" he teased.

She ignored that. "Listen, honey, I have to get out of here. Something's come up."

His eyes said it all: uh-oh. Now what. He knew her too well. "Yeeeeessss?" he inquired, releasing her and gathering up the spilled groceries from the counter.

"What say you," she proposed, "that we take a little trip?" It had come to her in a flash, the moment she'd gotten off the phone with her cousin. If the department was going to force her to take leave, so be it. They couldn't stop her from doing a little "research."

Michael was already out of the room, herding the children with one hand, expertly putting away toilet paper and laundry soap with the other. "A trip?" he called back. "What for?" He knew perfectly well they never took trips. He was instantly wary.

"I mean it!" she called after him in her most persuasive tone. He was now in the vicinity of the Florida room—the enclosed veranda/family room off the dining area—where he was refereeing a quarrel between Jackie and Sarah regarding possession of the TV remote. "I was thinking why not use the leave time and take a little vacation!"

Michael was silent for a long moment. "You've got to be joking," he finally concluded; Lena Bedrosian was not one to do things on a whim. Especially things that weren't work related. Which, he instantly realized, this probably was.

"Where did you have in mind?" he asked, cautiously.

"Tallahassee! We can catch the Florida State game!"

She had no idea which game she was trying to lure him with, or even which sport was currently in season. But the state university was so huge, there was bound to be something going on. Varsity diving, team table tennis, women's basketball, indoor softball—something. It didn't matter. Michael wasn't that discriminating when it came to sports. He'd probably go for it. Especially since he just happened to be an FSU alumnus. She was right.

"You mean it?" he blinked, doubtfully.

She was back in his arms, coaxing. "Yes. Just you and me. And the kids, of course," she added, catching Jackie's outraged look from across the room.

"All *right!*" he shouted, slapping his thigh, scarcely believing his sudden good fortune. Lena had never shown the slightest inclination to revisit her husband's alma mater before. They had met when she was at the police academy and he was a junior, and had married right after his graduation. She personally hated Tallahassee. But that didn't matter, just now. What mattered now, was to find out who killed her favorite cousin Marge. And why. Marge had been killed on state land, while protecting Florida's rapidly diminishing natural assets. Lena's instincts told her the answers—at least some of them—lay to the north. And following her conversation with Amber, she had a pretty good idea where to begin.

5

SATURDAY, LATE AFTERNOON

Lowell and Perry arrived at the Caloosahatchee River just after 4:00 P.M. The light was already waning at that hour in the Gulf Coast winter, and the air was cold enough to feel the bite. They had brought jackets in anticipation of the oncoming chill, as the sun set and the evening came on. Bedrosian had given them a few names. There was little else they could go by. She couldn't give them any authority, as she herself was out of the loop. But she had no intention, Lowell knew, of staying out of it entirely.

"You call me the minute you get there," she'd insisted.

"Lena, it's going to be the middle of the night in the middle of the woods. How'm I supposed to be calling you every minute?"

"I told you you should get a cellular," she grumbled.

"Sure. On whose budget, yours?"

"Just call me," she'd snapped, and hung up.

Lowell and Perry had driven both cars, in the end, figuring that the division of labors would inevitably separate them.

They left Perry's 4-Runner at the Days Inn where they checked in, and drove Lowell's Impala to the River Marina in Fort Myers. There they rented a leaky outboard motorboat and headed upriver by water, making the only noise on a beautiful, eerily silent late afternoon. Even the road that followed the river to the right was empty of traffic. Only the insects and water fowl shared their space, as they made their way inland, past miles of trailer parks, low-rent houseboat marinas, small dilapidated farms, and huge cattle ranches boasting signs saying Beef: Real Food for Real People.

"Gimme a break," remarked Perry. "I eat fish, does that make me a fake person?"

"No, just a communist sympathizer," replied Lowell. "Anyway, by 'real people,' they mean 'real men.' "

"Tell that to the fishing crowd."

Lowell spotted the landing from a quarter-mile downstream, and pointed ahead. It was nestled in a grove of huge oak trees, Spanish moss draped over the roofs, fences, and vehicles hidden in the lot among the palmettos that lined the property. "We'll dock up there, it has to be close!" he shouted, over the buzz of the twelve-horse outboard—the biggest motor available on a rental that particular late Saturday afternoon.

Perry nodded silently, wishing Lowell had let him bring his arsenal. Perry had quite an arsenal, and he sensed now that he might be needing it, before this was all over. Lowell would disagree, of course. Lowell didn't believe in weapons anymore. Perry considered him and his views naive, but lovable.

Patterson's Landing was a rambling wooden structure, half built on pilings out over the water, with a tin roof and a dock along the west side, featuring two old scows, a couple of runabouts, and a crumbling old houseboat. Also a gas pump. A couple of newer power boats were tied up in spaces marked "guest slips." Several cars were parked at random angles in the sand and dirt parking lot. A neon beer sign with two burned-out letters boasted "B   weiser." Lowell was in no mood for a beer. An aspirin or two, maybe. He docked the flat-bottom, tied it up, and swung ashore. Perry was right beside him.

A young man—barely out of his teens, Lowell guessed—approached them from the front of the building. He had short brown hair and a shell earring. He looked agitated.

"We're closed," he called, curtly.

"Can we just tie her up and use a pay phone?" Lowell inquired.

The young man hesitated. "What 'chall lookin' for?"

Lowell gave him a quick look of scrutiny. He was used to cracker sullenness, and hostility. The boy exuded plenty of both. But there was something else burning behind those fiery eyes. Something akin to sorrow. Lowell took a chance. "Listen, I'm here to see about an old friend of mine, worked down this way, heard she might be in trouble."

The young man's ears pricked, at that. He frowned, his eyes narrowing to slits. " 'She'? " he repeated.

"Name of Marge Pappas. You know her?"

The young man's eyes slitted some more. He took a deep breath. Perry tensed, as though expecting the youth to leap at them. The boy's face darkened, and the veins in his neck stood out a moment. Lowell calmly met his stare, and the boy blinked first. His shoulders sagged.

"You mean the Wildlife Officer, that who you lookin' for?"

"She's the one." Lowell feigned jocularity, hoping to learn something. It was possible that news of Marge's death hadn't gotten out yet, locally. If he pretended not to know of Marge's fate, he might gain some confidence with the locals. Or at least with the boy.

"You're too late," Billy Patterson said, bitterly. "She's dead."

Lowell feigned surprise, but his dismay was genuine. "Damn," he said.

"Yeah, well." The boy's voice rose, a mixture of rage and

despair. "She was a friend of mine, man, and she was just doin' her job!"

"Hey, I'm sorry," said Lowell softly, and meant it. "Name's Tony Lowell," he said, offering his hand. "I knew Marge. She was a good woman. If somebody killed her, I'd like to find out who."

"Lotta good that'll do," muttered the boy, barely audible.

"What do you mean by that?" asked Lowell.

"Nothin'. Just—" his voice trailed off. "Name's Billy Patterson," he changed the subject, unconsciously imitating Lowell's style. He reluctantly returned the handshake. "I live here. Pump gas, fix boats, run errands for the old man. She stopped by here once in a while for gas and stuff. She was a nice lady."

"This is my friend Perry Garwood," said Lowell, nodding in Perry's direction. Perry stood stock-still, eyes fixed on the edge of the forest, beyond the highway that paralleled the river.

Billy's eyes turned toward Perry, a mix of wariness and curiosity. "You Indian?" he asked, bluntly.

Perry shrugged. "Creek. So they tell me."

"Sorry," said Billy. "No offense, though there's some pretty prejudiced people around here," he added. "Like my old man. Not me, though. Y'all can use the dock, I guess." He glanced nervously over his shoulder. "If my old man asks, tell him you're payin' five bucks for the day. If he don't ask, it's on the house. The pay phone's around front."

Billy walked behind them as they rounded the ramshackle garage to the service area out front and the pay phone. Lowell sensed he wanted to say more than he'd said. He fiddled for change, patiently.

Perry continued to contemplate the thick pine woods across the road, already impermeable in the fading light. The trees were so close together you could hardly walk between them. A tough place to hunt, he thought. But a good place to hide.

"Hey man," Billy suddenly volunteered. "You need some wheels?"

Lowell acknowledged that, in fact, they could use a ride. He'd been under the impression they would be entering saw grass wetlands, hence the boat. He and Perry had argued about it the whole way. Perry had proven right. Lowell had one name and phone number that Lena had been able to provide: that of state Superintendent Dave Connors.

Billy glanced around once more, furtively. "Maybe I could drive you. I guess you'll be headin' for her camp. I know where it is," he volunteered. He seemed anxious to get away from the Landing, Lowell noticed. He glanced at the building. It seemed to stare back, windows for eyes, silent and menacing.

Billy led them to his aging Ford pickup on the far side of the lot, and drove them in silence a quarter-mile up the river road past a couple of stores and old cracker bungalows to State Road 29, a narrow two-lane highway that turned off to the right, and into the scrub oak flatlands. A few miles farther the land opened up, cleared as far as the eye could see as though by a huge scythe. A white sign proclaimed: Lejeune Farm and Ranch Company. The ranch went for miles, marked occasionally by "real people" signs.

Billy pointed up ahead. "Those used to be the largest stands of cypress in the world. Now there's only a few left, down in—"

"Corkscrew Swamp Sanctuary," Perry spoke up. "Indian country."

"That's where Marge bought it?" breathed Lowell.

Billy nodded.

"Some of those trees are seven hundred years old," said Perry. His face was somber, with a look that fell somewhere between pensiveness and awe.

They passed through the Seminole Indian hamlet of Immokalee, a dismal smattering of seedy bars and bingo parlors, turned west on a small county highway, wound past a few citrus farms and clear-cut subdivisions with rustic names honoring the land they'd just destroyed, like Forest Glen, and plunged into the forest. Tall stands of second-growth pine gave way to hummocks of cypress that loomed over them, Spanish moss draping the road, trunks thick, roots protruding in short pointed stumps that jutted eerily from the watery dusk-shrouded landscape.

"Those knobs are called knees," Perry informed them. "The trees breathe through those."

"I knew that," claimed Lowell.

"Up there," pointed Billy, toward the thickest grove of cypress yet. "Corkscrew Swamp."

As they turned down a narrow sandy track, they reached the abandoned campsite, set in a clearing beneath a thick canopy of trees. Spanish moss hung in heavy clumps, almost to the ground. Perry swung off the running board before Billy had even stopped, landing lightly on his feet. He turned in a slow circle, gazing at the darkening forest, listening intently.

"Hunters," he announced.

"Isn't this off-season?" asked Lowell, unpacking his battered but still-functional old Nikon.

Billy shrugged. "Small game only. But ain't nobody pays much attention, anyways," he said, with a wry note in his voice.

"Well, somebody's been shooting."

"There's a hunting club up along the river," said Billy, in confirmation. "But they shouldn't be down here, this is supposed to be a state wildlife preserve."

"They're here," said Perry.

Lowell looked around. The forest was silent, the air still. But he didn't doubt Perry's Native American instincts, if that's what they were. Or his commando savvy. If Perry said there were hunters out there, there were hunters out there. He just hoped that whoever they were, they watched where they sprayed their bullets.

Lena had been convinced Marge's killing had been a homicide. She didn't have much on which to base that supposition, other than something Marge had said to her sister. No question, hunters were notorious for shooting each other and others, with reckless abandon. Like that housewife in Maine who got shot hanging laundry from her own back porch. The court had ruled it was her own fault for resembling a deer, and the shooter was sent home with apologies from the judge. Presumably for having impugned his judgment—if not his eyesight and marksmanship.

On the other hand, Marge Pappas had been shot in the back of the head, according to the police report. While it could have been a hunter's stray bullet, it sounded more like an execution. Lowell took photos of the area using his 50-mm lens and fast 1000 ASA film. The cabin was empty but for a bunk bed—now stripped—the camp stove, and a few foodstuffs and utensils. Perry knelt down by the stove and opened the fire box. "Ashes are cold," he confirmed.

Lowell went back outside and examined the footpath that led in the direction of the creek. He spotted several sets of tracks. "Footprints," he called. "Looks like more than one set."

Perry joined him, along with Billy. "Could be cops," he observed. The kid didn't seem in any hurry to leave, Lowell noted. They followed the trail for some distance into the woods, alert for hunters. Lowell stopped, and knelt down. "Tire marks," he called out. He took photos from several angles. They reached a small clearing, where Perry suddenly stopped and held up his hand.

"Over there," he whispered, pointing at the ground near the edge of a swampy area. "A lot of broken grass and reeds. Somebody went down hard here."

They were several hardly noticeable, damp patches on the dark earth. Perry stooped down and sniffed the ground, tasted a tiny sample of the soil, and spat into the bushes.

39

Lowell looked at him, quizzically. "What is it?" he asked.

"Piss," growled Perry, irritably.

"Human or animal?"

"Who the hell knows?"

Lowell chuckled, knelt down, and scooped up a small sample, putting it in a plastic bag. There was no sign that the police had been in the area. He turned to Billy. "I don't understand why the area isn't cordoned off," he said.

"They didn't find her here," explained Billy. "She was found down by the creek."

Lowell looked at him, in surprise. Perry shrugged, doubtfully.

"That way," Billy pointed ahead toward a heavy thicketed area across the marsh. "We have to go around, though, and I ain't got time. Mr. Connors can take you in from the other side, but it's gettin' dark."

Perry moved farther along, and called over once again, urgently: "Lowell! Over here!"

Lowell hurried over to where Perry was kneeling once more, at the edge of the trail. "Animal prints," he announced. "Looks like a large cat."

They looked. Several sizeable paw prints were clearly visible in the damp soil. Some of the boot prints seen near the camp were also present.

"Panthers," breathed Lowell, clicking away with his camera.

"That's the she panther!" exclaimed Billy. They looked at him. "The one with the cubs!" He told them. He explained about his conversation with Marge the day before, and their shared secret.

"Looks like someone was after that cat," said Perry. "Maybe your friend caught them. Maybe they didn't like getting caught."

"That's presuming a lot," Lowell observed, somewhat annoyed. "Poaching panthers is almost unheard-of. Especially right on a Wildlife Officer's doorstep."

"I've heard of it," muttered Billy.

"You're the detective," said Perry, slightly miffed.

Lowell didn't reply. He was thinking about Marge Pappas. Wishing he'd had a chance to know her better. He shook it off. "Let's go," he said.

Billy drove them back to the Landing in silence, where Lowell called Bedrosian.

She answered right away. "Lowell? That you?"

"There you go again. What if it was Jeffries, or Michael?"

"Michael's here, Jeffries is up in Gainesville for the Law Enforcement Lobby Luncheon or some damn thing, and I've been waiting to hear from you! What have you found out?" She sounded anxious.

"Lena," he began. "I only just got here. I checked out her camp and took some photos. She may have had one or more visitors there before she was killed, but it'll take a forensic specialist to tell if it was last night or last week. It didn't look to me like the cops were even there."

"Maybe that's because they claim it was an accident. What else you find?"

"Nothing yet. We're on our way to the alleged site of the killing. I'm not Superman."

"This I know," she remarked. "Have you talked to Connors yet? Connors was Marge's superior, the deputy superintendent."

"No," admitted Lowell. "He's next."

"Then call me when you actually know something, all right?" She hung up.

Lowell glowered at the receiver. He looked at Perry, who was grinning. "What's so damn funny?" he demanded.

6

Dave Connors was visibly upset when they met him at the Ranger Station, near the entrance to the state campground. It was nearly dark when Billy dropped them off. Lowell thanked him for his help, tried to give him a twenty (which Billy refused), and waved as he drove away in a cloud of dust. Lowell had a distinct feeling the boy hadn't wanted to be seen with them.

Connors seemed a little perturbed that they hadn't called him right away, and also seemed taken aback by their means of arrival. Lowell suspected, from the way he looked at Billy, that they knew each other well. And why not? This was a rural area, and its small population was probably tight.

"She was a damn fine officer," Connors was saying. "It isn't right, to die alone out there like that, in the line of duty. And a woman at that, for chrissakes! What kind of cowardly son of a bitch would shoot a woman in back of the head?"

Lowell kicked a stick into the trees. "Pretty much the same kind of cowardly son of a bitch that would shoot a woman anywhere," he responded. "Know anyone like that?"

Connors snorted. "Couple hundred." He squinted at Lowell. "Who you say you were again?"

"Tony Lowell, Private Investigator. Lieutenant Bedrosian of the Manatee City Police Department is her cousin. She asked me to come down here and look around."

"Off the record?" Connors looked at him, shrewdly.

"Off the record." Lowell nodded. "Also, I knew the deceased. And she'd been worried about some threats. You hear anything like that?"

"No, but I met Lieutenant Bedrosian," Connors confirmed. "Seems like a good cop. If she thought something wasn't right I believe it. You fellas have a place to stay down here?"

Lowell nodded. "Fort Myers," he said.

"That's a ways." Connors lowered his voice. "I have to warn you two. I don't think you're gonna get a lot of cooperation from the authorities, hereabouts."

"Nothing new there," said Lowell. "But why is that?"

"They look after their own, know what I mean?"

Lowell nodded. "That explain why there were no markers out on the trail?"

Connors frowned. "Out where? They cordoned off where they found her."

"Show us."

"It'll take a half-hour to get there. We'll have to bring lights, it'll be dark."

"We have lights. Lead the way."

Connors drove them in his green Cherokee down a dirt fire road into the now dark forest, passing a single marker: "Entering Hondo County." He finally pulled over and parked at a turnout beneath a tall stand of conifers. A sign was posted that stated: Keep Out. And underneath, Property of Caloosahatchee Hunt and Gun Club. Connors opened the back of the truck and took out three Day-Glo orange hunters' vests, one for each of them.

"Better wear these," he advised.

"Isn't this all supposed to be state forest?" Lowell inquired, as they got out of the truck and looked around.

"That's right. The Club has a special lease. Most of the members are public officials, between you and me. We're told not to ask questions, so we don't."

"By whom?"

Connors shrugged. "You'd have to take that question up in Tallahassee. I just work here." The light was just enough to see the trail as he led the way along a well-traveled path that plunged deep into the woods. Perry stopped occasionally, shining his light into the trees, sniffing, or listening. Once a shot rang out, off in the distance.

"Who uses this trail?" Lowell asked, after a while.

"Just the hunters, mostly. And rangers." He paused. "Although I've heard rumors of some kind of militia on one of the large private adjacent tracts."

Lowell looked at him sharply. "Militia?"

"That's what I've been hearing. But aside from poaching endangered species, which is illegal anywhere, what happens on private land is out of my jurisdiction. Or," he added, after a moment, "Marge's for that matter."

"Any idea what it might have been about? The shooting?"

Connors eyes narrowed. "They said it was an accident."

"So what if it wasn't?" said Lowell.

Connors frowned and shook his head. "I don't know."

"No idea at all?"

"No sir. Marge was doing her job, I have no doubt about that. Which in large part consisted of protecting the wildlife. Sometimes it can be a pretty dangerous job. More than that I couldn't say."

"You have people out there hunting and shooting anything they feel like with impunity, isn't that right?" Lowell persisted.

"What I hear," commented Perry, "folks down here don't

45

worry too much about little things like impunity."

"He's right," said Connors. He didn't look too happy.

Lowell and Perry looked at each other in silence.

"Let's go," said Connors, with a weary sigh. "It's getting late." They headed farther into the scrub and palmetto flatlands. After another half-mile of picking their way along in the growing darkness, they reached a clearing where the trail forked. The more heavily traveled track continued north, parallel to the river. But the less used branch headed into the marshlands, to the west.

Perry stopped, and aimed his flashlight at the ground. "More animal tracks here," he announced. "No boot marks. They all go this way." He pointed south.

"They found her up there," Connors pointed ahead. "Another hundred yards or so." It was pitch-black by the time they reached the north edge of the swamp, across a quarter-mile or so of wetlands from the place where Billy had shown them the panther's paw prints. The trail intersected the one they'd followed up from the south here. Perry immediately picked up the boot marks, and more scuffling marks. Lowell took some shots using his flash attachment. Then they moved on in silence through the darkness, until they reached a clearing that had been recently and heavily tracked. There was no sign of yellow tape, or other police activity or involvement.

Lowell took a few more shots, first wide angle, then with the 50-mm lens. Perry scoured the ground. "Five or six guys, I'd say."

"No way to tell much from that. It was all mostly the cops," said Connors.

"You're right. They tracked it up pretty good," sighed Lowell, shining his light over the area. "We won't find much."

"Right over there, you can see the outline of the body," Connors told them.

Lowell examined and photographed the death site, the

taped markers, the last remnants of a once vital life, that had met its violent and untimely end here in a dank swamp. Bedrosian must have had a hard time of it, he thought. He looked at Connors, grim and determined, then at his friend Perry, thoughtful and thorough. Perry was tasting the soil again—a peculiar ability. He spat. "Blood," he confirmed. Lowell collected a sample.

"Let's go," he finally said. "I want to talk to the sheriff."

"I doubt," Connors told him, "that the feeling is going to be mutual."

Connors led the way back to the truck, and drove them back to the campground. A reception committee awaited them, consisting of two sheriff's deputies. As though in anticipation of Connors's prediction, both of them were courteous, if not cheerful.

"How's it goin', Dave?" asked the heavyset, shorter one.

" 'Bout as well as can be expected," replied Connors, unable to muster much cordiality of his own.

The taller, darker one asked Connors who his companions were. Connors let Lowell and Perry introduce themselves. The cops stated their names and showed their badges: Deputies Kohler and Vega, from the Collier County Sheriff's Department. Vega was the tall one. Ex-Miami, Lowell guessed. Probably right-wing Cuban connections. Pro-law and order and down with Castro, but don't touch the profitable, highly socialized sugar biz. An odd mix of contradictions, and therefore unpredictable.

"What brings you gentlemen to these parts, Mr. Lowell?" asked Vega, looking Lowell, then Perry up and down with just the slightest glimmer of a frown.

"All the great hunting and fishing you have here, what else?" said Lowell. Perry didn't say anything.

Deputy Vega tilted his head, and grinned cheerfully. "This is the wrong season. Maybe you should try Duval County."

Lowell raised his hands in mock surrender. "All right. All

47

right. It's clear there's no fooling you fellas. We're here about the Pappas killing. Lieutenant Bedrosian of Manatee City asked me to look around," Lowell continued, evenly. "She was a relative of the victim." He showed them his dog-eared license, which was mostly up to date. Except for the overdue license renewal fee. "I'm a licensed private investigator."

"She's paying you?" the other deputy, Kohler, could scarcely conceal his scorn and disbelief at that.

Lena wasn't paying him, actually. As usual. But Lowell decided the local cops had no need to know that. He just nodded, vaguely. Who knows. Maybe she'd get the department to reimburse him this time. Stranger things had been known to happen. Maybe they'd give him a medal if he found Marge's killer. Maybe Florida would have a change of heart and ban phosphates and condos. Maybe Rush Limbaugh would come out liberal.

"Who's your buddy?" asked Kohler, nodding toward Perry. Lowell made Kohler out as a classic ex-big-city-cop, gone country with all his might. Out to impress. Or if not to impress, then to intimidate. Big, but more flab than beef.

Perry looked at Kohler and his eyes narrowed slightly.

"This is Mr. Garwood, my associate," replied Lowell. Perry looked up at the trees, and didn't say anything.

Vega nodded, doubtfully. "It was a lousy thing, that happened," he said, after a moment. He shook his head sorrowfully. "Shooting a woman like that? Man!"

Lowell focused on Vega, deciding he was in charge. "So you have confirmation it was a gunshot?"

Vega blinked. "What else would it be? This is a hunting district. Somebody mistook her for a deer, it was late in the day."

"Maybe," said Lowell. "But Lieutenant Bedrosian said Officer Pappas had been receiving threats."

The deputies looked at each other, clearly surprised. Vega frowned. "We hadn't heard anything about that."

"Had you heard that Lieutenant Bedrosian has been taken off the case?"

Vega spread his hands. "Hey, look. Lieutenant Bedrosian may be a great cop, but she's from another county. And if she's family, like you say, that would be standard procedure."

"So you don't mind if we look around a little?"

Vega cocked his head, slightly, and shrugged. "I don't have any problem long as the sheriff don't. Just make sure you don't disturb any evidence, don't break any laws, and we should have no problem."

"What kind of evidence are we talking about?" asked Lowell, casually.

Vega grinned, and shook his head. "I'm just talking in general, Mr. Lowell. You walk straight, keep your eye on the road, you'll be okay."

Lowell decided to take a chance. "You want to tell me what you think happened out there?" he asked. "Off the record?"

Vega shook his head. "Officer Pappas was shot by hunters," he replied. "That's all we know at this time."

"But has anybody come forward?" Lowell persisted.

"No sir," said Vega. "They usually don't."

"We're checking around," added Kohler, "but don't expect no miracles."

"I understand the deceased received a gunshot wound in the back of the head," said Lowell. "Any objections if we take a look at the body?"

Vega hesitated, and scratched his jaw. "It's all right with me," he said, finally. "But you'll have to clear it with the medical examiner."

"Of course. Have they completed the autopsy?"

"Far as I know."

"The coroner said it was an accident," objected Kohler.

Vega gave him a quick look of reproval. "That's all right, Doug. They can ask him themselves."

49

"We'll do that," said Lowell.

Perry gave him a look—a combined look of admiration and warning.

The Cuban deputy maintained his cool, and flashed a smile as though attempting to break the ice. "Look, I realize that Miss Bedrosian—"

"Lieutenant Bedrosian," corrected Lowell.

"—has an interest in this investigation and everything, and I understand how she feels, the deceased being a family member and all. But the thing is, accidents do happen, and sometimes there's not a hell of a lot you or we can do about it."

Lowell returned the smile. "Then you wouldn't mind running us down to the morgue?"

Vega shrugged. "If that's what you want."

Kohler didn't look too pleased, but didn't voice any objections.

Lowell turned to Connors, who'd practically shrunk into the shadows. "Thanks for the tour," he said. "We'll see you around."

Connors couldn't wait for them to leave.

The county medical examiner, a surprisingly young and beefy man named Fred Barnes, met them at his office with uncharacteristic aplomb, mostly because he had nothing better to do this particular Saturday night. He waved off Lowell's credentials. "Lieutenant Bedrosian called. But I don't have any smoking guns for you, I'm afraid."

"I'll wait out here," Deputy Vega told them, politely.

Barnes took Lowell and Perry downstairs to the pathology lab, where the remains of Marge Pappas's nude body lay on her face on the cold stainless steel, spread-eagled, all privacy gone, exposed to the elements. Her head shaved and most of her skull missing. Just as well, Lowell thought, that Bedrosian wasn't here.

Barnes seemed resigned, and slightly defensive, as though he was being blamed for something. "You wouldn't believe how many of these come through here," he said. "I got 'em stacked up in the freezer like cordwood, and unless there's something in the police report to indicate malfeasance, it's pretty routine."

Lowell hadn't yet seen the police report, but Bedrosian had warned him that there wasn't going to be much to go on. "Mind if I take some photos?" he asked.

"I guess not. No one else has," replied Barnes, with a shrug.

"How close was the shot, do you figure?" Lowell asked.

"Hard to tell. The damage was massive, which would usually indicate high caliber." He pointed to the jagged edges of broken bone, which Lowell managed to look at. "The bullet exited through her eye, and we haven't found it. I estimate it could have come anywhere from three to fifteen feet."

"Isn't that unusual? I mean, wouldn't impact with the bone have caused some fragments?"

"Usually," acknowledged Barnes. "But not always. But there was one odd thing," he commented. "I didn't find any spatter pattern on her jacket front. That's unusual."

Lowell nodded, with a frown. "Can I see it?"

Barnes shook his head. "You'll have to ask the cops. They took it."

"Any postmortem lividity?" Lowell asked.

"Nothing conclusive. She died facedown, which is how she was found."

Lowell took stills from various angles with his flash unit, while Perry examined Marge's hands. "You got soil samples?" Perry asked, suddenly. "There's dirt under her nails."

"Not yet," admitted Barnes. "But I don't see—"

"You mind?" asked Lowell, with a glance at Barnes.

"It's highly irregular," said Barnes, defensively. "But go ahead."

Lowell took out his Swiss Army knife and extracted a sample from under each fingernail. He thanked the medical examiner, and nodded at Perry that he was ready to leave.

Deputy Vega dropped them off at Patterson's Landing without further discussion, and left, burning rubber. Lowell noticed that the parking lot was full. Not surprising, for a Saturday evening. This was probably the only watering hole between Fort Myers and La Belle. Kicking himself for not having come by car, he headed once more for the pay phone. He had just finished a long and animated conversation with Lena when he caught sight of Billy Patterson waving frantically from the floodlit dock.

"Over here!" he hissed. Perry nodded for Lowell to come, and stood waiting with Billy on the dock while Lowell wrapped up his call.

The boat was on the bottom of the river. The brown water was clear enough that Lowell could plainly see the cause. The bottom had been blown out by a shotgun blast.

"Welcome to Big Cypress," muttered Perry, ironically. "Told you we shoulda drove."

"It was like this when I got back here, I swear!" Billy insisted, fear in his voice as well as his eyes.

Lowell felt sick, thinking of his own boat, the schooner *Andromeda,* now also resting on the bottom. He knew better than to ask who might have done it. "What's going on inside?" he asked, instead, with a nod toward the building. Billy's look of terror increased.

"Nuthin'," he insisted. "I wouldn't go in there!" Billy's voice rose to a near squeal when Lowell took a step in that direction.

Lowell looked at the Landing, puzzled by the boy's reaction. "Why not? It's a public restaurant, isn't it?"

"No!" Billy stammered. "I mean, yes, but not now." Lowell and Perry looked at him. Billy's voice dropped until it was barely audible, and he uttered the dread words. "It's the militia," he barely breathed. "They're having a meeting."

Lowell was tempted to drop in anyway, but Perry convinced him of the benefits of discretion. Instead, he and Perry accepted Billy's hasty offer of a ride down to the marina in Fort Myers, where they'd rented the boat. "I know those guys," the boy assured them as he put some distance between themselves and the Landing. "The insurance'll cover it."

"Sure," said Lowell, evading a meaningful look from Perry, who had barely and with great difficulty managed to badger him into buying the insurance. Billy dropped them off at the marina entrance, and Lowell thanked him once again. Once again, the boy refused money. Lowell convinced Perry to deal with the boat people, and wait for him at the Days Inn. "I won't be long," he promised, and told him what he was going to do.

"Yer outta yer fuckin' mind," said Perry.

7

State Representative Bob Hathcock dozed in the back of his state-issued stretch limousine, as it sped south along I-275. He was worried. Things hadn't gone the way he'd anticipated, and now he was going to have to explain why to his constituents.

Bob Hathcock figured that 90 percent of his supporters were sportsmen, one kind or the other. Most hunted and fished, some both. Most had grown up within spitting distance of the glades or Big Cypress. It was their land, his land, and they'd sent him to Tallahassee a long time ago to protect their land. And their interests. He was still there after twenty-two years, still protecting it. He'd made sure his boys got their share of the revenues, and the state lands handouts, whenever a parcel went on the block. Such as now. Even with all the pressure from conservationists and other "extremist" types, Bob and his cronies always made sure the biggest chunks still went to the key ranchers and growers in the district. Who also happened to be his key campaign contributors.

Most state land was leased on a sweetheart basis, supposedly set by "market value." The ranchers, and their elected officials, had made sure to keep market value real low (unless, of course, they needed to sell some). Some parcels even found their way, every so often, into the hands of developers. Golf was a favorite, with the legislators. Most played, and they could call a golf course a park. Parks were rubber-stamped by the necessary state agencies topped by the State Land Trust. The main requirement was that the lands had to be used in "the public interest." That was where Luann Perla came in. With her help writing the necessary bill riders there was usually no problem, never had been. Especially once the lands were turned over to the counties. Bob Hathcock's constituents were all members of the public, weren't they? They were the ones who decided what was in their interest. It was Bob's job to make sure they got it, was all. And if they considered more golf courses in their interest, or marinas on the coastal wetlands, or hunt clubs, well by God, they got it. This was God-given country, for its possessors to benefit from as they saw fit, just like in the Book of Genesis. That's what democracy was all about.

There was another thing. Bob Hathcock was quite alert to the fact that government was out of fashion, that government agencies and regulators were being more and more perceived as the bad guys. Not considering himself to be a government official, except on payday, Bob Hathcock went out of his way, these days, to assure his constituents that he was on their side, and opposed to government meddling. He saw no conflict in taking this position. If anything, to his way of thinking, it helped justify the need to take lands out of the hands of government and turn them back over to the people. Especially his people.

But now all his carefully woven plans had gone to hell in a handbasket. All on account of Jack Kranhower, and one little ol' bill he'd intended to run through on the last voting session before the legislature was scheduled to close, the kind of bill he'd run through a thousand times before without problems.

He'd taken steps, of course, to mitigate Kranhower's influence. The man was a liberal dinosaur anyway, everybody knew. So to plant somebody on his staff to help write the legislation and facilitate its smooth flow had proven necessary and surprisingly easy to accomplish. Especially what with septuagenarian Senator Kranhower's diminishing eyesight and attention span these days, either Bob Hathcock or Luann Perla had been almost directly writing a lot of the legislation that supposedly came out of Kranhower's joint committee, and running it straight on through to the legislative floor whenever Jack was out of town. Or sometimes even out of the room. It was that easy. It was that easy because the state government, like any government, generated so much paper as a matter of due course, that most of it never got read by anybody. Usually, nobody read Bob Hathcock's bills except Bob Hathcock.

Until last week.

Last week somebody (and he had a sneaking suspicion who) had actually read Bob's budget amendment—the one that granted ten thousand acres of state land to Collier and Hondo Counties. Which would become a county park. Which would become part of the Caloosahatchee Hunt and Gun Club. Which would be for the use of its members only. For the benefit of the State Land Office it would be designated as a "public park." But the public wouldn't be invited. Ever.

Bob Hathcock's trepidation increased as his limo bore south toward Tampa, and beyond. Wearily, he leaned back in his plush leather seat and closed his eyes. He had a problem: He was en route to a fund-raising dinner this very evening at the Caloosahatchee Hunt and Gun Club, where he was expected to deliver a speech, and with it the goods. And now he was going to have to prevaricate. Or at least stall.

It had looked so simple, so easy, on paper. He had even

found a simple solution for the last-minute demands from the NRA and militia people: a state purchase of five thousand additional acres from some of the vast Lejeune Farm and Ranch Company's lease holdings, which would then be leased to the militia or whoever the hell they were for the nominal sum of one dollar fifty per acre, per year. "The way I figure it," he'd told Bill Naylor on his way into the Kranhower meeting, "if we can sway this guy, the county commissioners"—Club members all—"can come up with that, one way or t'other."

He'd asked his aides to find some good jokes for him, for tonight. They'd come up with three "new" nigger jokes, a new "environmentalist goes into this bar" joke, and a great new fishing joke. He'd had a couple of hunting jokes ready, too, but figured it would be in bad taste, so soon after the Pappas accident.

The limousine cleared Tampa with minimum delay, and sped south on the once again wide-open interstate. Bob Hathcock poured himself a Jack Daniel's from the state-stocked bar, and picked up the cellular phone. He dialed a number in Tallahassee, and waited a few moments. It was answered directly, by a gruff, weary voice.

"So, Jack, you come to a decision yet?"

"Bob, is that you? Where are you, I thought you were all-fired anxious to be finished with this business."

"Had to hit the road, Jack. Got a speech tonight at the home district. Anyhow, I thought we were finished with this little item. I'd been planning on telling 'em what a great guy you are. You disappoint me."

"I also disappoint my wife. It's the way it is," snapped Kranhower. "I don't like this land scam of yours one bit, Bob, I want you to know that."

"What scam?" protested Hathcock, sensing he was going to have to reach for his sleeve pretty soon. "This is a legitimate public park for the people of Hondo and Collier Counties, and they and I both agree that how they use it should be the prerogative of the citizens of those counties, not you folks up there in the capitol."

"I'm from Lake County, Bob. Not Tallahassee. I work up here exactly the same number of days you do. I take that back, I probably work double the amount of days you do, judging by your absentee sheet."

"You gonna penalize me for answering to the call of the voters in my district? You gonna penalize them?"

"I'm not penalizing anybody. Unlike you, apparently, I work for the state of Florida, and to my way of thinking, the rights and property of people of the state of Florida take priority over the special interests of a few sportsmen down your way."

Hathcock was furious, but not surprised. Kranhower always did have that damn liberal streak running down his back. "Can I quote you on that, Jack? Maybe before this week is out, you'll be hearing from some people in your own district, who might be worried you're gonna stop one of their chances to grow, too."

"What some people call growth, other people refer to as cancer," retorted Kranhower. "Hold on a sec, will you, Bob?" Kranhower reached for a little switch he kept on his desk, for just such occasions. He pressed it, and there was a loud, crackling electric noise, from a two-inch speaker. The thing was basically an old squawk box with a switch, tuned to static. He gave Representative Hathcock a blast of static, and then shouted over his blustering response with a broad grin: "Can't hear you, Bob, you're out of range!" Then he hung up. He looked up at the young woman standing in the doorway, still grinning broadly. "That asshole, trying to rip off some state trust land for a private club for his boys."

"I hope you'll be careful, Senator. Some of those boys are pretty powerful down there."

He shrugged. Kranhower had been deeply troubled about the killing of state Wildlife Officer Marge Pappas. His own legislative assistant's cousin. He wondered if it could be a coincidence. Or could it be a message, a sign of something far more sinister? Until now he hadn't thought of it in the context of any pending state business. It had been a hunting accident. Or so he'd been told. He'd given Amber Pappas his most heartfelt condolences and the rest of the week off, but she'd returned to work for today's committee meeting. Which had fizzled out anyway when he'd stopped Bob Hathcock and his supporters' little bill rider cold in its tracks.

The bill amendment had been simple enough, and Senator Kranhower was furious with himself for not having spotted it sooner. It forced him to wonder what else Bob Hathcock's cronies had slipped past him lately. He recognized the writing style, he'd seen it often before, and assumed it was that of legislative committee staff. He realized now that Amber Pappas had tried to warn him several times about little bill riders, and he'd dismissed her as an overeager, overly idealistic political novice. But she'd been right. He looked up at her, with reddened eyes from lack of sleep, and told her so.

Amber shrugged, modestly. "Thanks, Senator. I admire your courage in standing up to those people, too. I think that's what happened to my cousin."

He looked at her, and frowned. So she'd been thinking along those lines as well. He had never subscribed to conspiracy theories, and didn't want to start now. "Why? What do you mean?"

"I mean, some of them may be dangerous."

He shook his head, not willing, not wanting to believe it. "Miss Pappas. Are you implying that those people might have something to do with what happened to your cousin?"

"Somebody shot her. Maybe for the same reasons."

He just couldn't buy it. Not yet. It was too terrible to contemplate. "Amber, the police report categorically stated it was an accident."

"I think it wasn't," she said, stubbornly.

"Do you have any proof of what you're saying?"

"No sir, not yet. But my second cousin Lena is a police officer and she's convinced it wasn't. So please. Just watch out, all right?" She forced a smile, to replace his now-vanished one. "I don't want to have to go looking for another job," she finished, blushing as she said it.

He laughed, reached out, and patted her arm. "Somebody's gotta be a damn fool messin' with your family," he said. "Don't you worry about a thing, girl. Anyway, I got no reason to worry, I'm a public official." He laughed.

She didn't. "So was Marge."

He pondered that. Then looked at the phone, thoughtfully. "Amber, could you get hold of my wife? Tell her I'm going to miss dinner tonight. I've got to catch a flight down to Naples."

Amber stared at him, in dismay. "Senator, you're not going down there! All you have to do is not sign the bill, you don't have to talk or explain it to them!"

"I disagree, Miss Pappas. Good government is like a dialogue. Give and take, put all the positions, all the viewpoints on the table, and hash it out. Those people down in Collier— or Hondo, or wherever the hell they are—all claim to be God-fearin' taxpaying citizens. They need to hear what I've got to say."

Amber shook her head, knowing she could not dissuade him. Once Senator Jack Kranhower made his mind up about something, there was no holding him back. That was how he'd gotten elected five decades ago, before Civil Rights—which he later came to actively champion—was even invented. Now it was all property rights. Different strokes, from some very different folks. A lot more dangerous folks, she knew, than those freedom marchers. True, from what she knew about the Hunt Club they were all Chamber of Commerce types. But they also carried guns. And they tended to use them.

61

The Air Florida 727 jet took off—Senator Kranhower on board—arced into the still-chilly Gulf sky just before four-thirty, and banked south to Naples.

It was pitch-dark when the black limousine exited from I-75, and turned east on State Road 80, toward La Belle. Slowing at Patterson's Landing, the limo turned abruptly south on the unmarked macadam, and bore through the darkness toward Hondo County, and finally to the entrance gate of the Caloosa-hatchee Hunt and Gun Club. The gate was down, and an armed guard stood waiting. The guard walked slowly over to the driver's side window, one hand on the top of his side hol-ster. The window slid down with a soft electric hum. "State Representative Hathcock," Cedric, the Black driver, said curtly. The guard frowned at him, and said: "Open the back." Repressing his indignation, Cedric obeyed. The guard looked in, and recognized the legislator. "Sorry sir," he said, with a salute. "Just security precautions."

"Yes, of course," said the representative, with a tight smile. The gate lifted and the limo drove on through the darkness, until there was a sudden explosion of light ahead, and they emerged into the clearing surrounding the vast clubhouse lodge. The limousine glided up under the log portico, and a uniformed doorman stepped forward, to open the rear door.

"Welcome back, sir," the doorman said with a salute, as Representative Hathcock climbed out. He was overweight, and felt it, today. His back was sore from the long ride, and his mood was increasingly apprehensive. He hoped the evening would be mercifully short, and to the point. He would do what he had to do, but he was also aware that the way the members were going to see it, he had failed to do his part. For the first time in his long, undistinguished political career, he felt afraid.

He knew the members would not be in any mood to hear

that their bill had been tabled—by that hated liberal puppet Jack Kranhower. He had a way out, of course, though he hated to do it. What went around came around as the saying goes, and politicians, no matter how dicey things got in the hallways of the capitol, still had to watch each other's backs, it was just the nature of the business. But he had his own skin to worry about, tonight. He would simply throw Kranhower to the wolves. They would chew him alive before the next legislative session even opened. Assuming, of course, that he reopened the government. These ol' boys, he knew, liked having the government shut down. Less regulation. Less interference.

Of course, somebody had to make sure the block grants were handed out, those plush prison contracts, and highway construction plums, things like that. You couldn't have it both ways, he would have to tell them. You can't get rid of government (thereby putting him out of a job) and still expect all the goodies, all the services, all the corporate and agricultural entitlements they were accustomed to. They wouldn't want to hear that, though. Not coming from him. Better stick to the main point, he decided. That Jack Kranhower was holding up the land transfer. Then let the chips fall where they may.

Taking several deep breaths, Representative Bob Hathcock put on his best campaign smile, and went in to face his peers.

8

The hunter's trail ran for miles along the banks of the Caloosahatchee River, one of south Florida's once-pristine but still-beautiful waterways. Now it served as the east-west canal and conduit for the Intra-Coastal Waterway—kind of an Alligator Alley for boats. The river ran from Fort Myers inland past flat farm and ranch lands, trailer parks, and resort developments optimistically proclaiming "waterfront lots." Much of the land to the south was still wilderness. Here, despite the omnipresence of human encroachment, flourished an abundance of living creatures, all vying to exist in a lush, still wild, and seemingly hostile environment. Running east from Fort Myers, the river flowed past big developments and tiny fishing camps to La Belle, then on to Lake Okeechobee, through fifty miles of scrub and slash pine forest, saw palmetto, and saw grass wetlands.

The Caloosahatchee Hunt and Gun Club was about fifteen miles south of the river along a tributary called Punta Creek, situated on high ground that, were any archaeologists to happen into the area (probably at great personal risk) they would have recognized at once to be Indian mounds. The camp had been built in the 1930s as a hunting camp, intended for the rich and idle to bag big Florida game in the utmost of comfort. The main lodge, of red cedar logs and shakes, boasted a main common room with fifty-foot ceilings and vertical multipaned skylights. A solid teak bar ran forty feet in length, with African rosewood bar stools and Connelly leather seats. The walls were lined with big game hunting trophies from all over the world, not just Florida. The taxidermy was flawless. Fierce predators glared menacingly from every wall: a veritable pride of lions and tigers and bears. The latter including a black bear, a grizzly, a polar, and an enormous Alaskan brown. There were also two gorillas, a large rhinoceros, and dominating the room above the main arched entry from the lobby—poised in perpetual rage—towered an African bull elephant, with ten-foot tusks and trunk perpetually looming out into the room like a giant phallic symbol—something not lost on the Club's all-male membership.

"About forty grand in ivory up there," longtime member Everett Wilder once observed, as he lit a cigar, leaned back, and gazed fondly toward the hall entrance. "Helluva waste." The Club members used those tusks for the traditional hat toss, upon entry. You hook the hat, free drinks for the night. You miss, it's one round whoever's at the bar. Sometimes that could be a substantial tab. Luckily (for the membership) in the end, the taxpayers usually footed the bill.

Among the least-prized trophies, however, were actually some of the rarest: six mounted highly illegal heads of the nearly extinct Florida panther. Most had been mounted many years ago. A few were more recent, although the members spoke little as to their origins and existence, of course, because they were now a federally protected species, and the repercussions would be unpleasant. It didn't matter, though, because the members were all of like mind on this issue. All regulators and environmentalists, by Club (as well as local) consensus, were agents of the devil, here to undo God's work. Which was, in the words of member Reverend Sharples, misquoting his favorite Bible passage: "that God made earth for man's use and his pleasure." And herein was the rub: The Club had overgrown its turf, which specifically included a thousand acres of forest and swamp, under special "lease" from the state of Florida. Between the limitations of the seasons (basically November and December for big game, and January through February for small), and lack of free range, the take, or "harvest," as the members called it, had fallen off dramatically in recent years.

Environmentalists blamed poaching and overhunting for the decline, and were demanding that an additional fifty thousand acres of state land adjoining Big Cypress and Corkscrew Swamps be given the protected designation of a State Wildlife Preserve. Club members blamed "outsiders" and "excessive regulation" by the state, and were convinced they could manage it better than "a bunch of gov'ment bureaucrats." They wanted the land for themselves and felt strongly that they should have it.

And so they had sent their usual decree by appropriate messenger to the halls of the state capitol, and now under the hundred constantly watchful glass eyes of the world's preeminent big game trophies, predators far deadlier than those on the walls had descended on the forest in their Range Rovers and Cherokees in anticipation of the result.

The occasion was ostensibly informal: just some "good ol' rest and recreation, Florida-style." But this time, they had come for important business. The bar was abuzz with rumors from Tallahassee. And so, while the members were always elated to be here, always itching to get out into the woods and start shooting, on this particular weekend—actually a three-day holiday squeezed around Presidents' Day—they had come to hear an update from their Executive Board, and then from their man on the scene: their own member, state legislator Bob Hathcock of Naples.

In anticipation of their pending acquisition, and in order to assure security for their enterprise, the Club had already begun fencing off several miles of the land in question with barbed wire, and posting armed guards. And here, too, they had run into a snag. It was merely an unfortunate twist of luck, or (in the view of Club members) demonstration of natural selection, that the land in question, as it happened, was also the very same land—by coincidence—on which lived most of the few remaining Florida panthers. And every time Club members put up fencing, someone was trying to tear it down. Some of the members, especially Quentin Lejeune who also headed up the local militia, were getting pretty angry about it.

Having dined early on steak and venison, gator and crabs, and drunk prodigiously from a well-stocked beer list and wine cellar (hard liquor at the bar only) in the vast paneled dining room, the members were restless this Saturday evening, unwilling to sit through more routine, mundane matters. They listened with barely restrained impatience to the droning recitation of previous minutes, club finances, and other minutia from current Club President Lars Conyers. Lars had been president for two terms now, and remained popular. But he was notoriously boring.

"Come on, Lars, get to the point," urged Wilder, from the bar. This caused an oddly disturbing response from one member, Quentin Lejeune, that drew embarrassed laughs from the younger, more cultivated members. Quentin Lejeune was what only he might get away with calling a "self-styled token redneck," in that he was from a long line of rural Florida settlers. Quentin Lejeune had suffered the misfortune, many years ago, of throat cancer—no doubt merely coincidental to his grudgingly long-since abandoned plug-chewing habit. He was one of the richest and most powerful men in south Florida. But he could only speak in a deep, gutteral whisper. He had a mechanical voice implant in his throat, which he would occasionally use. But he hated the sound, and so used it but rarely. Most of the time he had the services of a spokesman, his farm foreman Rice Crawford. But in keeping with Club rules Crawford was not present. So when at Club functions, he rarely spoke at all. Just now, however, he had emitted a sound—a gutteral, rasping sound that old-timers knew to be a laugh. It made newer members' skin crawl.

Lars hesitated, self-consciously, still uncomfortable with the necessary obligations of office, such as those he was doing his best to perform if they would just let him. Lars owned a chain of tax consulting services, mostly in Lee and Charlotte Counties and had, as his buddies would put it, "done right well." But he was still basically an introverted accountant, and some of the more raucous members couldn't resist reminding him of the fact now and then.

"Sorry, Everett, I'm just trying to do my job," Lars replied, returning to his agenda. The grumble of dissent grew, as the wine flowed and the report droned on. Any of the other members of the Executive Board could have handled the task more easily, but as they'd often pointed out, since Lars had sought and won the office, it was up to him to carry it out.

In addition to Quentin Lejeune, the board included Everett Wilder, recently elected County Sheriff Doran Riker, and the absent Bob Hathcock, whose imminent arrival was eagerly awaited. They knew Bob as a major car dealer from Naples, as well as a six-term state representative, former executive director of the state Chamber of Commerce, and chairman of the powerful House Natural Resources Committee. Quentin Lejeune was a major citrus grower and cattle rancher from Arcadia. Among other things. Everett Wilder owned virtually all of the newspapers and most of the television stations in three central Florida counties. He also owned a dog track, and was chairman of the board of the First Bank of Florida.

A waiter approached the head table, and whispered in

Wilder's ear. Wilder nodded, and nudged Conyers's elbow. "Lars, he's here. Let's get to the business they've been waiting for."

Lars looked flustered. "Of course, Everett." He turned to the room, and announced: "Gentlemen, I'm pleased to announce that Representative Bob Hathcock has arrived." The room erupted in cheers. As the politician entered, beaming and waving to his friends, he wondered how long the cheers would last.

The horizon was an angry red glow out over the Gulf as State Senator Jack Kranhower climbed wearily down the steps from the commuter plane, and hurried across the tarmac to the small terminal building. A driver was waiting at the gate, thanks to Amber, with a car from the state car pool in Naples. It was a simple four-door Taurus sedan, but it would do. Senator Kranhower didn't give a damn about the symbols of power. He didn't need them. He had the real thing. And he'd had it for so long it had become wearisome. And yet he understood full well that now, more than ever before, he needed to wield it. There were forces at work that would strip him of what he held. And in so doing, would strip the state of Florida, the people of Florida, of much, if not most, of its remaining assets.

Senator Kranhower hadn't always felt this way, of course. He'd been a big supporter of free enterprise and the free market in his day. Problem was, there was no more free market. Everything was controlled one way or another. Either by government, or by huge special interests. And what Senator Kranhower had come to discover, very discomfortingly so, was that government was far and away the lesser of the two evils.

Unfortunately, he was headed for a meeting with a powerful group of people who disagreed. Vehemently. He did have one thing going for him, however: the element of surprise. He knew they were expecting Hathcock, their regular errand boy and local mouthpiece. He didn't think they'd be expecting him.

Senator Kranhower was wrong.

When Amber Pappas called long-distance from the senator's offices in the state capitol, someone was listening. Someone who's job it was to monitor long-distance calls through the state switching system. Especially calls made from certain offices. Amber had called her cousin Lena, followed by a call to the state motor pool, which had put her through to Naples. When the motor pool officer asked for the senator's arrival time and destination that evening, she told him: eight o'clock. The Caloosahatchee Hunt and Gun Club.

That was also the person on the other end of the line needed to know. He made a call of his own: also long-distance.

9

SATURDAY NIGHT

State Representative Bob Hathcock was finally beginning to relax. It had taken a couple of bourbons, sipped underneath the angry elephant head that ruled over the teakwood bar. He was now waxing effusive. "It all has to do with property rights, that's right," he nodded to Frank Bowers, a pending new Club member. The impeccable Everett Wilder listened, from two drinks over. Hathcock wanted Wilder to listen—Wilder controlled most of the mass media in this part of Florida. Hathcock was reasonably sure he had Wilder in his pocket. Wilder, looking at him in sage bemusement, was reasonably sure of the same thing. Wilder threw Hathcock a smile, and gave an imperceptible nod to Luke, the bartender. Luke beamed, and poured the representative a fresh bourbon. Wilder was buying.

Neophyte member Frank Bowers, his scalp visibly burned and bald on top, even though he wasn't yet forty, shook his head emphatically at what Bob Hathcock was saying. "If I may say so, sir," he said, frowning, "this is more than rights. Basic fundamental personal freedoms are what's at stake. They take away our golf courses today, they'll take our guns tomorrow. Then our land next."

"This," Hathcock reminded him, "is about the state giving away land, not taking it."

"But it's ours in the first place," insisted Bowers. "We the people, own the land. It says so right there in the Constitution of the United States." At least, he hoped it did.

"That's fine," interjected another member, Ron Thurman, farther down the bar. "The only problem is, how to divide it up."

"I'm going to talk about that very thing, tonight," promised Hathcock.

"I can hardly wait," said Wilder.

Bowers looked from one to the other, slack-jawed.

There was a bustle of activity at the far end of the bar. A messenger, one of the young Club apprentices, had just entered, and was speaking urgently to the bartender, who nodded in the direction of Hathcock and Wilder. He hurried toward the three men. "Mr. Hathcock," the young blond man said, breathlessly. "A message for you." He handed Hathcock a folded sheet of paper. The representative gave the young man a fiver from the bar and unfolded the message. He read it quickly, then looked up abruptly at the others, suddenly sober. "Senator Kranhower is coming," he announced.

" 'Tax-and-Spend' Kranhower is coming here?" gasped Bowers, scarcely able to contain his glee. "He must be a bigger fool than we thought!"

"I wonder," murmured Wilder, finishing his gin and tonic. He set the glass down and turned to search the room for someone sufficiently dignified to drink with.

Hathcock considered the implications. He'd been all set to blame Kranhower for the holdup on the land transfer. But if the senator was coming here, it might mean he'd changed his mind. He'd better hold off on the flaying and filleting until he knew more.

Frank Bowers, however—not yet even a member—had some other ideas. He waved to his mentor and membership sponsor, Club Marshall Quentin Lejeune, in his customary seat at the end of the bar.

"Mr. Lejeune, you're not gonna believe this," Frank shouted, waving for another Wild Turkey. He hurried over to tell Quentin his idea. Lejeune mulled it over, savored it a bit, and finally nodded, a glint in his steely eyes. Bowers let out a rebel yell and slapped his hand on the bar. "Eeeeeeee-haaaaa! Let's do it!" he announced. Several of the older members gave him disapproving looks, but he didn't notice. Soon word was spread through the Club like a prairie fire, and the members, chuckling and grim-faced alike, headed for their lockers, or their cars.

Everett Wilder watched them go, shaking his head. It was a harebrained idea, something the Young Turks would think up, but ultimately futile. They were lucky the rules forbade media, or he'd have loved to see the footage—let alone air it. Although it would have meant giving up his membership in the Club, he felt for a moment it might just be worth it. If nothing else, he was far too dignified to participate. "I'll watch from the bar," he informed Lars Conyers, when the Club president hurried over. "I can see better from here."

It was nearly eight o'clock when the Ford Taurus pulled into the parking lot, outside the Hunt Club. It was a chill winter night, and Senator Jack Kranhower could smell the hickory smoke billowing from the huge stone chimney that dominated the north wall. The big multipaned windows were ablaze with light, but too high to see in through.

The driver opened the door, and Kranhower wearily turned and set his feet on the ground. He felt his age, suddenly. But something more. There was something in the stillness, and the chill, that made him involuntarily shudder a moment. He looked up and caught his breath. The sky was sharp and clear, the stars brilliant and close. He stopped a moment to admire them, glittering above the forest canopy, oblivious to the foibles of man.

"Shall I wait, sir?" the driver asked.

"I'd appreciate it," the senator told him, and slipped him a twenty. He walked toward the entrance. They'd know he was here by now, he figured. The gatekeeper had called in over the intercom. But his hope remained that the element of surprise would still be with him, to the point that they would not have time to prepare a planned and organized welcome.

Once again, he was wrong.

He was greeted at the door by a brief hello from Lars Conyers, Club president, who informed him the members had just finished dinner, and he could speak to them in the dining room. Lars and another younger member held the double oak doors. Kranhower entered, and stopped short, feeling his chest seize up a moment, his pulse soar. He fumbled for his glycerin pills, and found one. A waiter standing nearby had the presence of mind to hand him a glass of water.

"I'm okay," Kranhower heard himself saying, and took a deep breath. He held his head up and walked to the podium, refusing to further acknowledge the manner with which they'd greeted him. What he'd just seen. He didn't look at anyone except the bejowled, grinning visage of Bob Hathcock up at the podium. He felt himself moving as though in a dream. A bad dream. He reached the dais at last.

"Hello, Bob," he said, and turned at last to face the expectant membership of the Caloosahatchee Hunt and Gun Club. All of whom were, at this very moment, demonstrating their constitutional right to bear arms. Each and every man held an authentic Continental Army musket in their right hand, butt on the floor, muzzle pointing upward. At a signal— this delivered by Quentin Lejeune—they all lifted their weapons. And aimed them straight at Jack Kranhower.

"Senator Kranhower," shouted Bob Hathcock, into the microphone. "We've been waiting for you!"

The sound of a hundred loud clicks echoed around the vast room. Kranhower turned toward the sound, and found himself staring down the barrels of one hundred and seven now cocked-and-raised flintlocks. The shock rocked him. If he'd been more lucid, less fatigued and stressed, he might have found it funny. Or have been amused by the fact that the "revolutionaries" he faced—in addition to being the well-to-do civic leaders of southwest Florida—were threatening to shoot him with approximately 1.4 million dollars worth of antiques. He recovered quickly, although his heart had taken another hard blow, and he could feel its rickety pumps racing. Logically, he figured that these card-carrying citizens would not take to murdering him, at least not outright in front of a hundred-odd witnesses (albeit most were also pointing guns at him). Surely insanity hadn't gone that far, even down here along the toxic (in more ways than one) upper western fringes of the Everglades.

The very notion of society's greatest beneficiaries taking to arms against their own government would seem absurd, were it not happening. It was the same logic, he concluded, whereby so many of his colleagues up in Washington could be a part of the government, and still denounce it and fawn and pander to reactionary armed militias bent on overthrowing it. While both hands remained deep in that same government's pocket. Even more strange, he'd always felt, was how these same spokesmen for "arming the people" against the government, were so vociferous about arming the military branch of the very government they professed to despise with bigger, better, and more weapons than ever. It didn't make sense, to him. Unless somebody knew something he didn't about the loyalties of the armed forces of the United States of America.

Trying not to let his hand shake, Senator Kranhower took

the microphone from Representative Hathcock, telling himself it was imperative that he ask those very questions of these folks, and what better time than the present. Perhaps sensing what was coming, Hathcock stepped back, wishing there was room to step back a whole lot more.

"You boys should be careful," said Kranhower, in his folksy Cracker drawl, as he looked around and met as many steely gazes as he could in those few moments. "Those things could go off." The "boys" (most of whom were gray-haired business executives) held steady, bent on staring him down. "This kind of reminds me of this boy back home," Kranhower continued, determined to hang in there no matter what. "He lights up this big ol' firecracker, and he's holdin' it and holdin' it there in his hand, until all his friends are shoutin': 'Throw it away!' 'Throw it away!' But he just keeps holdin' on, with this big ol' grin on his face like some of the ones I see out there, until finally he looks around and says: 'Hey! What's the problem? Ain't nothin' happened yet!' "

The room rippled with a groundswell of chuckles, led by Everett Wilder over at the bar—the only man aside from the help noticeably unarmed.

"Senator Kranhower! We the people hereby take back our government," shouted one of the younger members, in front.

"Get out of government, Kranhower! Your time is over!" shouted another, from the middle of the room. There were more shouts, a few of them overt threats, but most just attempts at intimidation.

"The boys, as you see, have a message for you, Senator," said Bob Hathcock, with an apologetic grin. "They wanted to make sure you got it."

"What would that message be, Bob, could you clarify it for me?" Kranhower said, trying to keep the sarcasm out of his voice. Not to mention the gnawing fear that he couldn't quite suppress.

"That the people want less government!"

"Then I tell you what, Bob," proposed Kranhower, hanging on to the microphone for all it was worth. "I would be more than happy to tender my resignation to the governor, if that's what 'the people' really want," he added, amid shouts of triumph, around the hall. "On one condition, which I'm sure you'll appreciate."

Hathcock looked nervous. "What would that be, Senator?"

"That you, as the presiding elected official at this little kangaroo court of yours"—he ignored the angry shouts at that—"resign along with me." More angry shouts. "We'll go fishin', and leave the governin' to these folks." By now most of the guns had already been lowered. If nothing else, Kranhower noted in amusement, the members' wrists were getting tired.

There was a snort of laughter from the direction of the bar, from one well-dressed gentleman armed only with a bourbon and water. A number of the expressions—until now steely gazes—sheepishly wavered a bit among the black-tie crowd. But the guns remained at the ready.

"This land you're standing on belongs to Hondo County, Senator!" shouted Frank Bowers, trying to regain the upper hand. "The state of Florida has had enough free usage. We want it back!"

"Free usage?" queried Kranhower, giving Frank a puzzled look. He glanced up at the high-molded ceiling, and the row after row of mounted heads. He figured they would love nothing better than to add his own to their collection, if they could get away with it.

Being young and petulant, Bowers wasn't quite beaten yet. "I speak for the defenders of the Constitution, Senator!" he shouted. "It is our intent and purpose to keep government in check. You may consider yourself under citizen's arrest!"

"On what charges, exactly?" asked Kranhower, no longer surprised by anything.

"For attempting to usurp the legitimate rights that belong to we the people!" shouted Bowers.

"Oh, please. Last I heard, we held elections in this state," said Kranhower, feeling anger of his own welling up. "And I for one was elected in a legal public election—"

"Not by us!" shouted Bowers.

"—by the people from my district, to represent all citizens of the state of Florida. Maybe you should read *our* Constitution. Then get out your dictionaries, and look up the word *usurp*."

"I think what the boys are sayin', Jack," said Bob Hathcock, hastily, "is that if you aren't gonna give them their land back, they're gonna take it back."

"That would be ironic, considering that it was never theirs to begin with," snapped Kranhower. He turned once more to face the hostile crowd.

Kranhower knew his brave front was not going to hold up much longer. His body was not going to hold up much longer. The hostility in the air was genuine, and tangible. These people believed their own rhetoric, that they did indeed consider themselves the new patriots, and he was representative of a newly perceived tyranny. But he had to finish what he came for. He just hoped the message he'd tried to get through, had in fact gotten through. And would be acted upon. Because if he allowed these people to intimidate him, the wolves that already prowled the halls of the capitol would be on his throat. Then he may as well let them shoot him here, and now.

"Gentlemen," he announced, gripping the microphone once again, trying to buy some time. "Your concerns are duly noted, and I'll take them up as soon as my colleague here, Representative Hathcock, sees fit to reopen the government. Meanwhile, I strongly advise you not to start cutting any trees."

Qeuntin Lejeune, in the back of the room, looked on in silence and shook his head in disgust. He would have spat if he could. The only thing young Bowers was accomplishing was to make a fool of himself. He himself had other gators to skin.

He kept quiet, eyed both politicians in amusement, and drank his Jack Daniel's.

"Put your toys down, fellas, you've made your point," pleaded Hathcock, sensing maybe he'd allowed things to go further than they should have. Those few remaining stalwarts obeyed, some sheepish, some sullen.

Frank Bowers was the last to lower his prized Gaston-Renault musket that he'd bought instead of a new roof for his house, last year. He felt angry, and confused. There were folks hereabouts, he knew, who wouldn't have backed down so fast. Who weren't afraid of the big bad government wolf. He wondered what had gone wrong.

"Okay, fellas, your unity of resolve here is impressive," the senator resumed, recovering his sense of calm, and purpose. "But misguided. Let me remind you of a little bit of history. This was all Indian land before any of you came along. Then came de Soto and ol' Ponce de León. Then the English and Spanish took turns sinkin' each other's ships and swappin' jewels and ownership along with a bunch of pirates, until the government, that's right, the government of the United States of America stepped in and purchased the whole territory from Spain. Of course the U.S. Army then had to come in and run out the Seminoles, which they did, and we became a state, back in 1845. 'Course then came the War between the States as y'all like to call it, which we lost, so we're still a state. Which I for one am glad of, otherwise what's left of it would've been turned over to the swamp peddlers a long time ago!" There was another angry murmur from the real estate and development contingent, and several muskets were cocked once again.

"Sorry, fellas," he continued, with a brief wave of apology. "Heat of the moment. So now you say it should be county land. But what you are really saying is that it should be *your* land. You see, my problem is, whether it's federal land or state land or county land, the one thing it never was, is your land. So, gentlemen, I'm sorry, but I just can't see handing out five million dollars' worth of state-owned land without a fight."

There was renewed uproar in the room, and once again the threat of violence churned in the air like a hot Okeechobie updraft. Suddenly there was a loud whistle, from the direction of the bar. It was Everett Wilder. All eyes turned toward him, and the room fell silent.

"Good Lord," he said, shaking his head. "I sure as hell wish I could've had a camera crew down here. You fellas might've handed Senator Kranhower here the next governorship of the state, with that little display."

"I don't think so!" shouted Bowers, and the uproar arose once again, but this time it was member against member, and many of the considered leaders were engaging Wilder or Bowers in hot discussion.

The attempted coup (if that's what it really was, the senator would wonder long afterward) was over. Under Lars Conyers's embarrassed supervision, the guns were carried out of the dining room in stacks. The Club had just settled down again to resume drinking when a shot rang out. Kranhower dived instinctively for cover behind the bar. Pandemonium reigned once again, for a brief moment. An older Club member in the back of the dining room bent over and sheepishly picked up the gun he had just dropped. "Sorry, fellas," he wheezed. The room erupted into laughter.

Kranhower had won. But what his enemies didn't know— couldn't know—was that he'd paid a stiff price. His heart was on the verge of failure. Helped to his feet by several Club members, now ready to resume civility and buy him a drink, he had to pull away, waving his hands in an apologetic thanks-but-no-thanks, dismissal. He just hoped he could make it back to the car before he collapsed.

He felt someone at his elbow, and a low voice. "Senator, if

you'll come this way." He looked up at the middle-aged busboy standing there. He had a sandy-colored ponytail, and a tanned weather-scarred face. He didn't look much like a busboy, actually, (he didn't look like a Club member either) but he wore a uniform and apron, and was carrying a tray. It had a Kirin beer balanced in the center and no glass.

"They told your driver he could go," Tony Lowell informed him. "I guess they thought they might keep you hostage or something clever like that. Luckily I have a car in the back."

Kranhower didn't hesitate. He turned, and followed the strange interloper into the kitchen, before anyone could react. His knees were already beginning to buckle. Lowell half-carried the old pol outside, helped him into his still-ticking old Impala, and took off. Kranhower's last thought before blacking out was he hoped his other driver was all right.

Lowell pulled over as soon has he had some distance from the Club, scrambled into the back of the car, and checked the senator's pulse and breathing. Both were erratic, but discernable. He fumbled into the senator's pockets, and found the little nitro pills. He put one under the senator's tongue, and the old man woke up.

"Son of a gun!" he gasped. "Where the hell am I?" He squinted at Lowell. "And who the hell are you?"

Lowell jumped back in the front and resumed driving, before telling him. "The name's Tony Lowell, Senator. It's a long story, but I'm working for a police officer, who also happens to be related to your legislative assistant, not to mention the state Wildlife Officer who was killed down here yesterday."

Kranhower shook his head, trying to get it all straight. "How did you get in there?" the old politician asked, breathlessly.

"Back way," said Lowell with a grin. "They don't want the help using the gate. Bad for their image. The service road isn't guarded."

"So much," said Kranhower, "for the security afforded by

a couple hundred loaded rifles." He threw back his head, and laughed and laughed. Which rapidly deteriorated into coughing and wheezing.

"Easy, sir, I think you just had a mild heart attack."

"It wasn't the first," said Kranhower, dismissing the subject. "I had another one the minute I walked into that place. You suppose those old firesticks were actually loaded?"

"I don't know." Lowell wondered the same thing himself. Typically, Bedrosian hadn't warned him about that part, when he'd called her the second time, shortly after she'd gotten a frantic call from Amber, her other cousin. On the other hand, he should have figured that any place that called itself a gun club probably had a few lying around.

"You own a gun, Senator?" Lowell asked after a while, as he sped onto State Road 80, and turned south to Fort Myers.

"You kidding?" laughed Kranhower. "I'd probably shoot somebody!"

Lowell, of course, felt the same way. "You're quite a man for a politician, Senator," he told him.

"Hell, I ain't no politician," gasped Kranhower, waving the thought aside. "I'm just a country lawyer tryin' to make a little sense out of chaos."

Lowell decided to override the senator's orders, and instead of dropping him off at the Hyatt Hotel near the airport, he took him straight into Fort Myers and the County Hospital. From there, he needed to call Lena, and check in with his friend Perry. Perry had a cockamamie scheme he'd cooked up with Billy Patterson for the next day, and wanted to borrow Lowell's camera. Lowell didn't like the sound of it. But he hadn't been able to talk him out of it. He just hoped he'd have a chance to do so now.

10

Superintendent Dave Connors wiped his ruddy, freckled brow in frustration. He was beginning to understand how his top Freshwater Fish and Game Officer Marge Pappas must have felt, her last day on Earth. He was supposed to be getting paid, even though he wasn't allowed to report to work, thanks to the budget impasse in Tallahassee. He didn't mind working. He just wished those clowns in the state legislature felt the same way. Always squabbling over the fine print, nickels and dimes, this and that little issue. All any of it ever had to do with was special favors for special interests, anyway.

While the shenanigans of politicians and their cronies never surprised him too much, he was bewildered by what was going on here in his own corner of the swamp. First, that horrible loss of Marge. That was really troubling. Even more troubling, was the official response. It was almost as though Marge Pappas didn't count, was expendable to larger matters. Like she had never existed. The investigating officers had disappeared faster than a falling rock in a swamp glade. There'd been a small article in a couple of Tampa Bay and Sarasota papers. But the local ones had buried the story in the Sunday obituary section. "Wildlife Officer killed in accidental shooting," read the Naples paper. As for the sheriff, he didn't even return calls.

The day of the shutdown, last Friday, and the day before he got word about Marge, Connors had been so upset about the budget impasse he had even called the local state representative's office. He knew the man slightly, from occasional brief encounters out on the "range," which is what local hunters tended to call their region of the state forest. State representative Bob Hathcock had sold the state a fleet of cars, including the pickups and 4 × 4 Cherokee he drove. He supposedly wielded tremendous influence on where state money got spent and on what.

He also belonged to the Caloosahatchee Hunt and Gun Club, where a lot of the biggies hung out, Connors knew. Connors stayed away from Club lands on principle: there was always a tendency for bullets to be flying, even though they were supposed to stick to the designated shooting range, outside of hunting season.

That was another reason he had a bad feeling about Marge's death. She'd been a little too far from Hunt Club property—in adjacent Collier County, actually—when she was found to have been a victim of a stray bullet. Forensics could probably have confirmed that, had there been any forensics. Instead, she'd been scooped up and hauled away like so much road kill. It wasn't right. In fact, it stank.

When he'd finally gotten through, state representative Hathcock's secretary told him the representative was out of town for a fund-raiser, but was due back for budget meetings next week, and yes, he was always happy to take questions from constituents.

"I'd like to know how long this damn work furlough is gonna last," Connors growled.

"Yes, sir, the representative is very concerned about that. He feels the ball is now in the senate's court, however. And if you would care to call the Senate Office, I'd be happy to give you the number—"

"Never mind," grumbled Connors, and hung up. Politicians. One thing he just couldn't abide, was politicians. It was one thing he and Marge used to argue about during their long routine patrols into Big Cypress, and the western Everglades. She was a big believer in the "system," as she called it. Talked all the time about "checks and balances." What checks and balances? The only checks he had were about to bounce. And as for balances, if this damn furlough didn't end soon, he wasn't gonna have one. Not in his bank account, anyway.

And now, he was getting the same runaround from local law enforcement in regard to what had happened to Marge.

It was cold this morning. A Canadian high had blown down out of Manitoba, pushing thin icy air across the Great Plains, south through the delta, and clear across the choppy turquoise waters of the Gulf of Mexico, penetrating like a frozen scalpel into the heart of the south Florida wilderness. Of course low forties counted as icy, hereabouts. But it had gotten down into the thirties last night, which had probably been hard on a lot of the animals. As well, Connors reflected, as a lot of the farmers. Oddly enough, a lot of them tended to complain to him, blame him even, as though he had any say in the matter. It was because he worked for the government.

He wondered about that guy Lowell that Marge's cop cousin from Manatee had sent down, the one with the Indian buddy. Lowell was a private investigator of some kind. Looked more like a hippy outlaw to Connors, but then you never knew who the good guys were anymore anyway, these days. If Lieutenant Bedrosian trusted Tony Lowell, he supposed maybe he could, too. He fished in his wallet for the tattered card Lowell had given him and walked across the ranger cabin to the only telephone. His phone line was dead. Damn! That meant a drive all the way up to Patterson's Landing, and the pay phone. Probably the weather front last night, he decided. The winds had been heavy as the moisture from the previous week's rainstorm had been pushed southward by the arctic air coming in. Gusts of up to forty miles per hour had probably knocked down a wire somewhere along the route. Connors didn't envy the line workers who would have to trace it and fix it in the cold.

On the other hand, Connors didn't envy what he was going to have to do either—with no backup. There was a certain county road a few miles south, that ran through Cypress Strand, part of the state preserve that was supposedly under his supervision. The wildlife and parks people had been desperate for years to get the road closed because it was being used as an expressway for poachers. Unfortunately, in Hondo, Hendry, and Collier Counties, poaching was a way of life. There was another problem that complicated matters. The road began in a county park, the Caloosahatchee River County Park, which served as a virtual parking lot for the poaching that was going on, on state land. The Hendry and Hondo County Commissions had for years turned deaf ears to the problem, until the state had finally demanded that they close the road to protect the wildlife in the preserve. The Hondo County Commissioners had voted six to zero to keep the road open. He'd gotten a report of an illegal gathering of hunters planned for this afternoon, at that same county park. So now, with Marge Pappas gone, it was Dave Connors's unhappy job to deal with it.

The sun was already low over the prairie east of the swamps when he took his sandwiches, loaded them into his backpack, and went out to the Jeep. He had just gotten the cold engine running when he noticed the black sedan coming along the two-track road toward the Ranger Station. The narrow dirt road was a one-way loop. The sedan was coming the wrong way.

Connors stepped out to wave the car down, and was met with a loud honk and shouts of derision as the driver gunned the engine. He barely got out of the way as four teenage boys sped past leaving a trail of dust, catcalls, cigarettes,and beer cans in their wake. Connors glared after them in impotent rage, and swore. Their hostility washed over him like a passing squall. But how the hell are the damn teens going to learn any manners, he pondered, let alone respect for the law, when their parents act the same way?

The Family Protection Patrol, as they called themselves, was enjoying a beautiful afternoon at the Caloosahatchee River County Park. The parking lot had been full for hours: mostly pickups, but also a lot of RVs, a few camper vans, even a few cars. Country music was the order of the day, blaring through portable low-fidelity speakers. Confederate flags flew from CB antennas on top of pickups, or were displayed like banners in rear windows, or on front license plate holders. There were no American flags flying, at this event. Sponsored by the local churches, it was billed as a "patriotic Christian family event," and they'd all come prepared. Most were from the Caloosahatchee Christian Church, but there were plenty of Baptists, Methodists, and even some Lutherans in attendance. It was planned as a "take back the park" event, jointly sponsored by the Christian Evangelical Churches of Lee and Hondo Counties, and the local chapter of the National Rifle Association.

"Take Back the Park Day," as it was called, had resulted from several complaints, in recent months, about Cubans, Blacks, and other undesirables from Dade and Broward or some of the Gulf Coast cities, who had been coming out here in increasing numbers, mostly to fish, but also to do, as the good White church people would say, "God knows what all else." The sheriff had already busted two carloads of tough urban teens, most certainly gang members according to Reverend Whitson from Christian Evangelical, in Fort Myers. The reverend had it on good authority that Black and Cuban street gangs were trying to gain a toehold in "God's Country," in order to peddle their drugs and commit crimes. And so the troops had been called out.

And troops they were. Nobody at "Take Back the Park" day had bothered to lock their cars or trucks, for good reason. Virtually everyone present above the age of fifteen was armed for today's church picnic. Camouflage clothing was, if not de rigueur, definitely prevalent. As off-duty Sheriff's Deputy Doug Kohler from neighboring Collier County slyly put it to his pals: "Let 'em try and steal somethin' from one of us. Just let 'em try." That had gotten a good laugh from the boys. Especially the reverend, who had a great sense of humor.

One Black family had just been starting a cookout near the north end of the lot, close to the playground, when the first of the church groups arrived. They left quickly, hurried along their way by a few harmless gunshots. Peggy Whitson was a little upset about that and complained to her husband, pointing out it wasn't a good example for the young folks, shooting at people with children like that, but she was overheard by some of the boys and hooted down. "Well, you do have a point," laughed Jerry Laker, a poor cousin of a major meatpacking family. "Now they cain't say we took the park back without no shots bein' fired no more, can they?"

The picnickers all had another good laugh at that, as they went about their business, firing up the barbecue grills. Reverend Whitson had brought a portable microphone and speaker, and had a few words to say about freedom and the importance of accepting Jesus as your savior. He then turned the podium (comprised of two cases of beer stacked on the end of the same picnic bench recently vacated by the Black family) over to Rice Crawford. Rice Crawford was head foreman for Lejeune Farms. And as everyone knew, Quentin Lejeune was just about the biggest big shot in the county, if not the state, because he owned forty-seven thousand acres of range land as well as twenty thousand more of prime citrus groves, but still considered himself a regular ol' boy. Also, while not actually here, Quentin Lejeune was the principal sponsor of the Hondo County Militia, run by Rice Crawford, his personal spokesman. And, as adjunct commander of said militia, Rice was here today actively recruiting new members.

"Frens, we got a crisis in this country, and you know it and I know it," Crawford began, to loud cheers. "It has t'do with too much gov'ment, too many damn taxes, and people tryin' to take your freedoms away and mine." There were lots of lusty cheers at his words, and a few shots were fired for emphasis. He went on, about the Second Amendment to the Constitution, and about how no gov'ment had no right to take nothin' away from no God-fearin' 'Murcan citizen. And so on. "We stand here," he told them, "against tyranny. But also against the ungodliness of globalism, and liberalism, and relativism, and humanism, and that new communist conspiracy, the New World Order!" He'd heard about that just last week on his favorite radio talk show.

"Amen!" shouted the reverend, and the crowd roared their approval. Finally, a fired-up Crawford surrendered the podium to the good Reverend Whitson. "Thank you, Commander Crawford," said the reverend. "Friends, you know and I know that we do God's work here, in our fight against government tyranny and the insidious workings of Satan. Just as Jesus did against Pontius Pilate, so do we against the tyrants in Washington, and Tallahassee! Now Satan," he went on, "would have you believe that government is good, that taxation is right, that a godless sinner has every bit as much right to walk this land as you or I. But let me tell you, my friends!" he shouted. "You know, and I know that it ain't so!"

They roared again, and drank some more, and Quentin Lejeune's illustrious spokesman Rice Crawford once more regaled the troops, while the Whitson family dug into their feast—thick-cut steaks, a whole fresh grouper, and two dozen all-beef Lejeune Farms hot dogs for any hungry kids who

91

might happen along. And the Whitson's table was ready way before anyone else's, thanks to the fresh coals—all ready and glowing like God himself had provided them—left behind by the Black family that had so quickly departed. The preheated grill was seen as sort of an honorary entitlement, they being from the church and so close to Jesus and all, the way the others generously figured it.

Someone in the back had a question. It was young Billy Patterson, who'd been busy taking pictures. He was standing beside a 4 × 4 that had quietly driven up. He was standing beside a suspicious-looking dark-skinned man, whom nobody had noticed up until then. "Mr. Crawford," shouted Billy. "Are you sayin' all this land should be given back to the people the government took it away from?"

"You got that right, son!" yelled Crawford, and the picnickers roared enthusiastically.

At that moment Billy's companion stepped forward. "In that case," announced Perry Garwood in a voice that stunned everyone into silence, "this land is mine, and I want all of you to get off now!"

It was as though someone had dropped a giant snowball on the whole picnic. There was instant icy chill, as all eyes turned their astonished fiery hatred on the dark-skinned interloper.

"What's that you say?" asked Rice Crawford, in disbelief.

"I say, this was all Indian land, before the government took it. So if the government is going to give it back, it goes to me and my people," replied Perry. "And since your ancestors have killed off most of my people around here, that leaves me."

Lowell had objected vociferously, when Perry had told him his plan, and then insisted on coming along. Perry had turned him down on both counts. "You'd just get in the way," he insisted. "Hell, you're a damn peacenik!"

Perry had accomplished his effect. Billy snapped one last frame with Lowell's Nikon, and looked at him with expectant admiration. Both knew they only had seconds, while the slower minds in the crowd summoned up a response, presumably from the now churning, beer-sodden depths of a hundred swollen bellies. There was a roar of rage, and surge of movement in Perry and Billy's direction. The two were into Perry's 4-Runner in a moment, tires spinning gravel into the faces of those who were upon them first. In moments they were out of there. Somebody fired a couple of parting shots after them, just to let them know they couldn't pull a stunt like that and get away with it without some kind of response from the local righteous.

A number of the boys wanted to go after them, as they sped away. But most were too drunk to find their car keys. "Let 'em go," ordered Rice Crawford. "We know who one of 'em is, anyways."

All eyes turned toward a bench near the woods, where Duvall Patterson felt almost overwhelmed by shame, mixed with rage. He'd tried to be a good parent, Lord knew. Tried to teach 'im good Southern family values. When to load, when not to load. When to fold, when not to fold. How to speak respectful to one's elders. Not to spit at the dinner table. And now this! It made him want to cry. In fact it did make him cry. Duvall Patterson's deepest darkest most shameful secret was the unhappy fact that he cried at the drop of a hat. Reverend Whitson's fiery sermons, talk radio's inspirational oratories, never failed to reduce him to tears. A good country song left him sobbing. What kind of a man could he be, to be so prone to tears? And now, in public! He felt his wife's eyes on him. She was stronger than he was, he knew, which shamed and humiliated him all the more.

Billy's presence at the picnic had caught him off guard. Billy had begged off earlier that morning, considering himself too old for picnics. But his real reasons for not wanting to go were entirely different. Duvall had reacted to his son's rebellion with typical indignation. "You think you're too good for a family picnic, is that it?" he had shouted, as Billy retreated.

"No, Dad, I just have stuff I gotta do," protested Billy, heading for the door. "I'm going to go look for a job."

"Like hell," swore Duvall. "You and them other punks got no respect for your elders, got no respect for God, or your own family! Besides, it's Sunday!" Duvall felt completely helpless in situations like this. His wife, Betty, had made him stop hitting children a long time ago, on threat of turning him in to child welfare. She gave him a warning look. "Now, honey, I'm just tryin' to—aw hell!" He started to protest. Instead, she reduced him to tears with a look. Trying to regain face, he'd turned once more on his son. Or at least, in the direction his son had just vanished. He screamed after him: "That does it, Billy boy! Don't be expectin' no favors from your old man no more, boy! And don't show your face no more unless you plan on workin' for a livin'!"

"That's what he said he was going to do," Betty said, softly.

This had happened that morning, while they were packing the big camper. Soon it was forgotten for the most part, as the picnic resumed. Duvall, once his dignity was restored, even tried his hand at volleyball, to get his mind off things. The church group had set up a regular volleyball court. The idea had come from the Perkinses, who'd moved here from southern California to get away from all the crime and "illegals." Bill Perkins was already a manager at Hathcock Pontiac and Chevrolet, over in Naples. Soon he and his wife, Kimberly, were busily teaching volleyball to the descendants of Crackers and Cajuns, people whose sports acumen had heretofore been limited to shooting, fishing, football, and golf (if they had any money). The kids took to it right off, spiking balls left and right in no time, although the beer drinkers began to get belligerent after a while—particularly the young males. They were just itching for somebody to show up and try to butt in on their park, their day. Especially somebody from Dade or Broward. Especially somebody with dark skin and an attitude.

Dave Connors approached the gathering with increasing

trepidation, and considered foregoing his planned intervention. After all, he was technically on furlough, why risk his neck for next to nothing? Yet in the aftermath of Marge's shooting, he felt duty-bound. Someone had to look after the parks and preserves or there wouldn't be any left before long.

He pulled into the parking lot, and spotted Rice Crawford's Range Rover. Crawford would be in charge, he knew, simply based on his stature. He was right-hand man to the man who literally owned most of the county. Maybe Crawford would listen to reason, and ask the boys to curb the poaching. But he doubted it. Crawford was a regular firebrand. Or more accurately, "firecracker."

Connors got out of his Cherokee, ignoring the barbs and comments, and sought out the militia commander.

"Afternoon, Mr. Crawford," he began, approaching Rice's table—strewn with the remains of a simple repast, he noticed, of hot dogs and chili.

"Was till you got here," quipped Crawford, with a wink to his usual crowd of sycophants.

"Listen, I'd appreciate it if you'd ask the boys to go easy on the wildlife," Connors began.

"Why, the gov'nor worried about losin' the only support he's got left down here?" retorted Crawford. The boys chuckled appreciatively.

Connors smiled politely. "It's the law, Rice. You oughta be able to relate to that, at least."

Crawford shrugged. "I read the Constitution and the Articles of Confederation," he said, surprising everyone within earshot. "My grandpappy worked for a man who was one of the founders of this state, in whose footsteps I have followed. I think I know a little bit about the law." With that he turned his back on Connors, and resumed eating. With a sigh, Connors walked back to his Cherokee, got in, backed out, and drove on into the woods along the fire road.

The day waxed and then waned, and the men got drunker,

satisfied with their outing but somehow at some visceral level wanting more. They began taking out their guns and wandering into the forest. The fact that the warden had just stopped by asking them to cool it only served to fire their appetites. The fact that hunting season was long gone, was irrelevant. This was their land, their park, their country, and they had a right to bear arms that was right there in the Constitution, which their own leader had actually even read. Some of the boys took to capping beer bottles, tossed out over the river or into the water. Soon a cacophony of shots and shattering glass echoed along the river banks, and far into the woods and wetlands.

At the radioed request of Dave Connors, a Florida State Highway Patrol officer named Nolan Higgins stopped by, close to dusk, and reluctantly asked the reverend to curb the shooters. But by then the reverend was too drunk to notice and cheerfully mumbled something about boys being boys. Higgins looked around in irritation for someone sober enough to talk to. The good Christians were just having a good time, and weren't hurting nothing, Rice Crawford assured him. Officer Higgins sensed a certain tension in the air, a murmuring of antigovernment attitudes. He was government, in the eyes of many of those present. Now he knew how Connors had felt. And maybe that other Wildlife Officer, too. The one who'd gotten killed.

Officer Nolan Higgins had a quandary: How do you get a large number of drunken men, already inflamed with rhetoric about the Second Amendment and government conspiracies and property rights, all of whom were in possession of firearms to stop discharging them (since there was no legal shooting range in the vicinity) and lay them down? Higgins knew that random bullets could be just as deadly as well-aimed ones, should they happen to come in contact with living flesh. But Higgins had no desire to take on a mob, and decided on discretion in favor of valor. Getting back into his patrol car, he quietly left the scene, calling his report in to headquarters by radio but taking no further action.

"You did the right thing, Nolan," dispatcher Angie Fuller told him. "Those folks can get pretty crazy."

"Well, they've taken over a county park, maybe you should mention this to the sheriff."

"I'll do that, Nolan, but I doubt he's gonna do anything. You better take care out there."

Duvall Patterson watched the trooper leave, with some satisfaction. He finished off the last of his blood-rare porterhouse steak, and hurled an angry belch in the general direction of his wife, Betty. Duvall Patterson had arrived at the park in a foul mood, which hadn't improved as the afternoon waned, after that incident with his son this morning, and now this, with that Injun character, whoever the hell he was. Billy would have to pay for this. It wasn't right, a grown boy to shame his father that way. Still, he knew that a man could only do so much. He glanced at his wife. She was looking at him again in that way that made his skin crawl. He felt the tears welling up, maddenly uncontrollable, and fought them back with inner rage. But her look was overwhelming. Because the truth of it was, she terrified him to the core.

When Jerry Laker and a couple of his other pals from the militia suggested they go shoot some "squirrels," Duvall was ready. He needed to escape the trap he was in, those walls of judgment and condemnation closing in on him as though from all sides. He quickly finished off the last of his six-pack of Miller Light and tossed the can into the river. Picking up his Remington 30-06, he growled, "Let's go."

Duvall put his mind to the hunt. It was the last great release, that confirmed and defined his manhood. He needed it right now something bad. There were whitetail in these woods, and a few gators left in the ponds. Good shootin' either one, if you got lucky. And if you got really lucky, who knows. There'd been rumors of panthers moving into this area from Big Cypress in recent months. The gov'ment said they were off-limits, but Duvall and the boys didn't give a damn about those bureaucrats and their regulations. A panther crossed his path, it was dead meat, period. Same's a nigger, or any meddlin' fuckin' government agent either, as several of the boys had drunkenly boasted to each other at one time or another, in the disquiet of recent times. They didn't say such things out loud anymore, of course. Not since that woman game warden got shot.

Officially, everyone knew it was an accident. But privately, opinion had been expressed at Duvall Patterson's and elsewhere, over beers at the bar or in the private company of friends, that Marge Pappas had it coming. She had just gotten too uppity, and had started to impinge on people's God-given rights. Of course, there were other conversations that were cruder in content, as the beer flowed and the day waned. Such as how Marge Pappas was a tease, and a flirt, and had it comin' in other ways, as well. Either way, the consensus that day at Caloosahatchee River County Park was she had it coming.

Nobody found anything much to shoot at that afternoon other than cans and bottles, and a few hapless raccoons and 'possums. Jerry Laker managed to wound a red hawk, but it escaped in a cloud of feathers, screeching with rage and pain. Someone suggested it was too bad there wasn't no more woman game wardens around, he could use a little "nooky." Nobody laughed, and the auto mechanic who'd made the remark clammed up.

If the boys didn't get lucky that day, nobody cared. They generally just left the carcasses for the scavengers anyway, since it was too much trouble—and too risky—to haul them out of the woods. The hunt was the main thing. The rest was just gravy. And Duvall Patterson, when he felt this way, he needed the hunt.

11

The Bedrosian family had driven for most of the day, north on I-275 to the junction with I-10 at Lake City, then another hour and a half west. They were all pretty cranky by the time they got to Tallahassee in the late afternoon. Lena had let Michael do most of the driving, since he insisted, and she hated freeways anyway. The whole Bedrosian family had made the trip in Michael's Dodge Caravan, and Lena had regretted her ill-begotten idea more and more as the hours passed. It had gotten perceptibly colder as the day went by, and a northern front pushed in from the Great Plains states bringing with it dark clouds and darker spirits.

Except for Michael, who was bordering on ecstasy. "I checked the schedule," he crowed happily, as he turned off I-10 at the Thomasville Road exit and headed south toward the city center and capitol district. "If we check in at the motel and grab a bite at Wendy's, I can make the Georgia Tech game. It's one of the conference semifinals, which will determine who goes to the NCAAs." He looked at her and his face fell as he sensed her mood. "If that's all right with you, of course, hon."

"Sure, sure, you go right ahead, Mike, that's what we're here for," she lied. "I'll put the kids to bed and watch TV." Lena hated TV, except for a couple of comedies, but was determined to make the best of the situation. Also, as she and Michael both knew, it was a rare opportunity for her to be alone with the kids. She had to admit they didn't get to see her all that often. The state offices were still closed anyway, at least until tomorrow when the budget squabbling was scheduled to resume.

Lena was anxious to talk to Amber. But that, too, would have to wait. No way she could talk to her with the kids around. Resigned, Lena dropped Michael off at the campus field house for the basketball game and drove directly back to the Hampton Inn, where they were scheduled to spend the next three days. It had been all her idea, she knew. What she didn't know, and was worried about, was whether the idea had been a good one.

With most of the Hondo and Collier County locals occupied elsewhere that afternoon, Tony Lowell decided to revisit Marge Pappas's campsite. He had a nagging feeling that something had been overlooked. The police had obviously made only the most cursory search, as he'd seen for himself and Dave Connors had confirmed. He took the same back road Billy had shown him, following the turns through the swamp from memory. For one thing, he wanted to take another soil sample.

The cabin had been vandalized, the foodstuffs and other incidental belongings scattered: whether by animals or humans he couldn't yet tell. There was a Dumpster at the end of the road, which the county was supposed to empty once a week. It was stuffed full, mostly with black plastic bags. Lowell remembered the same bags had been there yesterday, which meant the county services had also either been stopped, or hadn't gotten around to the more remote outposts yet. All waste materials generated on park and state lands were kept for recycling as a matter of policy, but he suddenly wondered why the bags hadn't been taken by the cops. Surely they'd at least look through them, he'd have thought. But when he looked for himself, after separating out the glass, plastic bottles, and cans, and just before dumping the remaining debris (mostly garbage and paper) into the trash bin, he found it: a crumpled hand-written letter on ordinary lined note paper. It was dated just before Christmas, with no return address. The writing was crude, plain, and threatening:

ATF state snoopers suck. You had yur chanc to prove you wer diffrcn, and couldn't even. So your gonna suck mine til you choke on it, bitch.

Marge must have loved that, he thought. She had enough trouble as it was, fending off the drunken advances of yahoos out hunting, or fishing, or just shooting bottles. And too many of them just couldn't take no for an answer. It wasn't even that she was an obvious babe or anything. She dressed like a man, usually in a law officer's uniform. She kept her hair up, out of the way, and was always careful to elicit no provocative words or actions, or even anything that an amorous moron could possibly construe as provocative. Ever. She had always been careful. But as Lowell knew from much overheard conversation in bars and cafés over the years, bottom line was: She was a woman. Period. That alone was enough to mark her in the eyes of some. That she was a government worker, a law enforcement official, all of those things were either irrelevant, or merely served to inflame certain unbalanced persons all the more.

Tony Lowell had a pretty good idea where to start looking for the letter writer. He took the soil samples he was after, then ate his irregular lunch: peanut butter sandwich and granola snack bar with a thermos of coffee, and thought about trying Bedrosian again. He'd tried her cell phone several times earlier from the pay phone at Patterson's Landing, and had gotten voice mail. That worried him. No one at the Manatee City police station knew where she was, either. "She's on administrative leave," the desk sergeant had informed him. That he already knew.

Lowell returned to the motel in Fort Myers just after sundown, and checked his messages. That was when he learned Perry had been shot, escaping from the church picnic. They'd winged his left arm just above the elbow, where it customarily stuck out the driver's side window, even during his getaway.

It wasn't serious. "Just a flesh wound, man," Perry reassured him, when he arrived in panic at the hospital where Billy had brought Perry: coincidentally the same hospital where Lowell had brought the senator the night before. That was his next scheduled visit. Meanwhile, he was very glad to see his friend alive and kicking.

"What other kind of wound is there?" he remarked. "A bone wound?"

"Probably wasn't even intentional," Perry insisted. "Probably just a warning," he said, in dismissal. "Those ol' boys are too good a shot to miss, if they'd intended any harm."

"They didn't miss," said Lowell.

"How'd it go at the gun club last night? Get any trophies?"

Lowell shook his head. "Senator Kranhower almost got to be one, though." He told Perry about his own narrow escape with the senator, who was now occupying a room the next floor up.

"That's nuts. Everybody's gone trigger-happy down here," said Perry, sorrowfully.

"It's the American Way," said Lowell.

Perry was going to be all right, the doctor assured them

both. Which didn't make Lowell feel any better that Perry had taken fire on his behalf. It wasn't the first time, either. Perry just insisted he was a professional soldier.

"You'll be taken care of," Lowell assured him.

"I don't assume you mean financially," retorted Perry, who knew his friend only too well.

"I'll have to owe you," acknowledged Lowell. "Anything else I can do in the meantime?"

Perry grinned. "Yeah, as a matter of fact." He signaled for Lowell to come closer. He whispered a request in Lowell's ear. Lowell grinned back, nodded, and promised he'd be back with the requested commodity, hell or high water.

Two hours later, Lowell had to sweet-talk a nurse into letting him back into Perry's hospital room when he returned from his errand. It was by then eleven-thirty at night: well past visiting hours.

"What the hell took you so long?" A tired-sounding Perry complained, as Lowell set his gunnysack down beside the bed.

"Minor details, like finding an open store, paying my respects to the senator, and trying to locate that kid. Where the hell did he go, anyway? He's got my damn camera!"

Billy Patterson, who'd helped bring him in (Perry had insisted on driving), had disappeared.

Perry shrugged. "Don't sweat it," he said. "He's gotta steer clear of his old man awhile. It'll turn up."

It had not been a good day, all in all, for either of them. Lowell apologized for letting Perry take the heat. "I think you'd better lay low for a spell," he proposed, surreptitiously opening his gunnysack and producing the manifestation of Perry's earlier request: a six-pack of Molson. Checking to make sure there were no nurses about, Lowell opened one for each of them.

"Here's to an early retirement," Lowell toasted his friend.

"Why? It was just getting fun!"

"Sure," Lowell sighed, after swallowing half his bottle. "It's been a bundle of laughs. I just can't handle you getting shot up every time you come along on a case."

"*You* can't handle it?"

"It's very hard on the nervous system, for your information. Not to mention the budget. You should have more consideration!"

Perry grinned. "Relax," he said. "I got health insurance. No deductible, covers everything except acupuncture." He thought for a minute. "That, and saunas. You ever try a good Swedish sauna?"

"You've got health insurance?" Lowell's eyes widened. He didn't have health insurance.

"Yeah, no sweat."

Lowell opened two more beers, and handed one over. "Perry, I'm serious. I'd feel a lot better if you'd just hole up back home in Manatee for a while, until the dust settles a bit. We've stirred up a damn fire anthill down here, and I'm not any closer to who shot Marge Pappas."

"How many people live around here?" queried Perry, slipping the prior empty bottle back into the cardboard container.

"I don't know. Hundred thou, maybe, including Fort Myers and Naples."

"That's great. You've narrowed it down to a hundred thousand suspects. What's your friend the cop doing?"

Knowing her, she was camped out at Manatee City police headquarters, nagging her superiors. "We're supposed to be acting on her behalf. That is, I am. So far, I don't feel like I've accomplished one whole helluva lot."

"I don't know," said Perry. "It's all relative. When you get a lot of people uptight about something, chances are, you're making progress. And chances are, you're looking at the right people."

"I don't like the way they look back," said Lowell.

"Well, here's looking at you, then," said Perry, and drained his bottle. "Hey. Did I ever show you my little self-defense maneuver you can do with one of these babies, in case of a frontal assault by two or more—" Just then the nurse came in, and launched into a loud burst of invective directed at both of them. Especially Lowell, who was summarily evicted from the premises for numerous and varied offenses she didn't have sufficient breath to express before he was gone.

"I'll call you tomorrow!" he managed to shout back as he was hauled away, along with the remainder of the six-pack. Perry was sorry to see him go. He was even sorrier to lose the six-pack, which Lowell wound up presenting to the startled security guard at the door. "For when you get off," he whispered, as the guard grinned and quickly whisked it out of sight.

Amber Pappas met Lena Bedrosian at nine o'clock the next morning at a popular coffeehouse on Duval Street in Tallahassee, beneath the shadow of the towering and now-silent state capitol, a block away. Lena had kept the kids up late watching cartoons on the motel cable, and Michael had come in late, in a dismal mood that didn't portend well—his beloved Seminoles had lost their basketball game in overtime. She'd fixed him a toddy on the little hot plate that came with the room, and he'd gulped it down, rolled over onto the bed with a mournful grumble, and gone right to sleep. She'd barely managed to squeeze in alongside him. And between the grunts and snores of a hard-core sports fan who'd drunk too much, the occasional whimpering of the baby, and her own jumbled thoughts about her dead cousin Marge, she already had just about all she could stand in the way of a vacation.

Yet it was Amber—ten years younger than her—who looked haggard, this Monday morning. Lena noticed it right off. Amber looked as though she hadn't slept in days. Lena, thanks to the wonders of modern pharmacology, had.

105

"Amber, are you all right, girl?" Lena asked at once, as she waved the young male server over. He looked smug and handsome. Probably a student on aid, with heavy fraternity fees to cover. Amber gave him a perfunctory flirtatious smile that was transparently halfhearted, and ordered black coffee. "Bring a pot, can you?" she requested, with all the authority, Lena recognized, of a well-placed state official.

They gave each other the customary greetings, and exchanges of routine family updates. Amber looked solemn. Lena asked her what was wrong. "Lena, I'm worried," Amber confessed, after the coffee and two hot egg-and-cheese croissants arrived. "The senator left here in such a hurry on Saturday for that meeting down south, and I haven't heard from him since."

"Is that unusual? I mean does he usually check in with you every day?"

"No, not necessarily," Amber admitted. "But this is different. He went down to Big Cyprus Swamp! The same place where Marge got shot!"

"I know, Amber, you called me, remember? I sent someone to look after him, I'm sure he's all right," said Lena, hoping she was right. She glanced cautiously around the coffee shop.

Amber's eyes were dark and sunken. The deep purple eyeliner hadn't helped. "It was all because of that stupid land bill Senator Kranhower held up. I tried to stop him from going down there, but—"

"Hold it! Whoa there, girl," exclaimed Lena, caught by surprise. She hadn't heard about any land bill. And surely it would have been news, with the legislature wrangling over the budget again. "You better start from the beginning."

"I know, I'm sorry. I'm not the only one with problems. It's bad enough, what happened to Marge. I always told her to find another job, an accident like that was bound to happen sooner or later, and—"

"It was no accident," said Lena.

Amber stared, and her jaw dropped open, her eyes squeezed shut a moment. "God, I knew it!"

"I can't prove it yet. They've taken me off the case, you know."

"I know."

"But I'm not sitting on my butt, Amber. Marge was shot in the line of duty, trying to do her job, trying to enforce the law. I'm sure of it."

"I'm sure of it, too. I don't know why, it's just a feeling. That's why I'm worried about the senator."

Lena told her the facts, so far. That Marge had been shot from behind. That the local authorities had slammed a lid on the investigation, "which stinks in anybody's book," Lena declared. "Also," she added, "she'd been receiving threats."

Amber caught her breath. "Then there's got to be a connection. These people came in here Saturday, demanding that the senator sign this bill transferring all this land to some gun club down there. I told him what was in it, because he can hardly read anymore. So he refused. Lena, you wouldn't believe how mad they were."

"So you were the one who alerted him to this—scam?"

"Scam is a good word for it," Amber laughed wryly, and blew her nose in a paper napkin. Lena's mind was spinning. She knew Amber was the state senator's legislative assistant, what used to be called his "Gal Friday." She also knew the senator was getting on in years, and that all those years of waging governmental warfare on the state capitol battlefront would take its toll on any man. Or woman. "How old is he now, Amber? Isn't he past retirement age?"

"Sure, but he's always been strong as a swamp cypress. It's not like him to disappear in the middle of the night. That's why I'm so worried!"

Now Lena was beginning to worry as well. Amber had called her in a panic Saturday afternoon, and Lena had asked Lowell to check up on Senator Kranhower at the Hunt Club. She hadn't been able to reach Lowell either, since then. She suddenly remembered she'd forgotten to recharge her cellular, what with the kids and Michael and all. "Damn," she muttered. "So you think somebody got to him?"

Amber nibbled her croissant, and took a thoughtful sip of coffee. "No. One thing about Senator Kranhower. Even in the few years I've worked for him, I've never seen him take any funny money, or let anybody bully him, like Representative Hathcock always tries to do. He never gave away nothing, either—"

"Anything either—," corrected Lena.

Amber stuck her tongue out at her older and actually less educated cousin, and continued crossly: "Like quid pro quo. He always stayed the course, no matter what."

Lena furrowed her brow, trying to see a connection. Her instincts were screaming that there had to be one.

"So you think," she said, "that there is a link between whoever shot Marge, and this sudden trip down south by the senator?"

Amber nodded, emphatically. "Yes, I do. I can't prove it. I don't know what, or how. I don't think Jack—the senator even knew Marge existed before she got shot. It's just that—I don't know, Lena! Things are so crazy nowadays!"

"I know. But you do have a point. So you think Marge and the senator somehow ran up against the same interests?"

"I don't know. It's just too much to be a coincidence." Amber seemed distracted, staring vacantly out the window, her brow a deep furrow that aged her a dozen years. When she spoke again, it was slowly, as though she were examining her words one by one, for clues. "Those people he went down to see, they're all these big shots, Chamber of Commerce types. Hathcock was there—!"

"Hathcock. State Representative Bob 'Hatchet Man' Hathcock?"

Amber giggled, in spite of herself. "That's what Jack always calls him." Her frown resumed. "But look, those people are all, like, public figures!"

"You're right," sighed Lena. "It doesn't sound too likely. It's not like they're a bunch of swamp rats or yahoos or nothin'."

"Anythin'!" corrected Amber, with a grin.

Lena scowled. "Maybe he went fishing or something, after the meeting. This is still only Monday morning. You haven't even been to the office yet, for crying out loud."

"I know, you're right, I'm probably making a mountain out of a molehill. It's just that I usually check the messages first thing on Mondays or when he's out of town, and there was nothing. That's the odd thing," said Amber, with a quick worried glance around the coffee shop. "But he's probably all right. Like you said. Went fishing or somethin'." She opened her purse and took out her compact, examined her face with a look of distinct displeasure.

Lena looked at her watch. Michael and the kids would be up by now, probably stir-crazy, wondering where she went. She'd left a note on the bathroom mirror, but they wouldn't find it until one of them went to the toilet, and even then they might miss it. Oh well, she thought. They're used to her absences by now. "I'll go with you," she announced. "It's ten o'clock, he'll probably be calling in any moment."

"You're right," agreed Amber, and waved at the good-looking server. "Check please!"

Lena pulled Amber over to a row of phone booths, on their way over to the capitol building. A gut feeling told her not to make calls from the senator's office. She instructed Amber to call the senator's pager from there while she made a couple of calls of her own. Amber agreed and took the nearest booth. Lena took the next available one down and called the motel, asking the operator to ring her room.

There was no answer. "Damn," she muttered. It meant that Michael and the kids had probably gone down to the motel coffee shop for breakfast. Next she tried the Days Inn at Fort Myers, for the third time since yesterday. "Sorry, he's not in," the motel operator told her. "I'll tell him you called." With growing frustration, she dug out her little black address book, and looked up a number in Manatee County. She dialed it along with her calling card number. It rang several times, then a squeaky, ancient answering machine kicked on:

"This is Lowell. I'm not real. Leave a recorded message, and you won't be real either. Bye."

There was a long beep tone. "Lowell," spluttered Lena, in irritation (she hated answering machines, especially with clever messages, and this was costing her prime-time long-distance). "That is such an asinine message. This is Lieutenant Bedrosian. I'm up in Tallahassee at the Hampton Inn. Please call me when you get this. It's urgent." She hung up, and rejoined Amber who stood fidgeting nervously on the sidewalk.

"I couldn't reach him," Amber told her, wide-eyed. "He always returns his pages right away."

"So we wait." They waited, and the minutes ticked by. No phone rang. After an interminable ten minutes passed, Lena looked reluctantly up at the twenty-two story state capitol, looming above them: a towering complex that housed the entire seat of power for the state, state offices as well as both houses of the legislature. It looked, thought Bedrosian, like something Darth Vader would have dreamed up. And there was little question, in her mind, as to which Force was in power up in there.

"Lena," said Amber, as though reading her thoughts. "I'm a little nervous about going in there, this morning. Would you go with me? Just until I can check things out, and find out what's going on?"

"Sure," said Lena.

They entered through the lobby, which was eerily quiet for a Monday morning. Amber adjusted her hair and managed to smile flirtatiously for the guards (still on duty) who waved them through, and led the way to the senate office wing and the private elevator. She inserted her key and they rode in silence up to the senator's floor. They got off and Amber led the way down the darkened corridor to Senator Kranhower's office suite. The first office was stenciled State Joint Natural Resources Committee. The second was State Senator Jack Kranhower. Amber unlocked the second door, and led the way in.

The office was a disaster: papers scattered everywhere, stacks of documents, reports, legislative bills, letters, transcripts—there wasn't a single flat surface in the outer, or (she quickly saw) inner office that wasn't in total disarray, with paperwork and debris strewn everywhere. Lena caught her breath.

"God, somebody's been in here and trashed the place!" she exclaimed.

"Yeah," responded Amber, sarcastically. "The senator. It's always like this in a crisis," she explained. "Why, did you think there'd been a break-in? Like Watergate or something?" She laughed, but it sounded hollow. She stopped abruptly.

Lena let out a sigh. "It crossed my mind."

"His schedule's in here," said Amber, leading the way into the senator's private office. "Somewhere."

Lena looked around. "Did he ever get any threatening mail, anything like that?"

Amber laughed again, wryly. "All the time."

"Any recently?"

"Sure." Amber gestured expansively around the office, then pointed at the desk that adjoined a computer table, all of which was buried in stacks of correspondence. "Take your pick."

Bedrosian looked at her cousin in annoyance. "You don't keep track of that sort of thing? Who, where, anything like that?"

"Look," said Amber, defensively. "The senator decided a long time ago, that if he was going to let the crackpots get to him, he might as well find another line of work."

"Maybe they're finally getting to him."

"Maybe. But I don't think so." Amber was adamant. Her boss was no quitter. And he didn't give in to threats or pressure from pressure groups.

"I respect that." Lena nodded. "But things change. Like you said, this world is getting weirder all the time." She thought for a moment. "Maybe," she suggested, "the senator should get himself a permit to carry a concealed weapon. I'm sure there'd be no problem getting one."

"There is one problem," said Amber, shaking her head. "The old coot would never carry one. I've asked him before."

"And what did he say?"

"He said he was afraid he might shoot somebody."

Bedrosian thought about that. "Sounds like somebody I know," she remarked.

Amber glanced up at her, then back to the hate letter she was scanning. "God spits on you, Liberal scum," it proclaimed. Bedrosian surveyed the office. "Do you have your own phone line? Separate from his, I mean?"

Amber shook her head.

"Do you have a copy of that land bill he turned down, before he left?"

Amber shrugged. "Sure." She went into the outer office, and over to a row of metal shelves that lined the wall. "It's right here." She reached up, and took down a thick sheaf of legal-sized paper, in a brown folder. She brought it back and handed it to Lena, who was busy jotting down a number from the capitol telephone directory.

"Thanks," said Bedrosian, looking at the document. It bore all the weighty appearances of government: tainted or otherwise. She hefted it a moment, then set it aside and reached for the telephone. "Get me the Capitol Police, extension 927," she told the operator, waving Amber to silence. A cheery male voice picked up on the other end. "Hello, Danny? This is Detective Lieutenant Bedrosian. Lena Bedrosian. From Manatee City? Yes, fine. Yes, about three years ago. Yes, it's nice to hear your voice, too." Amber made a face at her. Lena turned the other way. "Actually, I'm just up here a few days, taking in the sights with the family. No, I've been married for ten years, Danny!" She ignored Amber's smirk. "Listen, I need a favor. I need to run a wiretap trace."

12

The sun emerged from behind the cloud cover and the day began to heat up. Lowell was awakened by the Days Inn desk clerk, informing him that someone had dropped off a brown paper bag for him, containing a camera. He spent the next couple of hours getting the film developed, and examining the prints.

Around ten o'clock he tossed the last of his plastic foam cup of boiled coffee into the trash, left the motel, and unlocked his ancient Impala. He'd left it parked in what was then shade, and was now sun. Cursing the lack of a viable air conditioner in the old heap, he rolled down all the windows except the left rear one, which was jammed, and backed out of the lot. Turning west on Route 80, he sped back toward Fort Myers. He was hungry, and nearly succumbed to the relentless lure of the ever-present fast-food franchises that clawed at him with their garish displays, mile after mile. But by the time he'd got through the city to Route 41 and turned south toward the County Hospital, he'd lost his appetite. Which was just as well, since hospitals, as a rule, made him nauseous.

Now he had not one, but two people to see to in there, a situation he wouldn't have conjured up on bad grass. He circled the lot twice before managing to commandeer a rare shaded parking space underneath a clump of shedding royal palms.

Luckily, no one recognized him from the beer-smuggling incident the night before. The fact the this was the day shift and that had been around midnight probably helped. But he still felt somewhat sheepish as he slipped into the elevator.

Perry wasn't in his room. Lowell bypassed the unattended nurse's station and collared a doctor who was scurrying past, studying a chart. "Where's Perry Garwood?" demanded Lowell.

"Who?" the doctor glanced up briefly from his chart.

"Perry Garwood. About my size, part Indian, part bonkers."

"Oh, him," sniffed the doctor. "The GSW, Native American fella. He's fine."

"Of course he's fine. Where the hell is he?"

The doctor looked confused for a moment, then brightened. "Discharged as of this morning. I think he just checked out a few minutes ago, actually. You might still catch him at the business office downstairs."

Lowell hurried to the elevator and pounded the button. The car arrived, and he stood back while a gurney was rolled off, carrying a young man who was bleeding profusely. A female police officer followed the gurney out, and Lowell noticed a sheriff's deputy still on the elevator. The deputy looked familiar. Then he recognized him: Kohler, from Collier County. Kohler recognized Lowell at the same time and scowled, briefly. He seemed hesitant, uncertain. He stayed on when Lowell got on the elevator. "Another GSW," explained Kohler, nodding in the direction of the departed gurney. "Asshole ran right in front of a bunch of shooters, chasing his damn dog. I was just bringin' him in."

"That was civic of you, seeing as this isn't Collier County," observed Lowell, hitting the button for the second floor, where the business office was located. "And it's not hunting season. You going back down?"

Kohler barely nodded, distracted. The elevator was going up. "Thought I'd check in with a nurse I know," he confided, turning a little red. "Seeing as it's lunch hour."

"Eat hearty," said Lowell, and got off. He had the oddest feeling that the deputy had wanted to get off with him and decided not to as the door slid closed. The elevator continued up two flights, then headed back down. Lowell watched it go, wondering for a moment, then went to find the business office.

Perry was in the midst of an animated discussion with the powers-that-be, gesticulating wildly, when Lowell spotted him. "Perry!" he called, suddenly concerned. "Is there a problem?"

Perry looked up and waved, albeit painfully. " 'Course not. I'm just telling Maggie here about Indonesia. You ready?"

"You've been to Indonesia?"

"Couple times." Perry picked up the hospital bill printout, and stuffed it in his pocket. "Thanks, Maggie," he said, with a smile for the blushing blonde behind the cashier's window. "Hey, thank God for government insurance, right?" said Perry, with a grin. "Or I'd be up shit creek."

"You have *government* health insurance?"

" 'Course, what else?" Lowell had trouble keeping up as Perry headed for the exit. "Told you I did. Doesn't everybody?"

"You're such a comedian," said Lowell, with a grimace. "I didn't know you worked for the government," he added, trying to catch up. Perry never discussed his paying jobs—when he had them—and Lowell had given up asking. The answers were always vague, couched in innuendos and platitudes. Something about special services, whatever that was. Lowell was ready to believe practically anything. But the notion that his buddy was some kind of 007 CIA agent was a bit much. He secretly suspected Perry probably had a job appraising confiscated Jeeps for the General Accounting Office, or something along those lines. That would be sufficient to account for the insurance.

Perry didn't want to wait while Lowell went up to see the senator. "Gotta get out, man. I hate hospitals. Too many sick people."

"I won't be long," promised Lowell. "I want to talk to you about some of those photographs you took."

"They came out okay? I wasn't payin' too much attention to what the kid did."

"I'll tell you later. You can watch the talk shows on TV. They're a real hoot."

"No thanks," replied Perry. "Already got one headache. I'll meet you back at your place. I still gotta check out of the hotel. You said the weekend. This weekend is long gone, man."

Lowell grudgingly relented, watched his friend gingerly push the door open and leave, then turned and took the elevator back up to Senator Kranhower's room. The senator greeted Lowell like he was a long lost friend. Either that, or a last-minute rescuer from certain death and destruction. "Lowell!" he shouted, waving from his bed before Lowell had even entered his room. "Over here!"

"Everything all right, Senator?" asked Lowell, stepping in. He hadn't noticed a nurse, aide, doctor, or anyone since getting off the elevator. Lunch hour, he supposed. "Sorry I couldn't get here sooner."

"You're sorry?" growled Kranhower, waving his arms, dangling IV tubes right and left. Lowell grinned in spite of himself. The old senator did look pretty funny. "You ever been stuck in a hospital?"

"Once," said Lowell, but wouldn't elaborate. Too many bad memories. Which led inevitably to thoughts of Caitlin Schoenkopf, someone he didn't want to think about just now.

Some of the people he'd met lately, particularly at that Hunt Club, had reminded him of her father, the admiral. Lowell was still not on very good terms with the admiral. Especially after stealing his prized twelve-meter *Wellington,* that time. He brushed aside the cobwebs entangling his thoughts, and returned his attention to the business at hand.

"How's the ticker?" he asked. He almost said "old ticker," and managed to check himself.

Kranhower scowled again. "Still works," he grumbled, "which is the bottom line. Thanks to you."

Lowell shook his head. "No sir, I was just the delivery boy. Hopefully these folks have taken proper care of it for you."

"If you consider being tied up like a hog on a spit being taken care of they've done a helluva job," grumbled Kranhower, swatting and yanking at his jumble of monitoring devices and intravenous tubes until he was more thoroughly tangled up than ever. "You know how to disconnect these damn things?"

"No, I really wouldn't advise it," cautioned Lowell, nervously. "But I'll see if I can find a nurse for you."

"Find me a taxi, is what I want you to find. I've got to get back to Tallahassee."

Lowell shook his head again, and looked around the room. There was a phone on the wall, behind the IV stand. "You been able to call your family or anyone, to let them know how and where you are?"

"I called my wife," replied Kranhower, his voice like crushed rock. "Don't have a family."

"Sorry to hear it."

"She said she'd call my office." Kranhower actually succeeded in disconnecting one of his IVs. "Are you gonna get me that taxi?" he repeated. "I have to get back to the capital in order to kill that bastard Hathcock's little bill rider if it's the last thing I do!"

The man was serious, Lowell realized. "It might be, if you

pull that thing off," he scolded him. "But I'll see if I can find your doctor, and get his opinion."

"The hell with his opinion," growled Kranhower. "I feel fine. Never better." He coughed and wheezed for a moment, then stopped. "See?" he said.

Just then the wall phone rang. Lowell looked at it, glanced around, and hesitated. It was well out of the senator's reach.

"Answer it, would you?" gasped the senator. "Do I look like Spider Man?"

Lowell picked up the receiver. "Senator Kranhower's room. May I help you?"

"Who the hell is this?" a raspy voice demanded.

"This is the senator's aide," lied Lowell. "He's in the hospital, in case you weren't aware."

"I know that," snarled the voice. "You give him a message, pal."

"I'll do my best," said Lowell.

"You tell that sonovabitch, he should have heeded the people."

"What people would that be?" Lowell inquired, shaking his head at Kranhower in warning.

"The God-fearing people of Florida. Now he's going to pay the penalty."

"What kind of penalty?" Lowell wanted to know.

"The same one the bitch warden Marge Pappas paid," said the voice, and hung up.

The senator was grinning wryly, when Lowell put down the receiver, and stepped back around the IV stand. "What was that, another crackpot? I don't know how in hell they find me like that, but they do, every time."

"It was a death threat," said Lowell, sternly. "I'd take it seriously, Senator."

Kranhower waved his hands in dismissal. "Bah. I get 'em all the time. Comes with the territory." He had actually managed to sit up. "You see what those bozos did with my good shoes? I only got one pair."

Lowell checked the hallway outside the hospital room door. It was eerily empty. He ducked back inside. "On second thought, I think you're right, Senator. I think it might be a good idea to get you out of here."

"Then it's unanimous. Can you find my shoes?"

"They mentioned Marge Pappas. You know about her?"

The senator was pulling on his shirt, and Lowell could see he was in pain. He stopped. "There was something mighty strange about that," he said. "And one hell of an unfortunate coincidence. Did you know that she was related to my legislative assistant?"

Lowell nodded. Bedrosian had told him, before he went to rescue the senator from the Hunt Club. He was becoming a regular Rescue Squad, he thought, wryly. "Yeah, I did," he said. "Are you sure it was a coincidence?"

Kranhower stopped buttoning his shirt and looked up at Lowell, with a frown. "Amber said the same thing, but I don't buy it. What the hell else could it be? From what I heard, it was an accident."

Lowell shrugged, and shook his head. "Maybe," he said. "Accidents happen all the time. But it was one hell of a coincidence."

Kranhower managed to wiggle his wrinkled suit on, and reached for the telephone. "Then you won't mind if I call a damn taxi," he growled, and went into another coughing fit.

Lowell reached out and stopped him, gently. "Hold it." He checked the hall, once more. There was an empty wheelchair parked just opposite Kranhower's room. He stepped out quickly, and wheeled it in next to the senator's bed. "Get your shirt tucked in."

With growing concern for his charge's safely, he eased the old man into the chair as fast as he could, and set his feet on the little metal foot rests. "Easy does it," he said. "I've got my car."

"Now you're talkin'!" exulted the senator. "Just grab me some of them nitroglycerin pills, and let's haul some ass."

"So to speak," said Lowell, hurrying him down the hall.

Lowell made the two-hour sprint up I-75 without incident, keeping a close watch on his rearview mirror. The senator was feeling chipper at his escape from the hospital, as though that in itself was the key to good health. He actually did seem raring to go, as Lowell wheeled him out to the parking lot and loaded him into the front passenger seat of the old Impala.

"Nice car," the senator said. "Sixty-six?"

" 'Five," said Lowell. "Graduation present from my dad. My reward for shipping off to Nam. You're the first person in two decades to refer to this as a 'nice car,' incidentally. Most people prefer to describe it with four-letter words."

"So. You're welcome." Kranhower wanted to know about Lowell's dad, the former police chief of tony Palm Coast Harbor on the east coast, but Lowell didn't want to talk about him. So the senator spent most of the trip happily recounting tales about his adventures back in his youth—namely when he was Lowell's age (Lowell liked that part). He'd been in the navy, same as Lowell. They had something else in common, it turned out. Both had gone to the University of Florida in Gainesville: Lowell in the sixties, Kranhower in the forties; both had escaped with marginal grade point averages; and both had entered public service, in a manner of speaking. Both had tired of a long career in photojournalism: Lowell of taking photos and Kranhower of being photographed.

They stopped for coffee at a rest stop north of Port Charlotte. Krahower tried the pay phone but couldn't get through. "To the Gators!" the senator toasted with his paper cup, as they headed north once more, whereupon he instantly fell asleep in his seat with the most peaceful expression on his face since the invention of Prozac. Lowell, too busy driving to notice, automatically waved his own coffee cup in a return salute, spilling half of it. "Damn," he muttered, seizing the opportunity to clean up his language in the presence of elders, not to mention dignitaries. Asleep or otherwise. "Go Gators!"

He turned on the radio. Ever since his antenna got busted off a few years back by a low-hanging branch while he was chasing a delinquent teenage father down an old logging road, he didn't get very good reception. He finally managed to tune in a local country station out of Englewood, and caught the noon news. The second story, after the one about the continuing government shutdown in Tallahassee (generating lots of colorful language from the senator, who woke up and immediately fell back asleep), verified the incident Deputy Kohler had alluded to. A thirty-two-year-old man had been shot, while trying to catch a dog that had gotten off leash, in a county park. Police investigators were calling the shooting an accident.

"Sounds familiar," murmured Kranhower, waking up yet again.

Lowell exited the Interstate at Gulfbridge, honked as he passed the Clam Shack, and sped over the bayou bridge on still-undeveloped Mangrove Road. Five minutes later he turned into his driveway, glad to be home.

As he helped the senator climb out of the car, Lowell thought of Papa Hemingway, or Mark Twain. Dressed in white, all the senator needed was a white Panama hat, and a wicker chair to sit in in splendor on the lawn, gazing out at the bay with a mint julep in one hand, an unfinished novel in the other. Maybe there would be time for that image to come to pass one day. But not today. He had to get him inside, and call his office.

The senator, however, had other ideas. He took one look at the half-submerged schooner *Andromeda,* and stopped in his tracks.

"Son of a gun!" he exclaimed. "That yours?"

"Sort of," said Lowell, holding his elbow. "I'm working on restoring it."

"Helluva beaut!" beamed the senator. "How's she run?"

"Not too good," said Lowell. "She's kind of sunk. And you're not exactly shipshape either, Senator. I gotta get you inside."

The senator squinted across the sparkling blue water at the boat, looking more closely. "Son of a gun," he said.

"Actually," said Lowell, "I expect her to rise any morning now, and shine, shine, shine. After the planking finishes swelling, and I finish caulking the keel."

"Tough break," muttered Kranhower, as Lowell led him toward the house. "What about that one?" he asked, pointing at the little sloop, moored behind the schooner's transom, like a dinghy.

"Kind of a consolation prize," said Lowell. "I built it last year so I wouldn't forget how to sail."

"You built that?" exclaimed the senator. "Son of a gun."

"C'mon, you need to eat something, and get some rest."

"That mean we're not goin' sailing?" The senator grinned. "And here I was just startin' to like you."

They reached the back steps, and Lowell helped his new charge up onto the porch, and through the back door. "Make me feel like a damn invalid," muttered the senator.

"Tell you what," proposed Lowell, guiding Kranhower through the kitchen and depositing him onto the leather love seat. "You get well, get back to Tallahassee and clean up the government, then come pay me a visit, and I'll take you sailing."

Kranhower's eyes lit up. "In the schooner?"

"In the schooner," said Lowell, heating up some bean soup.

"Deal," said the senator, and fell asleep once more, snoring like a true sailor.

Lowell went to open some windows and let the Gulf breeze

in, when he saw the red light blinking on his ancient telephone answering machine. He realized he hadn't checked it in days. He played it back. There were several messages from Lieutenant Bedrosian, leaving a number in Tallahassee. She sounded anxious for him to call her. But there was also a message from Amber Pappas. "Hello, Mr. Lowell, this is Amber, Marge Pappas's cousin? Listen, I'm sorry to bother you, I got your number from Lena Bedrosian who said it would be all right. We're tryin' to locate Senator Kranhower. If you know of his whereabouts could you please have him call me immediately? Day or night, he has my home and work numbers. Thank you."

After a quick lunch of soup and half an old ham sandwich, Lowell looked at his guest, trying to decide between feeding him, letting him sleep, and letting his worried loved ones off the hook. He nudged him gently. "Senator, wake up. You need to call your wife and your office, and let them know you're okay." The senator grunted, blinked, and nodded. Lowell handed him his ancient black rotary phone to the senator, and invited him to dial. Kranhower meekly obeyed.

"Howdy, darlin'!" chortled the senator, instantly alert and perky once more, as the call went through. "How're we doin' up there?"

"Senator? Oh, thank God!" Amber almost screamed. "Where are you? Your wife called, said you were in the hospital, but by the time I got through they said you'd left. Are you all right?"

"Fine, fine, fit as a fiddle. I'm at my new friend Mr. Lowell's place, in—" He looked up at Lowell. "Where the hell am I?" he asked.

"Gulfbridge. Manatee County," replied Lowell.

"I'm in Manatee County. Everything's fine, what's going on?"

"Well." Amber sighed in relief. "The capitol is still shut down, Senator. Especially with you gone. But there is talk of

125

a joint session to settle this budget impasse as soon as a quorum can be reached. Possibly as early as this afternoon. But I don't think you should be up and about just yet."

"To hell with that!" he exclaimed. "Is that sonovabitch Hathcock back?"

Amber hesitated, not sure how much she should say, not wanting to agitate his fragile main pump. "Well . . . you know that bill you were considering, the funding bill—"

"Of course. The one he tried to railroad through with the big state land transfer tacked on. What about it?"

"Weeell . . . Representative Hathcock is using a parliamentary maneuver to bring it to the floor for a vote this afternoon. Something about passage by proxy."

He laughed, ruefully. "That sly ol' swamp rat. I'm the one who taught him all them damn tricks. So they plan to run it through in my absence?"

"That's about it, sir."

"Over my dead body. Amber, you find me a flight up there from—wherever the hell I am, and do everything you can to stall that vote. Tell the speaker and majority leaders they wait for me or they'll never get another bill out of committee till the turn of the century. You got that?"

"Yes, sir. But I still think—"

"That's an order!" He heard muffled voices over the phone line, talking in the background. Amber came back on the line. "Senator, I'm so glad you're all right. My cousin is here, Lieutenant Bedrosian. She needs to talk to Mr. Lowell about Marge."

"Sure, I'll put him on."

"Wait!" she exclaimed. "There's something else. I'm not sure I should even tell you, but the Lieutenant wants to know if you've had any more threats."

He hesitated. He'd almost forgotten the phone call at the hospital. "Why? Now what?"

She took a breath, bracing herself. "There's a message for

you here, sir, but I'm not sure I should tell you. I mean, with your heart and all—"

"The hell with that," he snapped. "Let me have it straight, girl, that's what I pay you for!"

"You promise I'll still have a job?" she teased.

"Of course, what the hell do you think, I wanna do all that work myself?"

She laughed. "No sir, it's just that—"

"What message, Amber? Out with it. This is long-distance!"

"Yes sir. Sorry. When I came in this morning, I found a letter on my desk. Sort of a letter. It's printed in block letters, like one of those ransom notes?"

"Girl, I can't take things like that seriously, if I did I'd never get any work done. If we let the lunatic fringe take over, all is lost. Somebody has got to take a stand, and as far as I'm concerned, when it comes to handing out state land and taxpayer's money, the buck stops here. With me."

"I understand, sir, it's just that this one is kind of, I don't know, prophetic?"

"Great. All right, what did it say?"

"It says . . ." He could hear the crinkle of paper as she picked it up and read it: " 'The senator's heart may not hold up next time. He should take the hint. He can submit his resignation and live. Otherwise, he may not.' "

"Oh for cryin' out loud!" Kranhower fumbled for one of his pills, furious that he should even be bothered by such nonsense. Lowell, seeing him turn pale, quickly fetched him a glass of water. Kranhower gulped it without even noticing, still clutching the phone. He took a deep breath. "All right, Amber. Don't worry about it. I'll be there as soon as I can. I'll put Mr. Lowell on now." The senator thrust the phone at him with a growl. "Damn women, always fussing about one thing or another. Somebody wants to talk to you."

Lowell took the phone.

"Hello, Lieutenant. Sorry, it's not like I haven't tried to call you. I've been out of touch." He held the phone away from his ear and grinned at the senator. "Okay, whatever. Look, I've been going over the details, and they just don't fit. Somebody went back to the camp and tried to remove evidence. I don't know what of yet, but I'm starting to think more happened there than we know about. I got some more pictures, and I also found a letter." He dug it out, and read it to her over the phone. Kranhower winced at the terminology.

"Better send it up here," she said. "I'll run it through the state forensics lab. Maybe if we're really lucky we can tie it to this note that came in up here. What else?"

"That's all I can tell you right now, other than he received a threat at the hospital, which is why I brought him up here. I have some lab work to do of my own. Look, call me first thing in the morning and I may have something more by then."

"You better," she complained.

"Gotta go," he said. "If the senator is coming home, I've got to get him to the airport like now. Tell Amber he'll be coming in out of Sarasota, she can page us there in half an hour. Oh, and tell her to arrange for some security!"

"You got it," she said.

He hung up, and turned to his guest. "We'd better go," he said. "You've got a government to reopen."

" 'Bout time," growled the senator, getting to his feet. "Lead the way, son. A fella can get stir-crazy, sittin' around all day."

Two hours later, the sun burned in all its glory, low over the water that danced and sparkled out on Manatee Bay. Back from the airport, Lowell did some rudimentary soil tests in his kitchen, then retired to his darkroom. He had just finished a set of blowups when he heard the familiar sound of tires on the crushed-oyster driveway, coming down from Mangrove

Road. He went into the living room, looked out the window, and recognized Perry's 4-Runner. The screen door slammed behind him as he hurried out through the kitchen onto his little back porch, and walked across the grass to meet his friend.

Perry parked, set the brake, and gingerly hoisted himself out of the driver's seat. "Damn," he muttered. "I must be gettin' old."

"Now what?" said Lowell, offering him a beer. "Just because somebody shot a hole in you, you got a complaint?"

"*Another* hole. I can't take too many more of these," grumbled Perry. He took a swallow of beer, wiped his mouth, and looked around. "Still sunk," he said, meaning the schooner. He swung his eyes back to Lowell. "You wanted to talk about those photos."

Lowell nodded. "Come on inside, I want to show you something."

"Sure," said Perry. "What's up?"

Lowell took Perry inside and showed him the blowups where they were still hanging in the darkroom. Perry studied the various shots of the campsite—the tire and animal tracks, the path, the debris; and the ones of the militia gathering—the picnic tables, the barbecues, the men aiming guns straight at the camera.

"You see anything odd here?"

Perry looked more closely. And looked again. "Yes!" he exclaimed. "In these shots of the picnic! All the women are barefoot and pregnant!"

Lowell scowled. "No, here." He tapped a blowup of the trail running from Marge's campsite.

Perry looked. "Mud," he said. And rocks.

"Exactly." Lowell showed Perry the soil samples from under Marge's fingernails, and the ones from the campsite. "This is peat. It's all around her camp. It was sandy, where they found her."

"So they moved her?"

"I think so," said Lowell. "Now what else do you see there?" He tapped the blowup once again.

Perry picked up a magnifying glass, and looked more closely. "Hmm," he muttered, finally. "Yeah. Those rocks, they look out of place."

Lowell nodded. "And check out these guys" he added, returning to the militia photos. "They're all there, just about everybody we talked to, including some of the cops around there."

Perry shrugged, noncommittally.

Lowell studied one of the group shots. "There's one guy in here, looks to be the leader." He tapped a shot of Rice Crawford, exhorting his troops.

Perry looked. "Yeah, he's the main man, man. The big boss. Top gun. Head honcho."

"You didn't happen to get his name, by any chance?"

"Well, I meant to go up and ask the dude, but by then everybody was shooting at me."

"Yeah."

"Hmmm," said Perry, after a while. "Maybe it's time you and me go back down there and join that there militia, and get to know this dude."

"You can't," said Lowell. "They'll remember you. Not to mention that they are about as racist as you can get. You see any dark-skinned faces down there?"

"Only one," admitted Perry. "When I was hauling my ass outta there and looked in the rearview mirror and saw me."

"So it has to be me," said Lowell.

"There's still a problem," observed Perry.

"What's that?"

"You."

"Me?"

"First of all, those xenophobic paranoiacs don't know you.

And if they did, they wouldn't like you. Second of all, you don't even believe in guns. Won't that, like, show?"

"Details, details," said Lowell. "I still know how to shoot one."

Perry shook his head, and wandered over to the kitchen window that looked out over the bayou, and bay beyond. "Hey, Lowell!" he exclaimed, pointing. "I think you might want to take a look at this." Lowell looked up from his contemplation of the militia photos, and joined him at the window.

"What the hell?" he muttered.

Out on the bay, a forty-foot solid oak, teak, and mahogany Herrshoff schooner was slowly rising from the bottom of the cove, like a creaky wooden submarine, simultaneously groaning in protest and relief at its long-awaited resurrection. It bobbed at last on the surface like a giant cork, awaiting its captain.

"I'll be a sonovabitch!" said Lowell.

They opened the screen door, and raced to the water's edge. Far across the bay, fishermen stopped work mending their illegal gill nets to listen, as an eerie distant sound came drifting across the water.

"Eeeeeeeeehaaaaaaaaaa!" they heard, a faint joyful holler, borne on the wind. Tony Lowell's ancient schooner had just been born again.

13

Morning came, sharp, crisp, and chilly. All the more chilly thanks to a curt, crisp dawn wake-up call from Lena Bedrosian.

"Yeahwuzzit?" mumbled Lowell, his head throbbing. He cracked his eyelids open partway.

"Good morning. You said call first thing in the morning. What'd you find?"

There was a long pause. He opened his eyes the rest of the way, and attempted to formulate a suitable answer. "This is morning?" Lowell finally managed to say. He sat up, and looked around. His head felt like it had split open. He wondered that his remaining brains didn't dribble out.

"I can't talk right now," he mumbled, mouth feeling like old plaster in a condemned building. "Call me back in a few days." He started to hang up.

"Lowell, this is long-distance!" shouted Bedrosian, in outrage. "And time is short. I need some answers."

"All right, all right." Lowell sat up slowly as the blurry overlays of double images all around him began to congeal and he fought off a spell of dizziness. "What was the question again?" Morning had come, ready or not.

Somebody was operating a loud buzz saw, down in his studio. It was a terrible sound, for six in the morning. He didn't like it at all. He told Bedrosian to either call back, or wait while he went to pee, and maybe throw up, and also shut that damn noise off in his living room. "I did find a couple of things," he told her, "if I can remember what they were."

Bedrosian wasn't pleased. "Just call me back," she told him and gave him the number.

The buzz saw was operating from the vicinity of Perry Garwood's somewhat reddened nose, where he had sacked out on the sofa. Lowell remembered now. He and Perry had celebrated the resurrection of his schooner until the wee hours, and then some. Lowell let him be, shuffled to the john, then went to the studio phone and dialed her number.

"So," he said, finally awake. "What's up?"

"You're the one who's supposed to tell me," she snapped. "You said you had to do some lab work."

"Oh," he said. "Right." He told her about the soil samples, and his theory that Marge had been moved.

"Send them!" she ordered.

He told her about the militia photos. How they had taken over a county park, and run Perry off.

"Did you send that letter you found in the Dumpster?" she asked.

"I was about to," he said. "The post office opens in about three hours. So if you'll excuse me, I think I'll go back to sleep now, and—"

"Tell me about this militia. Do you know who's behind it, what their goals are?"

"Not yet. But I was thinking of going down there and joining up."

"You *what?*" Bedrosian was appalled. "You are going to do what?"

"I don't know why everyone finds this so amusing," complained Lowell. "I'm going to infiltrate the Hondo County Militia. Is that so shocking?"

"You get in, that'll be shocking. You get out alive, will be even more shocking. You going to pack a firearm?"

"What for? I'll be outgunned a hundred to one anyway."

"Good point," interjected a newly awakened Perry, stretching and yawning across the room.

"You, Tony Lowell, are going to join a militia. Without a weapon," Lena repeated, in disbelief.

"Oh, thanks for all the support," he complained. "I can always borrow one of Perry's. Just for show."

"And accomplish what?"

"Find out who shot Marge Pappas. You got a problem with that?"

She sighed. "So you think it was someone in the militia?"

"Yes. Either there, or the Club. They are very different organizations, but they seem to have a lot of common interests. There may be another common thread as well. I want to find out who or what it is."

"And you know who the leader or leaders are yet?"

"No. That's what I want to find out."

"Great," she muttered. "So you've narrowed your list of suspects down to everybody in four counties and a guy named What's-His-Name."

"Hey," said Lowell. "It's a start."

Perry rummaged around in the kitchen and managed to come up with a pot of recently fresh Kenyan coffee and some frozen blueberry muffins Lowell had bought in Manatee City before all this had started, and promptly forgotten about.

"Breakfast is served," he announced, after a while.

"That was nice of you," said Lowell, drawn by the aroma of actual food drifting into his studio, where he sat contemplating the photo images now laid out before him.

"It was the only humane thing to do," retorted Perry, "inas-

135

much as your table is typically devoid of any organic or inorganic substances such as anything more highly evolved than a palmetto bug might find edible, thus putting us both at risk of nutrition deprivation, combined with the very fact that you had sequestered even a potential for something of this caliber of culinary magnitude indicating good intentions and a desire for change on your part, merely called for participatory acknowledgment on the part of me, your humble houseguest."

Lowell wasn't *that* awake. "Say what?" he asked.

They ate in silence. Perry seemed edgy. There was something in the wind, something blowing up from Big Cypress, he said. His shoulder ached. He felt very apprehensive about Lowell's stated intentions, down there.

"Maybe you'll feel better in the light of day," suggested Lowell.

Perry shook his head, gloomily. He was in one of his fatalistic, philosophical Native American moods. "I just don't like it. You gotta pack some heat, man," he said. "It looks cold out there. Real cold this morning."

"It's a cold, cruel world," Lowell agreed. He was not persuaded by Perry's violent visions or prophetic pronouncements. It was one of his character traits—or flaws, as some of his friends might suggest—that in matters of personal conviction, he tended to be stubborn. Even though it often led to sometimes rigorous lessons in life, also known as hard knocks.

"At least let me show you how to disable a guy holding a twelve-gauge at your back, without even—" Perry started in.

"Perry!" Lowell remained adamant on that issue, except that he had finally succumbed to pressure on one point: Since he was trying to insinuate himself into a gun club, he might oughta carry a gun. "For show," he conceded. "I'll be fine," he added.

Perry drove off to work, vague as usual as to the specifics. Tony cleaned up the kitchen, and put on the radio. The news buzzed about traffic and the unusually cold weather coming

136

in (lows in the upper thirties tonight), and the hoped-for re-opening of the state government. The legislature had met for a closed special session yesterday to discuss the budget, and was expected to meet again today. No specific bills were mentioned, only that people visiting state parks could rest assured the rest rooms remained open.

Perry had left an old Winchester twenty-gauge shotgun leaning against the doorjamb. Lowell picked it up on his way out, fending off the old memories it conjured up, and carried it to the falling-down barn that served as his garage.

Mist was rising off the water as Lowell drove across Manatee Bay, to Manatee City. He drove to the post office, where he stuck the photographs, the three soil samples, and Marge's threatening letter in an overnight Express Mail envelope, and addressed it to Lena c/o the Hampton Inn in Tallahassee. Knowing her, she should be able to ramrod them through the state criminal forensics lab in a day, off duty or not. Or if she couldn't do it, Amber probably could, if she was any kind of relative. Assuming the lab was still open, that is, considering the still unresolved shutdown. He hesitated for a moment, and considered keeping the evidence a little longer, to give to Lena when she got back in town. He'd wanted to study some of the photos some more. Also he hadn't had a chance to study the shots from the ME's office yet. The Photomat prints were useless, and he hadn't had much time with his own blowups. He might have missed something. He decided to keep the prints and send the blowups. In any case he was going to be too busy staying alive the next day or two for forensics.

Lowell left the post office feeling unsettled, picked up the Interstate at the Manatee Parkway entrance, and sped on south toward Fort Myers: a fast hundred miles of flat, open freeway through pine forest, saw palmettos, and low mangrove-fringed coastal wetlands. The morning was still cool. Another arctic high had pushed in during the night, and as a result the air was as clear and sharp as a Sanibel lagoon.

He reached Patterson's Landing just in time for the weekly gathering of the TV talk show contingent. The timing wasn't intentional, by any means. Far from it. It was just how it worked out. As he pushed open the flimsy double-screen door and entered the dark, smoke-filled room—lit only by a fuzzy big screen TV that was much the worse for a thousand hours of football and right-wing raves—fifty True Believers swiveled their heads his way. Their current talk show hero's expansive profile was crudely visible on the screen, a dark, lurking outline. Today's theme was the American flag, and how some foreigner in Florida had tried to show a foreign flag, and had been rightfully chastised by the local Southern patriots. Many of whom, Lowell knew, also flaunted Confederate flags on their own homes. Or vehicles. Lowell didn't catch any of the details, but it sounded similar to the time Rush Limbaugh had defended the guy in Louisiana who shot the trick-or-treater for the grave offense of being a foreigner. The crowd couldn't have been more pleased. Lowell guessed that he was probably looking right at the bulk of the Hondo County Militia at that very moment. And unfortunately, they were all now looking right at him.

Lowell feigned the role of a passing-through customer, and made his way among the snack food and gun magazine racks along the wall to the lunch counter. The heads swiveled back and the show went on. A heavyset, weary-looking woman came out of the kitchen, which adjoined the office.

"Kin ah hep you?" she asked.

Lowell offered her his best fake smile. "Coffee," he suggested. "Arabica blend, with milk and honey. River Jordan style."

She wasn't amused. She pursed her lips, and regarded him as a crank. "Ain't got no honey," she said. "No milk, neither."

There was a loud, raucous cheer in the room. The famed TV orator had scored another rhetorical three-pointer. The woman, presumably Mrs. Patterson, set down his coffee and

138

vanished into the kitchen, just as Lowell was bravely thinking about risking a chicken sandwich. He was distracted by a movement to his left, and turned sharply. He'd left the gun in the trunk, of course, where it belonged. Billy appeared before him, a fright to see even for a man that wasn't hungover.

"Jesus," muttered Lowell. "What the hell happened to you?"

Billy was one big, ugly bruise. He had a bandage on his skull that ran from his forehead to just above his right ear, and it was seeping. There were black-and-blue marks, contusions and lacerations on his face, neck, shoulders, and upper arms. Billy's lower lip was puffed and swollen. It trembled slightly.

"Nuthin', " he muttered.

"Yeah right, come on, kid, let's get outta here."

Lowell got to his feet, threw two dollars on the counter, picked up the little bag of snacks he'd just purchased, and moved toward the double doors. Billy stood frozen, where he was. His eyes said he wanted to come, but then they turned in a direction behind Lowell and the look changed to one of terror. Billy's smashed mouth remained mute.

"Billy," the woman called, from the kitchen.

Lowell shook his head at the boy emphatically, and edged closer to the door. "Just follow me out, don't stay around, don't say anything, just go. Run for the blue Impala," he commanded, in a low urgent whisper.

He reached the door, and made the mistake of glancing back. Everyone in the room was looking at him again. It was an endless frozen moment, which oddly reminded Lowell of a movie scene, from when he was a kid. The movie was *The Birds,* directed by Alfred Hitchcock. There was a scene when the main character, a long-forgotten Australian actor named Rod Taylor, walks out of a besieged café with a woman and child, and all these killer birds are up there on the wires, rooftops, still yet restless, just watching, watching, as though waiting for a signal.

Lowell could see one man watching him with special attentiveness. Mixed with dark hate and fury: Duvall Patterson, the proprietor, Billy's father. Lowell glanced toward the office door, just glimpsing the departing shadow as Billy vanished within. He pushed on the swinging doors and stepped out into the blinding sun. No one moved. The talk show raconteur ranted on in the background, for once unattended.

Lowell resisted, firmly resisted the desire to run for it, throw open the Chevy door, hit that starter, and burn rubber out of there. There was no sign of Billy as he reached the car, set the bag on the full-width seat, and ever so casually, ever so carefully started the engine. His eyes were fixed on the double doors, wondering who would follow, and how quickly. There was still no sign of Billy. He honked once, quickly, a short note of urgency. Still no sign of movement from the office, which had a separate outside door on the left side of the building.

Suddenly a face appeared in the driver's side window: Duvall Patterson. He must have come out the back and circled around, Lowell realized. Which meant he'd already underestimated the man. Duvall just stood there and gave Lowell a sad, woeful look that chilled him far more than any evil yellow-toothed leer might have done. Lowell hesitated, once again fought down the temptation to burn rubber out of there, and rolled down his window. He felt the tension escalate.

"Hello," he said.

Duvall regarded him through narrow, balefully slitted red eyes. Lowell was startled to see that the man had been crying. "You need somethin', mister?" Duvall asked, after a moment of mutually hostile regard passed by.

Lowell nodded at the paper bag on the seat. "Already got it, thanks. I left the money on the counter."

Duvall nodded, having watched his every move. "You don't need no gas?" he asked.

Lowell did, but not that much. "No thanks," he said, looking past Duvall at the office, still hoping Billy could make it, somehow. Maybe Billy still had some sparks of fire left burning in him. As well as some savvy, and would—could make his move. But Lowell knew Billy wasn't going to come out as long as his father was standing there. He needed to stall, on the one hand, and get rid of Duvall, on the other. There were two possible ways to do it. One would be to do it Perry-style: create a diversion, yell fire-murder-police, throw a tantrum like Hamlet, toss a firebomb on the roof. That might work, except he didn't have a firebomb. The other was to engage the man in conversation, keep his back to the office, and steer him back inside, somehow.

"Listen, I couldn't help noticing what y'all had on the tube inside," he said. "I'm kinda new around here, but I'd like to get to know some of the like-minded folks in the area."

"Like-minded like how?"

"Well, I heard y'all had a picnic down at the park last Sunday. Kind of sorry I missed it."

Duvall's face seemed to tighten, ever so slightly. "I wouldn't know about that," he said. "Will there be anything else?"

There was no sign of Billy. Aware that he was losing it, Lowell tried one last approach. "Well, yeah. Since I'm gonna be in the area, who should I see about joining your little club here?"

"This is a public facility," replied Duvall. "Nobody's stopping you."

Lowell had to admire that answer. "Thanks. I'll keep that in mind."

Lowell threw a final glance at the building, then at his watch, which told him the talk show was a wrap. Which meant the lunchtime crowd was about to descend on him en masse. He'd had enough of them one-on-one. It was time to go.

Reluctantly, Lowell nodded to Duvall, started the engine,

and put the car into gear. Pulling away from that gas station was as hard a thing as he'd ever had to do, leaving that boy behind.

Duvall never said another word, just stood and watched as Lowell drove off. He knew damn well who Tony Lowell was. He'd been seen talking to his son. Billy had finally broken down after some necessary persuasion, and told him all about it. It had hurt him as much as Billy: both the asking, and the answers. But there were times when a man had to go an extra mile to take a stand. Take firm steps to hold his family together, when it was all coming apart so rapidly. Like that general said, sometimes that meant destroying the village in order to save it.

Duvall wiped his eyes, blew his nose, shook his head at the sorrowful way his life was going to hell in a shrimp basket, and went back inside.

14

Lowell drove a quarter-mile or so around the first bend in the river. There were a couple of pickups and campers parked along the water's edge. Fishermen. He pulled over in front of the farthest vehicle from the Landing and parked. No one paid him any attention. Fishermen came and went here and everywhere along Florida's endless shores, day and night. He almost wished he'd brought a fishing pole. He might be here awhile.

He ate the lunch he'd bought at Patterson's Landing, a guaranteed heartburn special: overboiled coffee with powder whitener and white cane sugar; a prepackaged cellophane-sealed "wheat bread" tuna salad sandwich with no lettuce, a waxed, polished apple with a little smiley face sticker on it that he couldn't peel off, and a Mr. Peanut candy bar. Lowell had read that peanuts contained more pesticides per volume than any other agricultural product. Great. They'll kill you one way if not the other, he figured. And ate the bar.

There was a sudden whoosh of motion as the first True Be-

liever hurried by in his pickup, followed quickly by the rest—
returning to their construction jobs at the new housing developments, or the waste management facility, or the
numerous ranches around La Belle. Most drove trucks. Some
drove utility vehicles. Some of them were brand-new. Especially the Chevys, all sporting license plate holders that ad-
vertised "Hathcock Motors, Naples." Several boats droned
past on the river, disrupting the fishermen with their wakes,
drivers and anglers exchanging jocular hollers. They all knew
each other. He kept his head down, wishing he'd parked a little farther off the road.

Ten minutes went by. An immense, box-shaped old Cadillac sedan approached. He watched it come in his rearview
mirror. It was the same vintage as Lowell's Impala, from a time
when the creative energies of the nation were being applied
elsewhere than the auto industry. It took up most of the road
as it thundered past, blue smoke billowing from its dual
rusted tailpipes. Lowell almost liked it. He recognized the
driver: Duvall Patterson. Duvall's watery eyes were fixed on
the road straight ahead, and he seemed preoccupied. The
woman, presumably his wife, was with him. She threw a
glance at Lowell's car, but showed no sign of recognition. She,
too, seemed preoccupied. Lowell let them pass, and waited
awhile.

As soon as traffic had dissipated, he turned around, and
drove back to the Landing. It was as though a storm had
passed through, stripping the land and moorings of anything
that hadn't been nailed or tied down. The parking lot was
empty. The boats were gone from the dock, except the few rot-
ting, abandoned ones that probably belonged to Duvall. The
sunken whaler he'd rented had been towed away. There wasn't
a sound. Nothing moved except the treetops, the current in the
river beyond, and the waterbirds. Lowell spotted Billy's old
Ford pickup, half hidden in the trees back by the Dumpster.

He walked over to the office door, and knocked.

"Billy! You in there? It's me, Lowell!"

He waited a little longer. There wasn't a sound. He rapped again, this time harder. "Billy! Open up!"

The sign said Closed, which was odd, this being the middle of a weekday afternoon. On the other hand, the road was empty of traffic. He tried the door. It was unlocked. He pushed it open. It creaked, unexpectedly loud.

"Anybody here?" he called out again. "Hello?"

Finally, he heard it. A scratching, scraping sound, coming from the kitchen. He took a step in that direction, and paused. Suddenly a ghastly shape appeared in the doorway, pale and silent as a midnight apparition. If anything, he looked even worse than before.

"Hello, Billy," said Lowell.

Lowell led Billy to a chair behind the metal office desk, and sat him down. "Easy," he cautioned him. "Maybe I should get you to a doctor."

"No!" Billy almost shouted. "I'm fine. It's nothin'."

"The hell it is." Lowell found some paper towels and soap, and a sink in the kitchen. The sink was porcelain on metal, rust stains bleeding through. He fixed a poultice, and mopped and sponged until Billy seemed a bit cleaner, a bit more alert. He smelled of hate, and violence, and betrayal, of cigarette smoke, and greasy food.

"It ain't no big thing," Billy insisted, when Lowell finished his ministrations. "Just a little disagreement, that's all."

"How often do you and your old man have these little disagreements?"

Billy gave him an odd, shrewd look. "That ain't the problem," he said, in such a way that startled Lowell. "Anyways, it ain't nothin'."

"Yeah, so I see," said Lowell. "Listen, what say you and I go for a ride, get you out of here, go see a doctor—"

145

"No doctor!" insisted Billy.

Lowell nodded, reluctantly. "What about your Mom?"

"No!" The emphasis was sharp, and unmistakable.

Lowell frowned. "Okay, so how 'bout we go for a drive, I'll show you how a classic Chevy runs, you show me some more of the local sights. How 'bout it?"

Billy shrugged, listlessly. "Sure, why not?"

They drove in silence. Then the emotional logjam broke, and it began to come out. "Oh, Jesus!" moaned the boy. Then more emphatically: "Oh, Jesus!"

Lowell couldn't agree more, except he still didn't know what he was agreeing about, but knew enough to remain silent. They drove for a while.

"How're the panthers doin'?" he finally asked.

"Somebody shot one of the Texans." He sounded hollow, when he said it. As though all the insides had been pounded out of him.

"Texans?" Lowell was confused. "I don't understand."

"He said he was doing it to help the panthers, like for crossbreeding. That's how it was supposed to be."

"You'd better explain. Somebody brought in some panthers from Texas?"

"Cougars, actually. They're basically similar. But they lied about it. They got some kind of initiation, the new member has to shoot something big. Panther's as big as it gets, except for gators, and they cain't shoot Florida panther, so they bring 'em in from Texas just for the occasion."

"Wait a minute, slow down there, pardner. Who does this?"

"The Hunt Club, man, who else? Sometimes they get away and breed. I always root they'll get away, 'cause the locals can't breed no more."

"Panthers, you mean?"

Billy nodded. "At least they ain't shot Gussie yet."

"Gussie?"

146

"The one me and Marge found, with the cubs."

"Gussie." Lowell nodded. "Good name."

Billy looked at him sidewise. "She's okay so far," he said, snapping out of it some. "But not for long."

"Why do you say that?"

"Because now we got the damn militia. They're on patrol duty tonight, in the groves. Bivouac's at Lejeune's. That's where my old man's goin'."

"Patrol duty? What kind of patrol duty?"

Billy shook his head and wouldn't say.

Lowell wanted to talk to Superintendent Connors again, but that could wait. He also wanted to talk to Bedrosian again, if he could get hold of her.

"Billy, you knew Marge pretty well, right?"

"Well as anybody, I guess," came the sullen response.

"You know if she had any friends around here? I mean, the kind she could confide in?"

"Maybe just me," said Billy, after a while.

Lowell thought about that.

"You know if she had any lovers—you know, boyfriend, girlfriend?"

"Nothin' like that."

Lowell felt it best not to mention to Billy, just then, his own experience with Marge Pappas.

Lowell pushed back the feelings memories of Marge brought up, sensing that Billy, too, had some unstated feelings toward her, wondering how significant they were, how far they might have taken him, and in what direction.

"How'd them pictures I took turn out?" Billy suddenly asked, as they turned into the small shopping strip at the edge of town, and parked in a bit of shade around back, under two huge live oaks dripping Spanish moss.

"They were good. Here, let me show you." Lowell had kept the budget prints for this very purpose, and sent the blowups to Tallahassee. He took them out now and handed them over to Billy.

Billy looked at them a long moment, then surprised him with a request. "Can I keep them?"

Lowell hesitated, then shook his head. "Not yet. They're evidence."

"You should always make doubles. They only cost two bucks more."

"When you're right, you're right, kid," said Lowell, with a grin.

"Somebody wrote her a letter," Lowell said. That, he'd copied. He dug the copy out of his jacket pocket and showed it to Billy.

Billy read it, and turned pale. "Oh God," he said. "Could been anybody around here," he said. "Anybody."

Lowell folded the paper up again, thoughtfully. "Where you wanna go?" he asked, as they approached Immokalee.

"Let's get some pizza," Billy suggested suddenly. They'd passed a take-out restaurant a block earlier.

"It's lousy, but you can eat it. This ain't exactly Rome," observed Billy, wryly. Lowell laughed, and slapped his bruised shoulder.

"Ouch!"

"Sorry," said Lowell.

Lowell bought the pizza, and they ate it the car. He told Billy what his plans were, and asked if there was anybody in particular he should approach once he got in to the upcoming militia bivouac.

"You're crazy," commented Billy. "You ain't gonna get in."

"Not even at night, just wave my rifle and drive in, like I'm a regular ol' boy?"

"But you ain't," said Billy, shaking his head. "They'll know."

Lowell knew he was right. There would probably be armed guards at all the access points, who would be checking. They probably had a list. He wished he could get a copy of it. Still, he had to try. He got out the Photomat pictures again, and showed Billy the ones from the picnic. He pointed at the shots of the leader, talking.

"Billy, who's this guy? Is he the head man, around here? In the militia?"

"You mean like commanding officer?"

"Yeah, the general, colonel, head honcho, top dawg kind of guy."

Billy didn't have to think about it. "No. That would be Quentin," he answered, guardedly. "Quentin Lejeune. This is Rice Crawford. He's like the foreman, and, like, speaker—"

"Spokesman?"

"Yeah. Mr. Lejeune has a speech, whaddyacallit. Iped—"

"Impediment?"

"Yeah. He don't talk at all. This guy Mr. Crawford, he does all the talking for Quentin Lejeune."

Lowell was certain he'd heard the name before. "He live around here? This Lejuene person?"

Billy laughed. "Yeah, he's only like the biggest rancher and citrus grower this side of Okeechobee. Lejeune Farm and Ranch. Owns half of four counties. But you don't want to go there."

"Why not?"

"Because," said Billy, stubbornly. "He don't know you."

That seemed to be the problem with everyone around here, Lowell was beginning to think. God help anybody who was a stranger, hereabouts.

"What about Marge Pappas? Did she know Quentin? Or vice versa?"

Billy paled. He didn't like that line of questioning at all. "I don't think so," he said. "Not personally. Anyways, my dad told me Mr. Crawford always said Mr. Lejeune didn't like to hunt nothin' except niggers and spics. I can't see him shootin' a woman."

Lowell wondered if that was Quentin's view, or Crawford's. "Sounds like a regular all-American kind of guy."

"You don't want to go there."

Lowell did too, and said so.

"You're crazy," said Billy. But after some prodding, he reluctantly gave Lowell directions to the Lejeune ranch. "It's down near Devil's Garden," he told him. "You can't miss it."

"Wanna come along?" invited Lowell.

Billy gave him a drop-dead look, and shook his head.

"Let me out up there." He pointed ahead. "At the pool hall."

Lowell slowed, and saw that the place was a biker bar. A garish neon sign splashed its declaration across the front roof: "Billiards. Beer and Wine. Cuban Food." Well, he reflected. Sometimes you have to take your friends where you can find them. Bikers could even make pretty good friends at times. He knew from experience. He let Billy out, and drove on.

The temperature had dropped twenty degrees in the last hour, and was still going down. One of those rare, but exceedingly bothersome arctic weather fronts was barreling southward, straight down from the Great Plains, with nothing to stop it until it hit Florida like an ice ball in the face of an unsuspecting sunbather. The citrus groves were abuzz with activity, in anticipation of that coming cold front. Pickups and harvest trucks were tearing to and fro on the back roads, their drivers grim-faced. Migrant workers wearing startlingly bright colors scurried about as though their livelihoods depended on it. Which they did.

Lowell found the modestly discreet entrance to Lejeune Farms after following a row of orange and grapefruit groves that ran for miles, literally, along a back county road he would have never found but for Billy's directions.

The white wooden gates stood open. The fence was obviously more a formality than for any security purpose, and a two-track gravel road went straight ahead, vanishing into the distant belt of citrus trees. Lowell turned in, saw no one but workers laboring in the groves, and drove on ahead. One truck passed him on its way out, carrying a shipment of early, possibly slightly premature fruit. He had to pull into a small turnout to let it pass, but the driver paid him no mind, assuming, Lowell supposed, that he had business there. People came and went all day long with a big operation like this. Lowell hoped the resulting anonymity would help him get to Lejeune.

The house and barns caught him by surprise. He came over a low rise and a large clearing suddenly opened out before him. The house was a classic Southern Colonial, white, clapboard, two stories, Greek columns, and a wide portico in front. Out back rambled several rows of large prefab aluminum buildings, presumably for ranch operations and equipment. It didn't fit the image of a Cracker militiaman at all.

Lowell could see that some emergency was taking place. He parked the Chevy and got out, staggered momentarily by a sudden unaccustomed blast of chilly northern air. Dressed only in his usual faded jeans and navy T-shirt, he rubbed the sudden goosebumps down on his arms, and berated himself for forgetting his jacket. He remembered he might have an old woolen work shirt in the trunk, and found it partially wedged under the spare tire. Smeared with grease from some long-forgotten abuse, it was still serviceable and provided needed warmth. He walked toward the nearest building, where he could hear sounds of machinery and shouting voices. The double sliding doors were open to the cavernous darkness within.

"I don't give a damn how you do it," he heard a gravel-toned voice bellow. "Y'all get that fruit in or protect those trees. One or the other. Or you are history, boy!"

There was a mumbled reply, more shouts, and the scrambling of footsteps. "And get them pipelines working!" He heard one final epithet. An aluminum screen door slammed, and an engine revved. A big GMC pickup truck came speeding out of the doorway, roared past with two harried-looking men inside, vanishing into the groves on the far side.

Lowell walked in through the same opening. "Hello?" he called.

A young Hispanic man appeared before him, eyes questioning, and wary. *"Que quiere?"* he demanded. Lowell noted he had a sheathed machete in his belt, and was wearing a holstered pistol. He also remembered that there had been no Hispanic men or women at the church picnic last Sunday, where Perry had been shot.

"Buscando por el dueno," Lowell managed in his high school Spanish.

"Mr. Quentin!" shouted the young man, not taking his eyes off Lowell. *"Venga!"*

Lowell recognized him at once: from news photographs over the years, and from his night at the Club. Short, lean, a white brush haircut, beige chinos, and a heavy fleece-lined jacket. He came out of a partitioned inner office, looked at his employee questioningly, then his pale blue eyes slid over and settled on Lowell with a hunter's scrutiny. They bore the same icy intensity as the arctic wind that had just arrived outside. Lowell felt no more welcome than the cold front, as though he were being examined like an exotic species of prey. Lejeune didn't speak.

"Kin ah hep you with somethin'?" The voice came from behind him, startling him. Lowell turned to face Rice Crawford. The man from the picnic. He spoke with a tone of unquestionable authority.

Lowell looked back at Lejeune, who nodded briefly at Crawford, and walked out of the room. Lowell had his story ready. He hoped it was a good one. "Hello, uh, you must be Mr. Crawford? My name's Lowell. Tony Lowell. I'm doing

152

some research on citrus growing for the County Extension, and wondered if I could ask a few questions."

Crawford looked at Lowell like he was a loathsome fruit fly. Like he was accustomed to giving orders, not answering questions. "We're busy here. What kinda questions?"

"Well, for example, I noticed a considerable degree of activity in the groves today. Is this sudden cold weather likely to damage your crop?"

Crawford looked at him shrewdly. "Mister, you obviously ain't been payin' attention. We got a freeze comin'."

Lowell hugged himself against the cold, and grinned. "You don't say. I keep forgetting those things happen. Even in Florida. Say, this would be a wonderful opportunity for me to see firsthand the methodology for freeze prevention and management."

Crawford's lip curled slightly, then he shrugged, and turned away. "Sorry. If y'all excuse me, I got about a million bushels of crop to save. Maybe another tahm."

Lowell stayed with him. "Mind if I tag along? Just to see how it's done?"

Crawford stopped and faced him. He looked like something not that far removed from a rattlesnake ready to strike.

"Y'all got any credentials, Mr. Lowell?" He had remembered the name.

Lowell actually did. He had an old Sun Coast Community College faculty card, from his off-again on-again days as a college instructor. He handed it to the ranch foreman. Crawford looked at the card as if it was spit, and handed it back.

"College boy," he said, contemptuously.

"Faculty," Lowell corrected him. "Like I said, I'm doing research. For a course on environmental agriculture," he improvised.

Crawford stopped cold. "You one of them environmentalists?" His voice bore even more scorn than before.

Oops. Wrong approach. "No. Not exactly. Look, I don't want

163

to keep you from your business, but I won't get in the way. I'd just like to observe."

Crawford ran out of patience. "Mister, the only thing I want you to observe is the No Trespassin' sign y'all apparently didn't see along the boundaries of this propity. Which I want y'all to leave, now." He shouted over to the young Hispanic man. "Vega," he yelled. "Show Mr. Lowell the way to the gate."

Crawford turned and strode off in the direction of a mud-spattered GM flatbed, across the yard. The young man walked toward Lowell, hand on his gun butt. Lowell wondered if this Vega could be related to a certain sheriff's deputy he'd met at the shooting site. He smiled, spread his hands, backed out, and got back in the Chevy. Per Rice Crawford's request, he wasted no time leaving the premises. But unlike Crawford's request, he didn't quite leave the property.

About a quarter-mile north of the main gate, he pulled onto the shoulder of the county highway. The groves spread on both sides of the road as far as the eye could see: parallel rows, each one straight and narrow, round-domed trees loaded with fruit, mostly oranges, some grapefruit or tangerines, some lemons. The trees ran for miles. Each row was wide enough to drive a vehicle through, and each vehicle was visible for a considerable distance, until perspective eventually made the rows seem filled in.

Lowell picked a row just beyond one in which he could see the frantic activity of men and machines a couple of hundred yards distant. Heavy flexible black plastic pipes ran parallel to each row on each side, with T-connections at the ends and heavy-duty sprinkler heads for each tree. Must be a thousand miles of pipe here, thought Lowell. And water heavily discounted to Lejeune—the same water that the residential consumers of Florida were now paying dearly for, including himself. He parked on the shoulder, hopped over the token rail fence, and walked in the direction of the work crew, one parallel row to the north.

It was obvious the crew was already doing double time. Most were stripping the trees of ripe or nearly ripe fruit, others were repairing or installing aboveground sprinkler pipes, and others were placing smudge pots every hundred feet or so—the last resort against a freeze. He knew about the sprinklers. They were called microsprinkers, designed to keep the fruit and trees from freezing by coating them with ice, then keeping a flow of water above freezing temperature on the trees. It took prodigious quantities of water to do this, although usually the process didn't go beyond four hours or so. If temperatures got below twenty-five degrees for more than four hours, no amount of spraying would help, and the crop would be lost anyway.

Lowell also knew about smudge pots. Smudge pots were environmentally hazardous as well as expensive, and at the very least, were severely frowned upon. Few growers used them anymore because of fuel cost and pressure from the EPA. They were being set out in case all else failed. It was clear Quentin Lejeune was more afraid of Jack Frost than he was of public opinion. Lowell wondered what other bothersome laws or regulations Lejeune considered himself above, and what further extremes he might go to to defy them.

Deciding as usual in favor of discretion over valor, Lowell avoided confrontation with the crew bosses, whom he now recognized as being some of the militia members he'd seen at Patterson's Landing and the picnic. They were armed, probably trigger-happy, and under orders to keep nosy intruders such as himself at bay. He turned to make his way back to the car and found himself staring down the barrel of a twelve-gauge shotgun, held by an unfriendly-looking man of advanced years. He'd seen him earlier in the day at Patterson's Landing. The man recognized him, as well, but couldn't quite place him. He was in his late sixties, Lowell guessed, a face lined with a lifetime of outdoor exposure to the Florida sun. There were signs of melanoma on his nose and forehead. Lowell wondered if the man knew his days were probably numbered. It was a moot point. By the man's expression, his own days might be on a short list.

"Who the hail ah yew?" the man demanded to know, his Cracker voice a nasal snarl.

"State Department of Agriculture. Inspector Lowell," bluffed Lowell, flashing his PI license, knowing the man couldn't read it (if he could read at all). "You have a permit for those smudge pots?" Of course they didn't, but the question caught the man off guard. He frowned. "Ah think," he said, "y'all bettah tell me why ah shouldn't jes' shoot youah ass, mister, faw chespassin'.'"

"Well, that would be a clear violation of the first commandment, plus several statutes of Florida law," he replied. Lowell was ready for the next part. A call to Connors after leaving Billy at the bar had confirmed that almost all of this district was state land, leased by Lejeune Farms for ten dollars a year per acre. "Also," he continued, "I believe this land is the property of the state of Florida, sir," he bluffed once more. "And as a citizen taxpayer and employee of this state"—a semitruth—"I'm merely checking up on the people's rightful property. Now," he continued, as his inquisitor's eyes bugged out farther and farther with each statement, "who might you be?"

The man with melanoma almost lost his composure, and his grip on the rifle butt tightened. "Who ah am is the man who is gonna count to ten, aftah which ah intend to clean up this heah environment of some vermin that don't belong heah! One!" he raised the double barrels, and started counting.

There were shouts, from an adjacent row. Growing sounds

of discontent in Spanish, and harsh replies: "I'll tell you when you can take a goddamn break! We gotta get this done or there's no fuckin' tomorrow!" Someone else shouted, from an adjacent row: "Hey Lucas! Where the hail you at?"

Lowell decided not to find out if he was bluffing or not. He remembered where he'd seen this man before. It was in a photograph, taken from the same angle—the business end of a shotgun. Only that time, it had been aimed at a similarly retreating Perry Garwood and Billy Patterson.

"Just one last question, Mr., uh, Lucas," he said, backing away. "You make the same threat to Florida state Wildlife Officer Marge Pappas?"

Lucas's hand wavered at that and he lost count a moment. Lowell dove into the grove just as the gun went off with a roar.

"Goddamn communist agitator!" he heard the old man shout. "You go to hail!"

Lowell decided it was time to talk to Bedrosian. He drove back to Immokalee, and pulled over at the phone booth across from the biker bar where he'd dropped off Billy Patterson. With any luck, she was back in Manatee City. He hoped so. He dialed her home number. After eleven rings, he cursed, and hung up. Fumbling in the chill for his tattered notebook, he found the number for the Hampton Inn in Tallahassee, and dialed with his calling card. The motel operator put him through with typical southern cheeriness.

Miracle of miracles, she was in. "How're things up there in Noleville?" he asked, when Bedrosian came on.

"Lowell," she snapped. "Don't ask. I'm going bananas up here. If I eat one more Chuck E. Cheese pizza I'm going to throw up all over the governor's bougainvillea."

"What, Michael not showing you the sights? Taking you around to all his old haunts? Doing the old tomahawk chop

157

and Seminole war dance, painting the town red, cheering for good old—"

"Enough already!" she shouted. "If I wanted to be a cheerleader I'd a bought a baton. What've you found?"

"One hell of a lot of hostility, for one thing. It's hard to figure. All these people with more space per capita than ten average Americans, and it's not enough for them. They all have more chips on their shoulder than a woodcutter, and the personality of an alligator. What the hell are they so mad about?"

"Too much government interference, is what I hear."

"Like from your cousin Marge, is that what you mean?"

That gave her pause. "She was just a game warden, for chrissake!"

"Her official job title was state Wildlife Officer. And like you she worked for the government. The one everybody seems to hate so much down here. Part of her job was to enforce the laws."

"Look," snapped Lena. "Marge Pappas was not the type to go around depriving people of their rights!"

"All I'm saying is when people get angry, some of them overreact."

"Well then, your job is to figure out who overreacted. Period."

"I'm trying my best, Bedrosian. I'm just saying that Marge may have not only been up against some high-powered, well-heeled poachers with firearms, but also a gang of gun-toting militia who don't respect firearms laws. Those are not some really great odds for one woman alone in the woods!"

"Just get to the point, Lowell. You found anything else useful, or not?"

"Only what I sent you. But I'm looking for a connection between this local gun club, and whoever's in charge of state land acquisitions."

"That's easy. Senator Kranhower is. They've been after him to sign some bill that signs over a bunch of state land to those people."

"I know, he told me."

"So what about the local cops, what did they say?"

"What, you mean besides 'get out of Dodge'? "

"I see. You sure you're okay, Lowell?"

"I'm fine. Call me at the Days Inn as soon as you get the handwriting report. Oh, and ask them to confirm my theory about those soil samples, will you?"

"Slow down, what am I, a secretary? Listen, you're not going to go through with your harebrained scheme of crashing that militia, are you?"

He was tempted to bluster and bluff, but relented. "No," he admitted. "I know pretty much what they're up to, already."

"Which is?"

"They're bivouacking at one of the big citrus farms, Lejeune Farms, using the occasion to help their commanding officer fight the freeze," he explained. "Free labor for him I suppose, and they'll probably really get into it. Building fires, smudge pots, what have you. It'll be like a mission, except no time for shooting. Unless, of course, the workers try to take a break. Or maybe run for it."

"What do you mean?"

"I mean, he's using the militia to keep the workers in line. To them its probably a patriotic duty. To him, it's free labor enforcement."

"Jesus," she muttered. "I think you should talk to the sheriff, before you jump to any more stupid conclusions."

"And tell him what, that I work for you?"

"All right, touché."

"What worries me is that they gather for these talk show raves, get all worked up, until they're looking for someone to hit. I got a bad feeling about this, Bedrosian. I think this guy

159

Lejeune is pulling their strings, not just using them for field hands."

"What? You think he is pushing them toward some kind of Oklahoma City type thing?"

"I don't know. But it may have been something your cousin Marge ran into the wrong end of."

"Really, Lowell. Aside from being a totally loco idea, it sounds like one of those sixties' conspiracy theories of yours."

"Except backwards. Because in this one, it could be the government who are the good guys. It's the locals I'm worried about. You want me to solve this case, or not? The victim was a government employee. Another government employee, no less than Senator Kranhower, got shanghaied by a hundred self-styled high-powered Paul Reveres with muskets, one of whom was this same guy Lejeune. The same guy who runs this so-called militia, through his henchman, a foreman named Crawford who's straight out of the Bull Connor handbook. So far all, and I mean all, the suspects down here, of which there are dozens, hate the government. They're not too crazy about me either, if you want to know."

"Now that," she said, "does not surprise me. Call me tomorrow, and I'll see what I can do. Oh, and Lowell," she added, and her voice changed, ever so slightly. "Be careful, will you? I heard about your friend."

"No problem," he quipped. "I've got a gun."

Her astonishment was monumental. "I don't believe it!" she exclaimed. "Now you pack a weapon. Now that you're going to go up against a hundred rednecks all of whom are better armed and better shots than you, who would love nothing better than a good excuse, and you're gonna—"

"It's a joke, Lena," he chided her softly. "You're the one always told me I should carry a weapon. Perry gave it to me, my ever-protective pal. It's in the trunk."

"Better leave it there," she said. "Just be careful, will you?" She hung up before he could answer.

160

Lowell walked across the street to the biker bar to see if Billy was still there, before going back to the Landing for a long overdue chat with his father. Also, it seemed to him like just about the safest place around these parts to have a beer in peace.

15

Lowell generally avoided bars. When he wanted a few beers, like with his friend Perry (now sulking at home in Palmetto), they sat on the dockside deck of the Clam Shack, back in Gulfbridge. But this time, in a strange and unwelcoming town, he wanted to be around people. Especially people who were just living their lives, not hell-bent on some mission of righteous zealotry. He surveyed the dim, smoky pool hall, found a corner away from the crowd, and ordered a Kirin from a tired, bleached-blond mininskirted middle-aged waitress. Make that "server," as she informed him. As in "Hi, I'm Barbara, your server." What the hell, he figured. Whatever shucks your oysters. She had goose bumps on her overworked (although still fit) legs from the excessive air conditioning. He didn't envy her.

"Hello, Barbara," he said. "Do you have any Kirin?"

"What's that?" She didn't have any Kirin.

"Never mind," said Lowell, sadly. "I'll take a Molson."

She gave him a look like "you think you got problems," and

withdrew, vanishing into the haze. He listened to as much country music as he could stand, and made a play for the juke box. It had Bruce Hornsby and Willie Nelson: reasonable compromises for a blues fan. The server named Barbara found him, and handed him his beer. He paid, added an extra two dollars for a tip, and asked: "How's the food?"

"Darlin', you don't wanna know," she advised him.

He grinned. "Bring me your biggest Cuban sandwich. I'll take my chances." A "Cuban" was a meat-and-cheese sandwich that was grilled crisp then flattened with an iron. Or a sledge hammer.

She spared him a rare smile. "Biggest, or best?"

"Change that to best."

"I'll wake the cook up for this one," she promised.

The sandwich wasn't even half bad. The bikers and their mamas and wanna-bes, left him alone. A lot of them were Native American, he noticed. Probably Seminole, although some might be Miccosukee. He didn't see Billy anywhere. But then it had been hours ago when he'd dropped him off.

When the server named Barbara asked him if he'd like another beer, he nodded, absently. Somebody had found a Byrds record, on the juke. He felt his nerves loosening up a bit. Barbara hesitated a moment. He wondered if it was a come-on. He didn't discourage her, but had other things on his mind. He sat lost in thought, drumming his fingers on the table, when she came back.

"Everything all right?" she asked.

"Sure, fine," he said, miles away. He looked up at her. "You know a kid name of Billy Patterson, by any chance?"

Her reaction surprised him. "That kid." She shook her head, almost matronly. "Should get a life."

"What do you mean?"

"I mean, between you and me and the Miccosukee," she said, lowering her voice, "he drinks too much. Drank six beers and threw up in the john. I mean, I'm in the business of sellin' drinks, sure, but the kid can't handle it."

"Maybe he's got things on his mind."

"Yeah," she said. "I used to work for his old man." Again she lowered her voice, with a nervous glance around the room. She leaned toward him, confidentially. Nobody was paying them the slightest attention, except that when she leaned forward, her miniskirt rose up, and about ten grinning bikers stopped to admire her butt. "Don't quote me on this, darlin', but he was the most lecherous old bastard I ever come across, and I have met me a few, you can believe that."

"Yes, I can," Lowell agreed, watching the watchers. They were relatively harmless. For these parts. "I think I'd like to get to know this man a little."

She looked at him like she assumed he was joking. He wasn't.

"Kinda sad in a way," she added.

That caught his attention. "How so?"

"The guy. The wife, I've seen her, too. All locked up inside. All of them. Really sad. I'd hate to have to be that way."

He paid his check, and added another five. Which left him nearly broke, but she didn't have to know that.

She watched him go. He hadn't even touched his second beer.

It was dark by the time Lowell got back to Patterson's Landing. The frigid wind continued to build. The temperature had dropped forty degrees in two hours as the arctic air mass descended, and a major freeze was clearly imminent. He could see a steady stream of smoke pouring from the corrugated zinc chimney stack of the ramshackle establishment, blowing quickly away into the night. The car heater wasn't working worth squat. There was a crack in the hose he had procrastinated about fixing for about three years. He saw that Billy's truck and Duvall's Cadillac were both there. He parked alongside the few after-work customers' cars, buttoned his greasy red-and-black checkered work shirt to the top, and entered the building.

Duvall had a big Franklin stove blazing away in the center of the big room. Lowell hadn't noticed it that afternoon, because of the smoky darkness and the crowd. He warmed his hands by the stove a moment, then sauntered over to the counter and sat down. The Cuban sandwich was beginning to get to him. But then he'd been warned.

The woman came out and gave him the same sullen, empty look. He ordered an Alka-Seltzer. "Billy here?" he asked, casually.

"He's out back, asleep." Her glare deepened. "Listen, if you're one of his buddies from that bar he goes to, you better just turn around and walk back on out the door, because his father has had it just about up to here with all them low-life scum," she warned him. She turned and hollered: "Hey, Duvall!"

"Suit yourself," said Lowell. "I thought Mr. Patterson would be off with his militia buddies, over at Lejeune's."

Her eyes narrowed. "Too damn cold. Why, he know you?"

"We met this afternoon. The name's Lowell. Tony Lowell." He'd always wanted to say that, but it was wasted on her.

She frowned and gave him a look of reappraisal. She turned around and hollered in the general direction of the rear quarters. "Duvall!" she shouted. "Somebody here to see you!"

He came out after a while, his expression sour and gothic. His face was flushed, his footsteps unsteady. Like father, like son? Lowell wondered. Duvall frowned in recognition, and his expression changed from challenge to wariness.

"I know who you are, mister, you been talkin' to my boy. What you want?"

Lowell saw no point in beating about the palmetto bush. "Well, if you know who I am then you know what I want. I want to know who killed Marge Pappas. And why."

He heard a noise in the kitchen. Duvall's expression narrowed further. "Why ask me?"

"Maybe you know."

Duvall's fists clenched and unclenched. Lowell knew he was either way off, or right on the nose. Either way Duvall didn't like the question a whole helluva lot.

"Why you think that?"

"It's my job. Maybe you heard somethin'. Saw somethin'."

"Git out," ordered Patterson. "Now!"

Lowell held his ground. "One other thing. I don't care what kind of beef you have with your son. And I don't care if he's as big as you are. You don't beat on a kid. Ever. Because they don't get over it. Ever. And they will never forgive you, no matter how hard they try. Think about it!" He turned and walked to the door.

He heard a commotion behind him, and turned. Duvall Patterson had crumpled into a chair, face in his hands, rocking back and forth, wailing. Lowell almost went back to him. He looked toward the kitchen and saw the woman standing there, stony faced. He saw no comfort there. Now he felt worse for Billy than before. He felt sick in his stomach. Looking at Duvall Patterson, he'd seen his own father: a mean, angry weakling. He looked again at the woman, wondering. Something seemed to pass between them, husband and wife, and she was gone. Lowell wondered if he might be wrong. If maybe Duvall Patterson, in his own withered way, loved this woman.

He stopped at the door. "By the way," he said, turning back. "I thought you were going over to Quentin Lejeune's, to help him save his crop."

"Maybe I am. What's it to you?"

"Me? Nothing. How 'bout you? He give you a cut in the proceeds? Or is this all just public service on your part?"

Duvall wiped his eyes, and glared. "You don't know nothin' about it."

"I know Quentin's got millions on the line out there, Duvall. What've you got?"

"You go to hell, Lowell."

Lowell threw up his hands, turned, and headed for the door. "He's using you, Patterson!" he called back. "You and all your patriot pals, you're all just free labor for his citrus money machine. He probably gets federal ag subsidies bigger than your county budget. He gets insurance if the crop fails, price supports either way, tax write-offs either way, a windfall if he gets his crop in and the competition doesn't. I'll say this for your leader, he's got all his bases covered, and you're the ones covering them!"

Lowell was out the door. Duvall stared after him, his mouth wide open. "That's bullshit," he snarled and followed him outside. Lowell kept walking. "That's bullshit, mister! He ain't like that! You go on and git. Git out! Git out!"

Lowell stopped, and turned. "You know what I wish," he said. "I wish that just once, I would meet somebody around here who could at least be civil." He shook his head while Duvall stared, and got out his keys. The server at the bar, he remembered. Barbara. She'd been pleasant. He decided to go back and look for her. He hoped Billy was going to be all right, but there wasn't much he could do now, except wait. There wasn't much hope anymore of getting into the groves unopposed, nor was there much more he could learn there anyway. Bedrosian and Perry had been right. He hated it when that happened.

The icy wind bit into him as he unlocked the Chevy, and got back in. Shivering, he started the engine, backed out, and headed back to Immokalee. As he drove through the darkness, a new idea began to ferment in his thoughts, like a homemade brew.

Back inside, Duvall watched him go from the window. He reached under the counter, and pulled out a Browning 9-mm pistol. He hefted it a long moment, then slowly, agonizingly slowly, he raised the barrel, and pointed at his head. He held it there, his eyes squeezed shut, tears squeezing out the corners, fleeing down his face like rats abandoning a sinking ship.

"Duvall!" barked a loud, angry voice from the kitchen.

He jumped and threw the gun back onto the shelf with a cry of frustration. "Damn you!" he shouted. "Damn you to hell!"

Lowell drove back down State Road 80, trying to decide his next move. He saw the floodlights coming on in the groves. The forced march, or rather harvest, was under way. He shivered again in the chill, and drove on. He wanted to lose himself for a while, amid pleasures and comforts about which he had almost forgotten, it had been so long. The hot musky scents, warm night sweat, and sweetness of mouth and lips, breath tainted by beer but still food for a deep hunger; breasts that were hard and buns that were still firm, and he suddenly wanted her more than he cared to admit.

She'd been waiting for him when he returned to the restaurant, and she whispered to meet her in ten minutes, she was off at eleven. He followed her instructions, and followed her to her little guest cottage a few blocks away in seedy downtown Immokalee, where he told her that he just wanted someone to hold, and touch, and be held by, and that's what she wanted, too. But push soon came to shove, as she allowed him to undress her while she fixed them a bourbon nightcap to ward off the chill. "I don't have heat," she warned him. "I think you do," he said.

He stood behind her while she poured the drinks, marveled at her tight ass and well-preserved legs, stroking them up as high as they went, and higher, until she was wet, and turned, and tore off his belt, and reached for him. He stood while she sat, and took him in her mouth, then lifted her, kissed her neck and nipples, taking them between his lips until she moaned, and carried her to her bed, not very far away at all. In a moment he was deep inside her and trying to hold on, and she held him in a grip between those fine legs and strong arms, until they cried out together and collapsed.

Her name was Barbara, he'd remembered, and she'd been around. He didn't mind, it was something they had in common. And aside from the basic needs that had driven them together, probably all they had in common. She wasn't even from Florida, she'd moved here a year ago, she told him, from South Carolina. She was warm, and sweet, and made love as if she meant it, and so did he. They did it again after a while, with her on top, and finally fell asleep on the sheets, unmindful of the creeping chill.

Lowell awoke suddenly, at around 2:00 A.M., an urgent thought resonating in his head. Slipping out of bed, he kissed the sleeping Barbara, dressed, and left.

Out on the empty small-town street, he checked in his trunk for a vinyl shaving kit, containing two plastic bottles of liquid, and an empty spray bottle. Tossing the kit into the front seat, he climbed in, checked the backseat for thugs and monsters, and drove south, out of town, and on into the darkness.

He passed a state Highway Patrol officer, parked in a closed gas station lot at the last intersection before leaving town. He didn't know the trooper, whose name was Higgins, but tossed him a casual wave anyway. The officer didn't wave back, but neither did he follow him.

Lowell drove down to the county road that led into the cypress forest to Corkscrew Swamp, and turned into the sandy track that ended at Marge Pappas's abandoned cabin, now padlocked. He took out his four-cell flashlight and his camera, now loaded with infrared film, and circled the camp slowly, searching the ground. Some poachers had camped out here recently, and the ashes from their campfire included a considerable number of blackened beer cans. He moved on to the edge of the clearing, and the path that led into the swamp. The rain had washed away the remains of any tracks—Marge's or the others'. The ground was thick with mud, and Lowell had a difficult time making his way in the darkness.

There were some rocks along here somewhere, the ones that he'd noticed in the first photographs he'd taken. This was not rocky soil, no outcroppings were present, and any rocks were out of place. Two of them, a matched pair, looked like they may have been used to mark either side of the entrance to the trail. He had one of those photographs in his hand and checked it with his flashlight against all the sight angles of the now mostly obliterated campsite. He found the trail entrance, and shortly afterward, the first rock in the high grass just off the path. Very carefully, he studied the ground nearby. It didn't take long to find the shallow hole where the rock had been set, some time ago. Someone must have kicked it, possibly even fallen over it, perhaps running for their life or hellbent on murder, several days ago. He soon found its opposite and examined them both closely. He set them down, and moved on.

About thirty feet farther into the swamp he found another rock, the size of a grapefruit and pear-shaped. It was blackened on one side, and he recognized at once where it had come from: the fireplace. There was mud, of course, as well. But then he felt something else. Setting it down carefully, he took the shaving kit from his slicker pocket and carefully combined equal portions of the two chemicals into the spray bottle. Holding the rock by the edges, he sprayed it on both sides. The mixture was called luminol, and had a peculiar capability that shortly became apparent. A large area that overlapped both the burned and clean sides began to glow: dim at first, then more and more brightly. It was blood. Whether washed away by the rains or scrubbed by a human its visible traces, as with the unfortunate Lady Macbeth, would still be there, years, even decades later, and luminol would seek it out.

Lowell took photographs with high speed film, showing the rock in the depression where he found it. He also knew now that the mud on the rock would prove a close match to the soil he'd found under Marge's nails. There was no longer any doubt: here is where she'd died. He brought the rock back to the campfire. It continued to shimmer in the darkness like a silver meteor, a frantic beacon in the lonesome swamp where death dwelt. Lowell had found his murder weapon. Wrapping it in his last clean T-shirt, he locked the rock in the trunk of his car, got in, and drove away.

16

WEDNESDAY MORNING, 3:00 A.M.

As he left Marge's campsite, and the place where she'd been murdered, Lowell made a left turn back onto the county road, and drove north toward the river. He wanted to call Bedrosian about the rock, knew she would appreciate the news, but not being called at this hour in a motel room with a sleeping husband and three kids. It would have to wait.

He had another idea, which had to do with the Club. The Caloosahatchee River Hunt and Gun Club was the social gathering and weekend retreat for the local honchos and well-to-do "sportsmen," as they liked to call themselves. One of whom was Quentin Lejeune. If Lowell couldn't get into Lejeune's militia, maybe he could get back into his Club.

Lowell never could understand blood sports. What kind of "sportsmanship" could be involved in the killing of usually harmless unsuspecting animals from safe distances, just for the "thrill" of it? But they were a tight knit, powerful group, with enough clout to pull strings in Tallahassee, and even challenge a man like Kranhower head-on. They were no militia. They were accustomed to using government for their purposes, not confronting it. That Kranhower incident had been a pretty radical action on their part, and one they probably regretted right away. Quentin Lejeune was the one common link, other than an affinity for guns, between the Club and the militia. Lowell began to wonder just how much influence Lejeune might have at the Club. He decided this cold, dark night might be a good time to try and find out.

The main entrance was gated and locked, as he knew it would be. But the service entrance, a half-mile farther east along the county road, remained open and unattended. Lowell didn't know if there was a full-time caretaker on the property, but figured there was a strong likelihood of one. He also figured such a person might very possibly belong to the County Militia, and he was willing to bet they would probably be out in the groves trying to help save Lejeune's multimillion-dollar crop.

Lejeune Farm and Ranch Company, must have more than forty million dollars at stake tonight. Give or take a few million. He wondered what else was at stake.

He decided to take a chance and try to find out.

The temperature continued to drop. Lowell parked on a fire road, not far from the service entrance to the Club. Lights off, he hunkered down to watch awhile, in case anyone was returning from the groves. He tried to stay warm. The inside of his windshield began to fog up. He didn't dare turn on the radio. The old battery was likely to give out at any time. He waited.

Thirty minutes went by, and no one came down the service road, and he couldn't wait much longer. He gambled that the caretaker or caretakers had gone.

He'd soon find out. Lowell started his car, pulled quietly out of the fire road and onto the main road, before turning on his lights. He almost hit it before he saw it: a quick blur of feet and fur—a Florida panther. He recognized the little tuft behind the shoulders, the distinguishing flecks of white, even in that fleeting moment. Then it was gone.

He wondered how long it would last, in these parts. It had been Marge Pappas's job to protect such creatures. And with her gone, there was a pretty good chance no one would. Not Connors, he was too short-handed and short on fiber. Billy Patterson? Maybe. He seemed to care about the critters. But he couldn't even protect himself. Lowell wondered if the de facto removal of the panther from protection could have been someone's intention. Enough so to remove Marge? He wondered who would benefit. Maybe the answer would be found at the Caloosahatchee Hunt and Gun Club. If he could get in.

He followed the road using only his parking lights, aided by good night vision. The Club grounds were completely dark except for a scattering of hundred-watt light posts. One lit the driveway by the outbuildings; one was by the back entrance; and another in a window at the back of what Lowell construed to be the staff residence building. It was separated from the main clubhouse by a clump of pines, which would shelter it from sound and view, once he gained entry.

A motion sensor triggered as Lowell glided to a stop alongside the two cars that were present. A bright light came on. Both the neighboring cars were vintage American heaps, akin to his own. Maybe his Impala wouldn't be noticed if someone came back. Or came out from one of the buildings. It fit right in.

Lowell held his breath and waited. There were no shrieking sirens. No skyrockets, or *whup whup* of assault helos, or clicking of a hundred muskets being cocked. No one came out. Since the light was on and would only stay so for one to three minutes, he moved quickly to the back of the clubhouse, out of range. At least of that sensor.

The Club—a gang of millionaires, by all accounts—had

been too cheap to install another motion sensor. Or were too arrogant to bother. He waited, still, and listened to the night. The arctic wind had died down, but it was still icy for Florida. He guessed the temperature to be below freezing. Which meant the Hondo County Militia should be hard at work, saving Quentin Lejeune's millions for him. The ol' boys wouldn't get to vent their defiance with gunfire, this night.

The farm workers would be working at a desperate pace for the next ten hours. Not until the temperature in the groves got back to a safe level, 32 degrees Fahrenheit or higher, would they be able to relax. Which would not happen until the sun rose again. And if Lowell's surmise was correct, the militia would be out all night.

Lowell had just begun to congratulate himself on his good timing when he heard the dogs. He'd had run-ins with guard dogs and other canines on more than one occasion. It came with the job. He just didn't feel like another such encounter tonight. The first barks raised the alarm. It became a chorus, rapidly coming closer, searching for his trail. Dobermans, he thought. Shit. Prompted by a new sense of urgency, Lowell picked up the nearest hand-sized stone, and threw it through the nearest window—which turned out to be the laundry facility next to the clubhouse kitchen. The night was rent by the sound of shattering glass, but it didn't echo far, swallowed up by the wind-rustled pines and palmettos until it vanished into silence. Then the barking resumed in earnest.

The dogs had a target now, and streaked toward it: him. They were a hundred feet away and closing fast. Lowell gave up on all pretense of dignity, yanked out the one jagged piece of glass on the bottom edge of the broken window, and dove through headfirst. He almost got stuck. His butt, he was ruefully reminded, was not as small as it once had been. And while still smaller than the width of his shoulders, it was less bendable. The first dog barely missed his crotch in a flying leap and crashed into the side of the building with a yelp. The second dog actually took a piece out of his running shoe. Then he was in.

Lowell landed on his extended hands, then elbows, then face in a heap of soiled table linen. Probably there since last weekend, this being strictly a weekend club. Which meant somebody was sluffing off on the job. Which was lucky for Lowell because it meant he didn't break his neck. He heard a snarl behind him as the first dog jumped onto the window-sill, fangs dripping. Lowell threw a tablecloth over the dog's head, slowing it just enough to give him time to run out of the room and slam the door.

Quickly, he assessed the damage. No fractures, sprains, or deep bruises. Maybe a little bit sore here and there. There was a new rip in the work shirt, that had caught on one of the re-maining shards of glass. He was in a large pantry. The dogs were in the laundry room now but could go no farther. They sniffed around, whined a bit, then climbed back out and trot-ted off, back to wherever they came from.

Lowell had the whole place to himself. He looked around. That was when he discovered that he was bleeding. It wasn't serious, he decided. The same shard that had shredded the wool shirt had also done a number on his arm. Luckily, it was his upper arm, a flesh wound, which would have been a lot worse but for the extra padding and heavy seams in the shoul-der area of the heavy wool work shirt.

Lowell tore off the shirt and his T-shirt underneath, and washed the cut in the pantry sink. He found a rest room nearby, with a first-aid cabinet, and managed to pull the cut edges of his flesh together, and tape them down. There was no hemorrhaging and no more bleeding.

A long row of lockers stood against the opposite wall, with a rack of white aprons for the dining and kitchen staff. A number of miscellaneous hats and jackets hung on wooden pegs. Lowell traded in his tattered shirts for a clean cotton dishwasher's shirt and a tan fleece-lined jacket. He would re-

177

turn it as soon as was feasible; meanwhile survival prevailed. The temperature in the building was barely higher than outside.

Using his penlight when necessary, but aided by the towering big windows and skylights and a nearly full winter moon outside, he surveyed the building, wondering what to look for, and where to find it. He wanted to find evidence of conspiracy, if any existed. Something that might connect Marge's death to the Club. He wondered about the Club's relationship with Bob Hathcock. Hatchet Man Hathcock.

He entered the dining room, and saw the classic icons of the Old Boy Great White Hunter: the row upon row of trophy heads. There was a time in history when those heads, he reflected, would probably have been human. Then again, maybe the human race hasn't come all that far since. He looked at them in the low moonlight—light enough to see their glass eyes sparkle, a glimmer of memory, perhaps, transmitted by another of nature's limitless forces, from the star and moonlight above.

Then he saw the panther heads. He whistled, quietly. He could tell that most were old. But there was one that wasn't. He looked for a ladder, or something on which to climb for a closer look. The closest thing he could find was a bar stool—a precarious perch for a close scrutiny. After a few wobbly moments, he gave up on the idea. He decided to ask Bedrosian, at soonest opportunity, if panther heads were legal to own. Probably, he figured. And who's going to write the ticket, if they aren't? He'd heard Collier County Sheriff Riker was a member of the Club. It might be interesting to find out. Billy had mentioned an initiation. It was possible this was one of the Texas cougars he'd alluded to. But if that head was recent, and was indeed a panther, a crime had been committed: the shooting of an endangered species. Which panthers had been for years. He wished he'd brought his camera with him, although it might not have survived his dive through the window in any case. At least not much better than he had.

He wondered what Marge would have done if she'd known about the panther heads. Gone ballistic, probably. He wondered if it were possible that one of these people would shoot a wildlife officer to avoid arrest if he was caught poaching panthers. What would be at stake, besides a relatively small fine? Public censure? Hardly. And hardly grounds for murder. But she was an authority figure, a government official, in a time when that alone, to some people, might be a killing offense. She and Dave Connors were the only two people in this part of southwest Florida who would have, could have, enforced either the antipoaching law, or the Endangered Species Act. So what about Supervisor Connors? The panther head was evidence a crime had been committed. He had no way to know how recently. That would take some lab work.

And then there was the state land deal. Could one or more members of this Club be so arrogant that an uppity female who got in their way would be highly expendable? They wanted to hunt in a bigger area, that was apparent and Marge would have opposed that, he felt sure. Maybe she had. The Club surely had plans to grow and expand. Growth was the goal of businessmen, economists, politicians, developers, manufacturers—overcrowding, water shortages, nothing would stop them. They didn't care how few cypress trees remained, or how little wildlife survived.

Lowell found the Club office with no trouble. It was a small room just off the main entrance to the "log castle," as he thought of it. A discreet door, marked with a brass plaque: Office. It was locked, of course. But Tony Lowell had been a private investigator long enough to have learned how to open simple interior locks. He slipped into the ten-by-ten oak-furnished room and checked the one window. It was covered with miniblinds and heavy velvet drapes. The drapes had a light-proof liner to keep heat out, and together with the blinds, would keep any light from escaping. Even so, he didn't dare turn on the desk lamp or any of those on tables.

As he began to explore the office, his flashlight batteries suddenly dimmed and flickered, about to run out. Just before the light dimmed to black, he found the desk drawer, but there were no batteries. Then, as the first twinge of panic came with the sudden onset of absolute blackness, he saw the little red light, down along the baseboard. It was a rechargable emergency light.

Silently blessing the foresight and wisdom of whoever's office he had invaded, Lowell pulled the light from the recharging unit, and switched it on. He was almost blinded by its brightness. He scanned the room, hooding the beam with his left hand.

A wall plaque and several framed photographs of well-groomed family members revealed the name of the office's current occupant: Lars Conyers, Club president. In addition to the desk with its four drawers, there were also two five-drawer filing cabinets and a wall-size walnut bookcase full of outdoorsy tomes and publications. There was a row of trophies, hunting prizes, awards for shooting competitions, and just good guy awards in a glass cabinet. One particular name appeared over and over again, going back years and years: Quentin Lejeune.

Lowell knew now what he was looking for, and found it in the large bottom desk drawer. It was a large legal-size manila folder, the accordian kind with the attached rubber elastic. Inside was a stack of legal papers. The cover page described a certain house bill from the current state legislature, with a certain docket number. A smaller file, in a smaller manila folder within the larger one, was a smaller document: a "Rider To" the larger bill. Lowell read the author's name on the bottom: State Representative Bob Hathcock. He scanned the rider first, and it confirmed what he already knew: Bob Hathcock had a vested interest in the net benefits of his own legislation;

namely the free acquisition of ten thousand acres of state land.

Then he saw the handwritten addendum marked: "additional purchase." It called for the purchase of an additional five thousand acres of adjacent land, by the state. This land, he read, was supposedly to be purchased with state tax monies at "prevailing market value," to establish "additional park land for Collier and Hondo Counties." In finer print, the designated park "proprietor" was to be designated as none other than the Hondo County Militia, a "private, tax-exempt nonprofit organization." Then he found the kicker: the seller of the land in question, to be purchased by the state and handed over to the aforesaid organization, was none other than the Lejeune Farm and Ranch Company. Of Lee, Hondo, and Collier Counties, Florida. Lowell put the file on top of the desk, and took several deep breaths, before resuming his search. What he wanted now was handwriting samples. He was not surprised to find that none of the signatures in the damning file matched that of the letter to Marge he'd found. The letter had been crude, an unlikely product of a Club member. But that could have been a deliberate deception.

Lowell located the membership list in the same desk, top drawer. Bound in gold-trimmed leather, it had a full dossier of every member. It was virtually the Committee of One Hundred for all of Collier, Hondo, and Lee Counties. The business files were next, he decided. There would be billing records, but also possibly signature files of each member. Possibly even copies of signed checks or W-9s.

A chilly breeze blew through the cracks in the log walls, rattling the casement windows. He wondered how the freeze fighters were doing out there. Was Quentin Lejeune out there fighting alongside his troops? Or sipping sherry in his elegant salon, awaiting the outcome? Quentin Lejeune was a cypher. Why would one of government's largest beneficiaries lead a frontal assault on its institutions? It didn't make sense, yet it was happening throughout the country. He tried to fathom all the possible agendas he could think of for Lejeune's private militia or his allegedly "public" hunt club. Again and again, he kept coming back to the obvious: personal gain.

His flight from the Dobermans had made him thirsty. He put down the files and went to find a drink. Surely, he figured, there would be some orange juice on the premises.

He found a reasonably fresh plastic gallon jug in the bar, helped himself to some chips and beer nuts from the wall rack, left his last dollar on the plate, and went back to the office. He had gone through quite a stack of documents, but so far had found nothing conclusive. Nothing pertaining to Marge. Even the incriminating panther head proved nothing. And even if he found something there was no way to make copies, or take photographic copies, without some risky lighting. Once again, he began to wish he'd brought his camera with him.

Still no handwriting match. He hadn't really expected to find one here, unless from one of the employees. But he wanted to be certain. There were no signature cards, but the files and wall cases soon revealed a wealth of possibilities: letters, pronouncements, and proposals, over the years from and to various club members and the "management." After an hour, he began to get edgy. None of the handwriting matched that of the letter, let alone its simplistic style. He decided it was time to quit while he was ahead. But how to get out? He could circumvent the motion detector, but what good would that do? The dogs would hear him, and be after him in a flash of snapping teeth. There had to be another way.

He looked at the telephone. He was fairly certain no one had heard or reported his arrival, or entry. Maybe he could just call a taxi, and bluff his way out. Or maybe call Connors, or even Billy Patterson. Yes, that was it. Duvall would be at Lejeune's with the militia boys. Billy would in all probability be at home, nursing his bruises. He could get here in twenty-five minutes, or less.

He found a phone book and looked up Patterson's Landing. He dialed. Then he heard a metallic clicking sound behind him. Slowly he turned, sensing and dreading what was there.

17

Lowell hadn't counted on the cops. The ones who now stood in the doorway, aiming their police issue 9-mm Glock pistols straight at the place where indigestion begins, along with sick and sinking sensations.

"Well looky here," growled sheriff's deputy Doug Kohler to his partner, Mario Vega, as they closed in on Lowell. "If it ain't the private dick."

"B and E plus trespassing." Vega nodded. He had the same steely eyes as the man at Lejeune Farms. They had to be related, Lowell figured.

"Possible grand theft," said Kohler, picking up the stack of files from the desk. "Careful. He might try and jump one of us, and make a break for it."

"That would be a shame," said Vega. "Then we'd have to shoot the son of a bitch."

"Take it easy," said Lowell, slowly raising his hands. He nodded at the documents. "Those are public records, you should read them for yourself. That's a copy of a legislative bill as submitted to our state legislature in Tallahassee."

"Then what the hell's it doin' here?" demanded Kohler.

"Now you, you guys are really perceptive. Because that's exactly what I was wondering," said Lowell. "It's pork barrel politics in action, assuming it's even legal. So with your permission, I'd like to return it to the state legislative office where it belongs." He had a sudden feeling that these two had only a limited perspective on what was going down on their beat. And the feeling was a bad one. That they took orders from someone who wanted that bill passed bad enough to bend the law. Or maybe smash it to bits. He hoped he was wrong. That his stomach was wrong, that it was just the Cuban sandwich, acting up. Maybe these two cops did care about truth, justice, and the American Way. Maybe he could just ask them to call Bedrosian, and she'd straighten them out. Maybe hell was about to freeze over.

That's when he remembered that these two were from Collier, not Hondo County. He wasn't even in their jurisdiction. His stomach didn't like that thought one bit.

Maybe he could still bluff his way out. But Lowell was beginning to suspect they had other purposes than a mere breaking and entering arrest. "Or maybe you'd like to read it first. We could stop by Kinko's in Fort Myers, grab a cup of coffee, discuss politics."

The two cops looked at each other. "You're a pretty funny guy, Lowell," said Vega. Lowell looked at Vega, and saw something in his eyes that chilled him a lot worse than the frigid night. "No, sir," said Vega. "I think you better put that back where you found it. That's private property."

"Not really. But if you insist."

Vega insisted. With the wave of his gun. Lowell obeyed.

"Now move it," said Kohler, gesturing toward the door.

"Hey, am I under arrest?" asked Lowell, hands raised, and moving as slowly as possible. "Because if so, I think you boys

186

may have made a wrong turn, you see, you're in the wrong county. I'd be glad to loan you a map—"

"Shut up!" barked Vega, silencing him with a blow to the solar plexus.

Well, thought Lowell, gasping for breath as they snapped on the cuffs. At least I won't have to worry anymore about the dogs.

Now he just had to worry about staying alive.

Officer Nolan Higgins of the Florida Highway Patrol picked up the call, while on routine patrol out on Route 80. A reported trespasser at the Hunt Club. A sheriff's deputy responded, and said they would handle it. It all sounded routine enough. He didn't give it any further thought for a while, as he turned at the 7-Eleven in La Belle, cruised watchfully past Patterson's Landing, and headed back toward Fort Myers.

A big tanker rig whooshed past, and the radar pegged it at ninety. Ninety on a curvy two-lane highway, at night. Normally, he would have done a full one-eighty brake-and-turn, and been after the son of a bitch in a flash. But tonight he had his mind on other things: things that had been happening here on his lifelong home front. Things that were starting to bother him. They had all been isolated incidents, or so he'd thought, at first. His daughter, Lisa, was getting flack from her peers at her high school. Not for being the daughter of a cop—a time-honored profession in the South—but for being the daughter of a "state official." That was, "like, gov'mint," as she'd put it. Worse than being a liberal. Or a hippy, in the old days.

Funny how things had turned, so. His wife, Terry, she was getting shunned, too, by the church women, among others. All his life, a believer in Law and Order, Nolan had been accustomed to being the good guy. Even, sometimes, the hero. Now he was being looked down on, treated like dirt, even by his law enforcement colleagues at the Sheriff's Department. He didn't understand it. Except that he was beginning to feel some connection to the Old West. When the locals ran things, enforced by their own sheriff, the federal marshals were unwelcome outsiders, and there was nobody in between except outlaws. Well, he was no federal marshal. But he was beginning to understand how it must have been, back then.

He turned up the heater as he passed the county road that ran down toward Corkscrew Swamp. That was where that Wildlife Officer Marge Pappas had bought it. Another symptom of the topsy-turvy things that were happening out there, these days. People no longer had any respect for the law, not even a lady wildlife officer, for God's sake! He could see fires burning out in the groves to the south and east. He was sure glad he wasn't one of those farmworkers out there, like he'd seen all along the highway tonight. Hovering by those oily smudge pots, working feverishly to save the winter crop from the freeze. Even with his thirty-two thou and his wife getting twenty-seven for her teaching job, they barely got by. But those poor people out there! He wondered if it had been some migrant laborer who had come across Officer Pappas, maybe trying to shoot a deer for dinner, and panicked when she surprised him. Desperate people did desperate things. He couldn't understand how the Sheriff's Department could close that case so quickly, with no proof. He knew Riker, it wasn't like him. But those two deputies, they were brownnoses from the getgo. Personally, he didn't trust them, and there was something about them—Kohler's coldness, and Vega's hard eyes—that bothered him.

Something in the back of his mind, just a glimmer of doubt, made him reach for his radio handset.

"Central, this is one-oh-seven," he called in.

Angie, the dispatcher at DeSoto Barracks, picked him up right away. "Ten-four, Nolan, you staying warm out there?"

"So far. Listen, Angie, you pick up a call on a B and E at the Caloosahatchee Hunt Club a few minutes back?"

There was a crackle of static. "Yeah, affirmative. I think it was one of those silent sentinels."

"You know if anybody's gone out there?"

"I'll check." There was more static. Higgins pulled the cruiser onto the shoulder, and waited. "One-oh-seven. I got a response on that. A sheriff's patrol went to investigate."

"You know who?"

More static. She came back. "Nobody at HQ knows. They responded by radio."

"Just for the hell of it, would you ask Howard to check on his deputies? It might not have been them."

"Okeydokey, Nolan."

Kohler and Vega. There was something weasely about them, that had always bothered him. His hunch was getting stronger by the minute.

Angie called back. "Nobody from Hondo County Sheriff's picked that up, Nolan. Coulda swore somebody did, though."

Interesting. "Thanks, Angie. Ten-four." He switched off, and started his ignition. Sometimes he had nothing more to go on but a hunch. A lot of times those hunches were right on the money. He had a feeling this was going to be one of those times. But he had another feeling as well. Not exactly a hunch. And it wasn't a good feeling. It wasn't a good feeling at all.

Turning the big state highway cruiser around, he headed back up Route 80 to the county road, made a sharp right, and headed south. Toward the Gun Club.

As the two deputies shoved him out the front door, Lowell wondered how they had gotten in. And also where the dogs were. Aside from the question of jurisdiction, police were no more authorized to enter buildings than he was. Not without a warrant. "Where're we going?" he asked

189

"Shut up," he was told. Again.

Lowell's stomach was twisted in knots, and he felt sick. It began to dawn on him, with horrible comprehension, that this might be it: the time of times when, for no good reason, no damn good reason at all, it was all going to end. His whole less-than-fulfilled life. His long all-too-often hopeless lifetime struggling as a latter-day Don Quixote. He wondered if this windmill was the one that would finally trip him up. Or take his head off. He began to fear it might be so. Sometimes there are forces, things so dark and powerful, one man's will cannot affect them, cannot turn the tide of events or alter the course he has set upon. But Tony Lowell sure as hell would give it his best trying. He'd keep on tilting until the windmill quit, or swept him away.

"Hear you got something against guns, Lowell," Kohler remarked conversationally, as they shoved him into the back of their patrol car, and got in the front. Kohler got behind the wheel. Lowell didn't say anything.

"Answer the question, wise guy," Vega warned him.

"You said to shut up."

Vega hit him again. This was getting old fast, Lowell thought, rubbing his jaw. "Only when they're pointed at something. Or someone," he finally replied.

"Like you?" Vega, half-turned around, grinned at him from the shotgun seat. Lowell didn't like his grin, or the cold unsmiling eyes above it. He liked the Glock pointed at him even less.

"I have a problem with people who shoot people," said Lowell. "For no good reason. Like my friend Marge Pappas."

"That," repeated Kohler, as though reciting the party line, "was an accident."

"Her cousin, Lieutenant Bedrosian, doesn't think so, and neither do I."

Vega turned around fully. "What difference does it make?" he asked. "The bitch is dead." He made it sound final.

That was when Lowell knew they were going to kill him. The least he could do, he figured, was find out why.

"So, did you guys shoot her after hitting her with the rock? Or before? Either way is pretty extreme, just to protect a bunch of poachers. Or did she catch you doing something really nasty?"

They didn't say anything. Which didn't make him feel any better. Or wiser.

The patrol car pulled onto the county road, and turned north toward Route 80.

"So who are you working for? I mean really. Lejeune?"

"I said shut up," snapped Kohler. So much for that approach. Something was fundamentally wrong with the whole picture. Lejeune, a multimillionaire, wanted to expand his personal empire. Fine, but why resort to murder when he was accustomed to getting his way by legal means? But then the militia didn't make much sense, either, other than for grunt work. Again, not grounds for murder. Yet a murder had been committed, these two police officers had some involvement, he felt certain, and seemed determined now to silence him. Why? Lowell felt his hourglass hemorrhaging. The sand was running out fast. He'd better come up with something to plug the hole even faster: one of his winning feints, one of his life-saving tackles, one of those bottom of the ninth homers he never hit.

The patrol car slowed. Lowell's pulse quickened. Up ahead he recognized the black gash in the otherwise seamless forest on both sides of the road: the same fire road he'd parked in earlier. The car slowed further, and turned in. Kohler killed the lights at that moment, and they were plunged into momentary blackness, except for the parking and instrument lights that remained on, but were not yet visible in that moment of blindness.

Now or never, thought Lowell. His hands were cuffed behind his back and there were no door handles, as was normal in a police vehicle. He was going to have to do it with his feet, or his wits. At this moment, his wits weren't helping much, and he was already starting to see his life pass before his eyes. Or at least the advance previews.

"Why are you going kill me?" he asked, hoping to buy another minute, another second. "It doesn't make sense. You're giving yourselves away. Lieutenant Bedrosian isn't just going to let this slide, you know." He hoped. "I report to her daily. She knows you guys are on the take," he lied. "And who from."

They looked at each other. Vega was edgy, as though itching to get it over with. His eyes were narrowing, focusing on the kill. Kohler seemed suddenly less confident. He turned to look back at Lowell. "You don't know nothin'," he stated.

"You're wrong. You'll find out when they take you in for two counts of murder one, not to mention conspiracy to defraud, destruction of evidence, obstruction of justice—"

"That's enough," snapped Vega. "I'm doing him now," he told Kohler. His released the catch, and Lowell could see his grip tighten on the butt and trigger.

"You're gonna mess up the whole car," Lowell warned him. *Now* he saw his life pass before his eyes. An instant later, he saw a flash of dazzling white light. It was exactly like he'd always read, always heard it would be. Not a sound, just that flash of white light and—wait a sec. He thought. And with that thought, he realized that he was still thinking. Which meant he still had a brain. Which meant he probably wasn't dead.

Officer Nolan Higgins of the Florida Highway Patrol had been ready and waiting in the fire road entrance. After blinding them with his brights and searchlights—all thrown on together—he switched on the loudspeaker.

"This is the Highway Patrol. You fellas having a problem?"

Kohler and Vega both froze. Lowell sensed, as though in a

slow-motion dream, that this was one of those pivotal moments for all three of them.

The deputies could now either fight it out (particularly if they knew it was two against one), try to run for it, which of course would be futile, or bluff their way out. Lowell knew what they'd admitted, which wasn't much. And whatever he knew, nobody was going to believe anyway.

But the two deputies didn't think of that. All they could think of was that they were trapped, and had to get out. "Shit!" shouted Kohler, still blinded. He finally had the presence of mind to throw on his own brights, which might have evened things up somewhat. But by then Higgins was out of the vehicle, and leaning in Vega's window with a flashlight.

"You're out of your jurisdiction," stated Higgins. "What's goin' on?"

Vega stiffened momentarily, then slowly lowered the Glock.

Higgins shone his light on Lowell a moment. "Who's the prisoner?" Higgins asked Kohler. "Looks familiar."

"Listen, Higgins. We're on a legit police investigation," Kohler protested. "Sometimes it takes you out of your district. You know that."

"Wait here," said Higgins, curtly. "I'm gonna call the sheriff. And ask him what you clowns are doing up here."

"Ask them why they turned into the fire road with lights off!" shouted Lowell.

"We wanted to talk to the prisoner first. We had some questions," responded Vega, with a sideways look at Lowell that said, This ain't over.

Higgins hesitated. "They read you your rights?" Higgins asked Lowell.

"You've got to be kidding," said Lowell.

Higgins looked at him again, trying to recall where he'd seen him before.

"I'm a PI from Manatee County, working for Lieutenant

Lena Bedrosian on the Pappas case," Lowell told him, urgently. "Call her and check it out!"

"That's bullshit. We picked him up busting into the Hunt Club," said Vega. "We were just bringing him in."

"By way of Shangri-la," said Lowell. "Or a snake pit in Big Cypress. They were about to shoot me."

"Oh, come off it," said Kohler, sounding almost convincing.

Higgins frowned, skeptically, and looked at the other cops. He couldn't believe that, of course. He'd never known a cop shooting a prisoner, except on TV. It just didn't make sense.

"You know that's ridiculous," Kohler went on, anticipating Higgins's thoughts.

"That's right," said Vega, smoothly. "We just wanted to interrogate the guy. He wasn't cooperating, which is why we were gonna just stop here and talk with him a little."

"Yeah, right," said Lowell. "They as much as told me sayonara. These guys are nothing but hired guns, officer. They don't want things known about that I happen to know about."

"That's bullshit!" snapped Kohler. "He doesn't know nothin'."

"You still haven't explained what you're doin' up here," repeated Higgins. He suddenly felt uncomfortable, wishing he'd called in for backup. Something was seriously wrong here. This wasn't like Sheriff Riker, not at all. "Maybe you better release the prisoner," he told Kohler. "I'll take him in myself until I get hold of Hondo law enforcement."

Kohler hesitated, unable to think clearly. "What is this, Nolan? We got it under control."

"I don't think so," said Higgins, reaching in and seizing the keys, to Lowell's immense relief. He unlocked the back door. "Get out," he ordered Lowell. "And you," he turned back to Vega, "Please put your gun on the floor."

"Like hell," said Vega, his eyes blazing defiance. "You got no right to interfere with us."

194

"Just call it legal instinct. I'm relieving you of duty. Just put it down," Higgins repeated.

At that instant three things happened. The first was, Vega lost his cool. "Look, why don't you go write somebody a ticket and leave the law enforcement to us," he snapped. The second was that Higgins lost his cool. "You son of a bitch!" he exclaimed, and made a grab for the gun. The third thing that happened was, almost by reflex, Vega tried to jerk the gun away. In a moment the two law officers were fighting over the gun, while Lowell looked on in horror. Then Vega yanked free and shot Higgins in the face. It was over in an instant.

Acting far more from reflex than thought, Lowell dove out of the patrol car and scrambled into the bushes.

"Shit! Get him!" he heard Kohler shout. Another shot rang out, tearing a branch away an inch from Lowell's head. He kept moving, crawling through the impossibly thick undergrowth of vines and thickets, brambles and saw grass, finally rising to his feet, running for his life. Unable to keep balance with his hands still locked behind him, he fell again into the thorny undergrowth, picked himself up, and ran again. Another shot rang out.

There was the sound of a car on the highway. "We gotta move him!" Kohler shouted. Officer Higgins's blood-spattered body was sprawled against the side of the patrol car, head still wedged partway in the front passenger window.

Vega had to push him aside in order to get out of the car.

"Hurry the fuck up!" screamed Kohler. "Get the keys!"

"I have to get the other guy," said Vega, finally managing to shove the body out of the window. It slumped to the ground.

"Somebody's comin', they'll see him!" screamed Kohler. Lowell noticed that now that they had reached the point of no return, it was the cool, calm Vega who was the man of action, with a panicked Kohler trying to assume command.

195

The oncoming car rounded the curve, its lights splaying off the trees, coming closer. They could hear the roar of a big engine. Lowell, now a couple hundred feet away in the scrub, stopped to catch his breath and gather his resources. Now that he wasn't dead, maybe he could come up with a plan that worked. He stayed low, and waited see what was about to happen.

"C'mon, c'mon!" screamed Kohler. "There's no time!"

Vega ignored him. Higgins still had Kohler's keys clutched in his hand. Vega pried them out and tossed them in through the window. He just managed to drag the trooper's body into the bushes as the car rounded the last curve and raced toward them, brights flooding them like searchlights.

The driver slowed down perceptibly, but with the sudden braking of a guilty speeder, not of a knight to the rescue. He was an African-American tile salesman from Fort Myers, late from a sales meeting in Immokalee and rushing to get home before his pregnant wife disowned him. He passed by with extreme caution, curious at all the police lights but sensing it to be police business, not his. He drove on, glad not to be under pursuit.

Cool as a snow cone, Vega was ready to finish with Lowell now, and said so. But Kohler had lost his nerve.

"Enough's enough, Mario! Nobody's gonna believe him anyway," he insisted. "Even if he can make it out of here with them cuffs on. Let's go!"

Vega scanned the area one more time, listening and staring into the darkness, a hunter searching for his prey. Crouched in the undergrowth two hundred feet to the east, Lowell didn't even breathe. Kohler started and revved the engine, and Vega finally backed into the car, gun still ready. Reluctantly, he closed the door, and leaned back into the seat. Kohler spun the tires, screeching back out onto the road.

"Don't worry," Kohler insisted, his brow dripping with

sweat. "He's fucked. We know who he is, where to find him. He's a dead man."

Vega closed his eyes and didn't bother to respond as Kohler sped away.

Lowell rose to his feet, fighting back his instinctive fear and revulsion at the things that crawled on him in the night: the dark creeping things he was unable to brush away, the wet slithering things, the things that bit, and stung, and stabbed at him in the blackness. But they wouldn't kill him. He knew now that he would survive.

He rose, finally, in the pitch blackness of the forest, using the minute glimmer of starlight from overhead, the moon now shrouded in clouds, to grope and claw his way back to the fire road. He couldn't find Higgins, now hidden in the bushes. He managed to fumble the patrol car door open, and, lying on his back, worked his way into the driver's seat. Still handcuffed, twisting like Houdini, he reached behind his back for the radio handset, managed to get it, dropped it, and finally started hitting and pushing every button and switch he could find. He managed to hit the squawk button once, and got the flash lights going. He couldn't drive, but got the engine running, for the heat.

The radio crackled. "Central to one-oh-seven. Where are you, Nolan?"

Desperately, Lowell fumbled for the handset, and got it. He pushed the talk button. "This is Private Investigator Tony Lowell," he gasped. "From Manatee County. There's an officer down."

Lowell called Lena from the Highway Patrol barracks where they brought him, on Route 80 outside La Belle. They hadn't

197

wasted any time with him. They'd loaded him into the first car that arrived, and Officer Higgins's body into the ambulance. The sheriff had called, and demanded custody of the prisoner. Lowell was beside himself with outrage. "Don't you understand that they are the ones I witnessed do the shooting? If you clowns had half the guts Higgins did for standing up to those bastards, you'd at least check the tire tracks where Officer Higgins got shot. You'll find a match to Deputy Kohler's patrol car. Which will also match the tracks found at the site of Wildlife Officer Pappas's murder. You do a ballistics test on Vega's weapon, you'd find a match to the bullet that killed Higgins. You'll find Higgins's prints on their vehicle. If you guys would go out to the Hunt Club and check my car, a sixty-five Impala, there's a rock in the trunk with bloodstains. I'll bet you the pink slip forensics will prove it was Marge Pappas's blood. Which means she wasn't shot where they said she was, in some bogus hunting accident! Will you wake the hell up and smell the bullshit?" But they ignored him.

Officer Earl Calvin, the gray-haired mild-mannered veteran who'd brought him in, was still waiting for a transcript of Higgins's last communications. Meanwhile, FHP Major Taylor had his hands full, and had called the state Department of Law Enforcement for help. They didn't have anybody in the area, though, and wouldn't until later that morning.

The arresting officers, while dismissing Lowell's wild story, had been vague as to how they thought he could have shot Officer Higgins while his hands were handcuffed behind his back. Or where the gun was. But even if he wasn't the perp, he was sure as hell a material witness. And so he had been read his rights and summarily locked up. Bedrosian was his one phone call.

"You're lucky," she told him. "We were just checking out of here."

Sarcastically, Lowell told her just how lucky he was, and how lucky Highway Patrol Officer Higgins had been.

She whistled. "Are they charging you?"

"Not for the moment." And even if they did he didn't figure it would stick, at least if there was at least one sane person at the arraignment, assuming it went that far. Problem was, he was meanwhile stuck in jail. They wouldn't even let him call a bail bondsman, he told her.

"Lowell, you need a lawyer," she advised him.

"I don't need a lawyer. I just need you to confirm to these morons that I was conducting a legal investigation," he snapped. "On your behalf," he added. "For no pay, as far as I can see," he further added. "And you might ask them to get a hold of Riker in Collier, about what his deputies were doing up here in Hondo County!"

"Actually, I'm not sure how legal your investigation was, since I couldn't authorize it. Officially speaking," she pointed out.

"What?" he shouted.

"I'm just saying you have this really unfortunate tendency for getting caught at the wrong time in the wrong place. Not to mention the fact that on this particular occasion, you were also caught in the act of the commission of a crime. I can't be responsible for that. How may times have I told you—"

"Bedrosian!" he bellowed, turning all heads in the barracks in his direction. He lowered his voice again. "Those guys were in the wrong county! I was doing investigative work. For you, on behalf of your late, lamented cousin. I would appreciate a little support here!" He lowered his voice, urgently. "Lena. I witnessed two deputy sheriffs murder a state police officer. They were trying to do me at the time."

She still couldn't believe it.

He looked up. The officer named Calvin was coming for him.

"Fine," she sighed, at last. "I'll get down there as soon as I can."

"Lena, wait!" he shouted quickly, then lowered his voice.

199

"I found the murder weapon. It's in the trunk of my car."

"You what?"

"Also, I saw the land bill. Even assuming it's legal, it's incredibly unethical. Tell Amber the senator was right to stop it."

"Wait a minute! Is there a connection here, Lowell? What murder weapon?"

"A rock. I'll tell you when you get here."

"Wait a minute! I thought she was shot!"

"I'll tell you when you get here. She was definitely killed at the campsite and moved to where they found her. I'll explain later."

"One more minute," Calvin interrupted.

"Well, I have some news for you, too, Lowell," she said. "That letter you sent up?"

"Time to hurry it up," Calvin told Lowell.

Lowell waved him off, urgently. "You found a match?"

"Yes. From motor vehicles. Somebody with a strange kind of history. Not a criminal record to speak of. But I think somebody you need to stay away from."

"Shouldn't be hard, I'm in jail," Lowell snapped, as Calvin reached for the receiver in his hand. "Who?" he shouted. But her answer was obliterated by the sound of Calvin hanging up the phone.

Lowell kicked the wall in frustration. Lena knew who the probable killer of Marge Pappas was but she'd been cut off before she could tell him. Her strange reference to someone with a history but not having a record could be anybody. Why the hell did she have to be so damned cryptic? Was it the deputies or not. Somehow he felt uncertain despite what had happened. Now he would have to spend the next few hours waiting to find out. Was it Lejeune? Could Connors be a closet sexual harasser? And what about Billy, the sudden alcoholic, who'd as much as admitted he admired Marge? Or Duvall, the melancholy redneck? Or how about the entire Club membership in some ancient pagan hunting rite? Oddly, nobody at the barracks who happened his way seemed all that concerned about the fact that two state law enforcement officers had been gunned down in the area in less than a week. Or that the only reason he was here was because he'd been called in by a police officer to investigate.

The wizened old Black civilian porter who brought him breakfast told him that two sheriff's deputies from Collier were on their way in, to request custody. "You're a popular guy, Mr. Lowell," he said. "But I sure don't envy you. No sirree."

Lowell didn't feel too enviable, himself.

18

Before leaving the motel, Bedrosian stopped to call her cousin Amber one last time. She told Amber about the note, and who wrote it, and that she was on her way to Naples to bail her investigator out. "Be careful, Lena," Amber had said, her voice taut with concern.

Amber had almost fallen over herself in relief when the senator had returned to work yesterday afternoon, although she fussed and fumed over his health. She'd called his personal physician, who'd demanded in vain that Kranhower come see him, and when that failed, came to the senator's office. Aside from a scolding and quick checkup, along with a vain prescription for bed rest, the doctor left without having accomplished very much. Lena stopped by late in the day and found them cheerfully cleaning up the offices. The senator seemed in good spirits, in his element. No mention had been made of any pending or missing legislation. Apparently the issue had been dropped like a red-hot cannon ball. For now. She wondered why.

Amber had been a bit more enlightening when she stopped to see Lena after a dinner meeting with the senator and Bob Hathcock. "It's amazing," she confided. "They are acting like best friends, like nothing happened at all. Everything is going as smooth as glass."

"Does that mean the government shutdown is over?" inquired Lena.

"Well, not exactly. They are still at odds over this finance bill. I learned one thing, though," sighed Amber. "From now on, I read every piece of legislation that comes across that transom. Orders from the top."

"Good idea," Lena told her. "Somebody ought to."

"Hey, cheap shot!" said Amber. "The senator always used to. Still would, but he's just so overworked. He just won't admit to his own limitations. And some folks have been trying to take advantage."

"I've heard of people like that," said Lena. "You sure you're okay?" she asked.

"Oh sure, hunky-dory. Everything is back and running as smooth as it's gonna run, anyway. Now, if we could just do the same with this damn government!"

"My best to the senator," said Bedrosian. "I'll be in touch."

"Sure," Amber had replied. "He says to say hi to your friend Mr. Lowell."

"I'll do that."

Now, having told Amber where she was heading, Bedrosian hung up, and checked the room one last time. Fortunately, Michael had finally tired of playing the archetypal alumnus Seminole booster, and was ready to leave. He had gone down to the car to finish packing it. The kids were beyond stir-crazy. They had been whining relentlessly for two days now, about the cold, about the lack of a major theme park, about the food, about the lack of food, about not enough TV, about all the wrong TV. Lena was fit to have her tubes tied (actually, she'd already done that the year before).

She glanced at her watch, increasingly worried about Lowell. Calling her from a Highway Patrol holding cell, ranting something about killer deputies. That was too crazy, he must have been talking in code or something. And a rock for a murder weapon? Marge had been shot! Lowell must've gone off the shallow end and hit bottom a little too hard. But she needed to get there fast, and warn him.

Bedrosian hadn't been to Naples in years, but remembered she had a friend down there in the department. Maybe she could get him to check up on what was going on until she arrived. She was confident she'd have Lowell out as soon as she got there this afternoon. But then the question remained, what to do next? Her knowledge of who wrote the note was significant, but not necessarily enough to convict. The one who wrote that letter may have been an entirely different person from whoever killed Marge. Marge's death had opened a hundred Pandora's boxes, raised a hundred questions, and provided few answers. Greed, hate-mongering, zealotry, poaching, all were possible motives in that troubled region of the state. Any or all of them could have played in her death. And now Lowell was claiming that the same cops who had investigated Marge's death had shot a highway patrolman. She had wondered about the way they had altered, or ignored, forensic evidence. The way they'd moved the body. That, she'd already figured out for herself, from the soil samples. At first she'd simply been appalled at the incompetence. But now she realized Lowell may be right. And if he was right, he was in danger.

Lena had been fighting a gnawing, growing fear, that had been eating at her lifelong confidence in the righteous inevitability of justice. But now that fear took on a very real, very strong possibility: that this case might never be solved. Because when cops committed crimes, and she ruefully had to admit it sometimes happened, all too often the public never learned the truth.

No, she told herself. That will not happen. That must not happen. This killer must be stopped. And punished. She had to get to Collier County, and fast.

A quick call back to Amber, who went through the senate travel office to get her a flight to Naples, and another good-bye. Kranhower was more than glad to help. He'd become rather fond of "that young sailing enthusiast," as he'd put it. He was even threatening to pay Lowell another visit when his health and schedule permitted.

Michael wasn't pleased about having to drive back alone with the kids (she didn't envy him that), while she flew on to Naples, and told her so as he dropped her off at the Leon County Airport. She apologized like a dutiful police officer, to her ever-patient family. They kissed each other good-bye, and she promised she'd call when she got there.

"Thanks for the vacation," he told her. "I know it was probably no fun for you."

"Not at all," she fibbed. "I had a great time."

Bedrosian's concern for Lowell increased as the Air Florida flight dipped down and settled into its final landing pattern over the pristine barrier islands north of Naples. The early chill had burned off, finally. It looked like a typically glorious south Florida day as she stepped off the sleek Gulf Stream jet into the fresh southern breeze, coming in now off Florida Bay.

She had a hired rental car waiting—she'd insisted on paying for her own, not being a believer in government largess—and called her friend Buddy Clarke of the Collier Sheriff's Department, from the rental counter.

"You get anything?" she asked him.

"Well," he told her. "Your friend by all accounts is being held as a material witness, and possible suspicion of murder."

"Is he still at DeSoto Barracks?"

There was a moment's pause. "I think so," he said. "But they usually turn prisoners over to the local sheriff for booking at county. Why?"

"Buddy," she said, earnestly. "Whatever you can do, don't let anybody from your department get to them. See if you can get somebody, anybody, to stall, over there. I'm on my way."

"Why?" he demanded. "Lena, what's going on?"

But she had already hung up and was out the door.

Lowell was near exhaustion. Only adrenaline kept him going, waiting for Bedrosian. Two hours went by. He'd finally convinced the old Black porter to listen, when nobody else would. The porter had overheard that two sheriff's deputies from Collier were coming to get him, and had warned him. But there wasn't much he could do if they got there before Bedrosian did. Hopefully, Bedrosian would have a good lawyer and a bail bondsman with her. What had he been thinking with his scornful denunciation of lawyers? If nothing else, a lawyer—preferably a nice fat one—would offer a shield between him and those two killers when they got here.

He looked at the clock. Eleven-fifty. Lunch break in ten minutes. That's when off-duty cops did unofficial business. Also, the ominous significance of high noon wasn't lost on him.

An idea occurred to him. He went over to the barred doorway. "Hey Calvin!" he shouted to the officer who had locked him up. Officer Calvin was getting ready to go off duty, and was closing up his desk across the large operations room. He looked up, uninterestedly.

"How about you get hold of the sheriff, and ask him if he has an arrest warrant before turning me over to those two deputies!"

Calvin yawned. "Take it easy, Lowell. You're the only witness to who shot Lieutenant Higgins. They probably just want to put you under protective custody."

"Exactly my point," shouted Lowell. "What does it take to get through to you people?"

"No need to get offensive, Lowell," said Calvin, reaching for his jacket. "I'm just doing my job, same as everyone else around here. The fact that you are talking like a raving lunatic isn't helping anyone's situation, including your own."

Calvin turned to go. At that moment a sheriff's patrol car tore into the driveway and skidded to a stop directly in front of the entrance. Two doors slammed, and footsteps raced to the door. Calvin turned in annoyance, as Collier County Sheriff's Deputies Vega and Kohler pushed in through the entryway.

"You can't park there," Officer Calvin informed them in irritation. He glanced doubtfully back at Lowell, a flicker of doubt in his eyes.

"We're here to pick up a prisoner," Kohler stated, all business. Vega surveyed the room. He seemed satisfied that the only occupants were Officer Calvin, someone running water in the kitchenette, and the man in the holding cell: Tony Lowell. Vega gave Lowell a cheerful grin.

Calvin stood firm. He didn't like these two, he decided. Never had. Too pushy, too cocky. Tended to bend the rules a little too often. He couldn't believe what Lowell had told him. But all the same . . .

"You fellas have an arrest warrant?" he asked, in his most businesslike tone.

Kohler's expression turned crafty. "The sheriff just said to pick the guy up, he's probably got all the paperwork," he said.

"Let's call him, to make sure," said Calvin, reaching for the phone. Normally, he would have taken them at their word. But there was something about them, about Lowell, that made him hesitate. Nolan Higgins had been a friend of his. He wanted to make sure that justice was done. And that meant going by the book. Making no mistakes, such as would cause exclusionary dismissal. Like had happened with all too many miscreants in recent times. Scumbags of all types, getting away with you name it on account of procedural mistakes.

"Sorry," Calvin decided, with an apologetic shrug. "I can't release the prisoner without a warrant. You should know that, deputy."

Vega turned away from Lowell, and turned his steely glare on Calvin.

"Calvin! Remember what I told you?" Lowell shouted. "Look at them. They have no authorization, and they know it. Call the sheriff!"

Calvin took a deep breath.

"Don't listen to him, man," Vega urged him. "He's a criminal, man!"

"So you say," said Calvin. "But I need a warrant."

Sensing trouble, the porter came into the room. He looked at the two deputies and back at Lowell. His eyes widened. There was no doubt in his mind. He'd seen these two guys working over poor people, migrant workers, friends of his, once too often. He felt himself begin to shake with fear.

"Come on, we ain't got all day," Kohler snapped at Calvin. "You gonna cooperate, or what?"

Calvin stood firm. Vega bore into him with his scud-missile eyes, and reached for his side arm. Calvin's hand was already on his.

At that instant, the door flew open, and Police Detective Lieutenant Lena Bedrosian burst in. She had state DLE Captain Tom Watson with her. She'd convinced him to come with her, thanks to her friend in Naples.

"What's going on here?" asked Watson. The two deputies froze.

"They don't have a warrant," Calvin began.

Vega seemed to snap. "Give us the fuckin' prisoner," he suddenly screamed, pulling his gun. "Or you are all dead motherfuckers!"

He made a grab for Bedrosian, but she pulled away. He aimed the gun at her in fury and squeezed the trigger. A shot rang out, a tremendous boom in the closed-in space. Mario Vega's face disappeared in a spray of blood and bone, cartilage and brain.

Everyone turned in shock. Calvin, his hands shaking, pivoted his Smith & Wesson revolver toward Kohler, who was pale as a snowbird, his hands raised. "E-e-easy," Kohler stammered. "Easy, there. I didn't do nothin'."

Once Kohler started talking, there was no stopping him. Vega was the one, he insisted. Vega had done it all, and threatened to kill him if he so much as peeped.

"Done what all?" Watson wanted to know.

"Shot that patrol officer!" said Kohler.

"What about Marge Pappas?" demanded Bedrosian, still feeling the shock of the shooting.

"I don't know nothin' about no Pappas," insisted Kohler. He then clammed up and demanded a lawyer.

Bedrosian immediately requested Lowell's release on technical grounds: There was no legal arrest, he'd been handcuffed when found, and anybody with half a brain could figure out there was no way he could have shot Higgins and hid the body in those circumstances.

"You'll be lucky if Mr. Lowell doesn't hire a lawyer himself, and sue you all," she said.

"I wish," sighed Captain Watson, "that somebody would tell me what the hell is goin' on here."

Lowell finally had an audience. He gave Watson an edited version of what had happened to Officer Higgins. Marge Pappas he wasn't yet ready to discuss. Watson shook his head in dismay. So did the porter, whose name was Kendrick Jackson. "What're they complainin' about," Jackson mumbled to a badly shaken Calvin, but mostly to himself. "I'm the one gots to clean up the mess!"

Captain Watson wasn't too happy about letting Bedrosian take Lowell, but once he'd gotten their statements he didn't figure he had much ground for holding him. Nor could he hold Kohler, merely because his partner had gone berserk and gotten himself killed. There were enough witnesses, including himself, to exonerate Calvin, who was now in a state of shock.

Watson filled out a report, Bedrosian did the same, and initialed what he wrote on the bottom: "self-defense, and defense of a fellow law officer." He then took a report from Kohler, who seemed less and less cooperative by the minute, and waited for the medical examiner to take Vega's body away.

Lowell had the presence of mind to insist that Vega's weapon be bagged for evidence. "I think you'll find a perfect match to the bullet that killed Officer Higgins," he told them. Watson, who hadn't slept well, mumbled something inaudible. He then turned his attention to Kohler.

"Deputy, I don't know enough to comment on Mr. Lowell's statements yet, which is lucky for you. I could hold you as as accessory to this shooting."

"Hey, I told you, it was Vega—"

"So what you are going to do is, go home, and stay there while I call your sheriff, and talk to all these other people. If you leave the county—your county—I will issue a warrant for your arrest. Are we clear about this?"

"Yes, sir."

"All right then. Get the hell out of here, and don't do anything stupid, got that?"

"Yes, sir." Kohler gave Lowell one last look, and left. The look said that it wasn't over yet.

"Shoulda wrote the son of a bitch a parking ticket," muttered a still-shaken Calvin, watching him go. Watson placed him on paid administrative leave pending the outcome of the automatic internal affairs investigation.

"Don't worry about it, Earl," Watson assured him. "You'll be all right."

Lowell and Bedrosian finished their reports, and agreed to return, if needed, for the inquest.

"Now beat it, before something else happens," growled Watson, showing them the door.

"All right, Lowell," Bedrosian grumbled, as soon as they were out of there. "Now what the hell was all that about?"

"Your cousin Marge, what else?" said Lowell. "Now, do you or don't you want to hear about the rock?"

"What I want to hear about is how the hell you managed to wind up in jail looking like leftovers from a buzzard banquet."

"In that case," said Lowell, "you are going to have to spring for a cup of very hot, very fresh coffee, and a very tall stack of blueberry pancakes." At which point he got into the passenger seat of her rental Buick, and fell sound asleep.

19

WEDNESDAY AFTERNOON

Bedrosian let Lowell sleep for a while in the car while she made some calls. Then she drove him over to the Denny's in LaBelle for breakfast. After a double order of pancakes and coffee Lowell was revived somewhat, and Bedrosian took him to the county impound lot to get his Chevy out. It was still tied up in red tape. Bedrosian managed to badger the attendant into allowing a search of the vehicle, and Lowell showed her the blood-stained rock he'd found, and told her where he'd found it.

She sighed, after a while. "That explains the fracture patterns." He looked at her. "My friend at the state lab," she explained. "He said there was an interrupt in the pattern."

He looked at her blankly.

"From the photos you took at the ME's office. Her skull fractures," she went on. "Usually a bullet will create a radiating fracture pattern. But a blunt object like this rock causes a different, more jagged pattern. He'd noticed some irregularities which didn't make sense at the time, based on the report."

Lowell dug quickly into the glove compartment, and found the almost forgotten envelope of Photomat prints. He shuffled through them and waved one. "Here!" he exclaimed. "I should have caught this right off." He showed her the photo. She flinched a moment, then looked. "Look there," he said. "These are the lines from the bullet fracture—they come from a much higher velocity impact. But see here, how they stop abruptly? The first impact always causes the primary pattern. The fracture lines from the secondary impact—in this case the bullet—always stop when they intersect an existing fracture." He pointed out several such lines. "Here, here, and here."

She stared at him. "So the rock did come first!"

"Indubitably," said Lowell, in triumph. "The bullet may have been to finish her off. Or possibly as a crude attempt at a cover-up—that would fit in with the two deputies' involvement, and their claim that it was a hunting accident."

"So what the hell was their involvement?"

He looked at her. "You haven't told me who wrote the letter yet. You first." She gave him a look, carefully bagged the rock, and placed it in the trunk of the rental car. On the road again, she told Lowell what she'd found out. That the handwriting had matched Duvall Patterson's driver's license application.

"Sorry son of a bitch," he muttered, shaking his head. "It probably never even occurred to him that stalking your cousin was a crime."

"Maybe. He didn't bother to cut out block letters, like most of them would," she conceded.

"Of course not," he replied, sorrowfully. "To him, it was probably a love letter. The angry response of a jilted suitor. He wanted her to know who wrote it."

Patterson's Landing seemed uncharacteristically deserted, listing out over the river's edge like a ship already abandoned by its rats. They parked out front, jumped out of the car, and approached the building cautiously. Bedrosian banged on the door. "Open up!" she shouted. "Police!"

A battered shutter slat was lifted, and a heavy face looked dully out at them. "What do you want?"

"Easy, ma'am," said Bedrosian, holding her hands up. "We just want to ask your husband some questions, is all."

She opened the door a crack. "He's gone," she said. Her voice sounded dead, but her eyes were firm and steady. She was wearing a greasy yellow nightgown. She looked like hell.

"Do you know where he went?" Bedrosian persisted.

"Why should he start tellin' me now?" She sounded bitter. "He ain't never told me before. He ain't here's all I know."

The stillness of the afternoon was shattered by the sputter and roar of an outboard engine starting up, close by. Racing around the side of the building Lowell reached the dock just in time to glimpse the old skiff as it disappeared around the bend in the river, a shriveled, sun-blasted man hunched over the wheel. Duvall Patterson was on the run.

Bedrosian, slowed by her street shoes, caught up to Lowell a moment later. "Was it him?"

Lowell nodded.

"We'll get him," she said, grimly, reaching for her police cellular.

"But can we hold him?" Lowell asked, stopping her. "Just because he wrote a letter doesn't mean he killed her."

"One way to find out," said Bedrosian, "is ask the sonovabitch."

Lowell had another idea. "Let's ask Billy," he said. "The son. He's been acting pretty spooky since I've met him. I think he's carrying some heavy weight around. I think he knows a lot more than he's been sayin'."

"Lead the way," said Bedrosian, a slight note of irony in her voice.

They went back to the front door, and rapped once again.

"Mrs. Patterson," shouted Lowell. "We need to talk to you."

She faced them and stood waiting, this time a small-caliber handgun gripped tightly in both hands. "This is mah home. Ain't you people done enough to mah family? You git out!"

Lowell threw a quick glance at Bedrosian, wondering what she was thinking. "We'd like to talk to Billy," he said. "Is he around?"

She seemed to come alive for a moment, at that. The look in her eyes turned to one of fear. "Whaddya want him for?"

"Just a few questions, ma'am," said Bedrosian, gently. "Please put the gun down." She could understand her worry. Having a husband like Duvall was hard enough to bear. She even felt uncharacteristic pity for the wretched woman. "We don't want to arrest him. We just need to talk to him. We need his help."

"He's a good boy," insisted Mrs. Patterson, lowering the gun. "Duvall, he treats him like dirt, says he's good for nothin', but it's Billy does most of the work 'round here. Him and me," she added. "Duvall, he always had this inferiority complex, you ask me. Always needed to find somebody to blame for every damn thing. I let him get away with that way too long," she said, sadly. "It's my own damn fault, puttin' up with him, and his philanderin', I reckon. Just tryin' so hard to prove hisself manly, but he never could. But Billy." And here her expression turned earnest. "Billy, he's a good boy. And he don't need no more trouble than he's got."

"So can we talk to him?" Bedrosian persisted.

She hesitated, then shook her head. "Reckon ah can't stop you," she said. "But he ain't here, neither. Stays away from home more 'n more. Cain't say's I blame him none."

"So do you know where we might find him?" asked Bedrosian, exasperated. The woman shrugged, as though trying (and failing) to shed a great weight.

"I think I know where he is," Lowell said to Bedrosian. "Let's go." They turned, to walk back to the car.

"Don't be lookin' for him in no bar, he ain't no damn Hell's Angel," Mrs. Patterson shouted after them. "Billy's a good boy!"

Sheriff's Deputy Kohler knew his days were numbered. Even if they couldn't pin anything specific on him other than accessory to the Higgins shooting, it was just a matter of time before he was going to have one hell of a lot of explaining to do. At the very least, the sheriff would take his badge. Sure, he could sue, due cause, and so forth. But if he did, Riker would rake him over the coals like a clam in a clambake. Better to cut his losses. He figured he had a few hours, at least. Maybe more. It would give him time to do one thing, anyway. Get the satisfaction of vengeance. There was one person too many in this county. And that one person had ruined everything he'd worked for, striven for, those five long years in the department. He vowed to himself that before Doug Kohler disappeared into the sunset, he was going to leave something to be remembered by. Namely, one very dead private investigator who had messed up other people's business one time too many. And he knew just who would have no choice but to help him out.

The freeze had passed. Rice Crawford had good cause to feel satisfied, if bone-weary. He'd saved his employer, Quentin Lejeune, almost the entire citrus crop, thanks to the desperate labors of a thousand migrant workers through two days and a night, noses kept to the grindstone by Rice and his hundred-odd loyal militia followers. He'd sent them all home at last, with free coffee and doughnuts, paid the migrant workers their $2.74 an hour net pay after expenses and deductions, and bussed them back to their camps. And he'd sighed a huge sigh of relief as the last truck drove out the gate with a heaping load of nearly ripe oranges that would get a nice coat of paint and nobody would be the wiser.

217

It was time to celebrate. He walked to his bungalow, out be-hind the main house, thinking about what Chavez, the cook, might have ready for him. Chavez liked to surprise him when he thought the occasion was right. This occasion would do fine. A good meal, a couple of drinks by the fire, and a well-earned rest.

He knew Quentin would be needing him in his other role as company spokesman when the wheeling and dealing began in earnest with the processors and commodity people, come morning. He looked forward to that. Lejeune Farms had never been in a better position to dominate a market than now: Their competition had been nearly wiped out overnight. True, Mr. Lejeune would get all the profits. Forty million they'd pull down from this crop; not bad for a night's work. And with any luck at all, they might just parlay it into eighty mil, or even a hundred. People needed their orange juice in the morning, it was as simple as that. It was nice to have that kind of power. Nor did he feel any resentment toward Lejeune. This was Lejuene's land, his empire, which his forefathers had plowed and sown, and fought the Indians and damn Yanks to keep. Rice had no complaints on that score. He'd have himself a spread like this one day and would expect the same lion's share of the rewards. Meantime, he'd get a tidy bonus on his next paycheck—damn near enough to get that new S-10 pickup he'd been admiring at Hathcock's.

"Hey, Chavez!" he shouted, as he walked in the back door and tossed his hat on the rack. "Get me a bottle of Johnnie Walker Red, on the double!"

He stopped short. He had company.

20

The sun was low, wide shafts of bright yellow light slanting between the trees from the west, as the hunched-over man in the dugout skiff made his way among the sandbars and mangrove hummocks into the south fork of the Caloosahatchee River, and the entrance to the lower Caloosa Canal. As the panic subsided, and with it the tears, he forced himself to concentrate. He knew where he was, and which way to go. That traitor Kohler was headed there, running to Big Daddy for help, just because he'd messed up big time. And now Kohler was going to pin it all on him. He'd heard, from the boys in the Room. It was amazing how word got out, about things like that. But it always did. The Room was more than just a meeting place. It was also an information exchange. Jerry Laker had come in just at the end of today's talk show, ordered his usual Bud, and pulled him aside. "Y'all better keep your head down, Duvall. I just heard Vega got shot, and Kohler is gonna squeal. I'd watch my ass if I was you."

That had worried him. It was like Jerry knew what was between him and them two damn deputies. That was something nobody alive should know about, besides that fool boy Billy. He didn't dare ask Jerry what he knew, though. Jerry gave him a sly wink. "Looks like Mario Vega's gonna be the perfect fall guy for Marge Pappas and that hahway patrol ossifer."

"I don't know nothin' about that," Duvall had snarled, panic setting in. His mind was in a fog, he was trying to see things like they were, but wasn't quite able.

"Ah was you, ah'd be outta here," Laker added, all casual like, like he didn't have a care in the world. Which he probably didn't. He pulled out a plug and bit off a chaw.

Duvall wiped his hands nervously on his overalls as Jerry drawled on: "Yes, sir, if ah know Deputy Kohler, he ain't the type to take no chances. Probably set up Mario to take the heat, and now there's just one person left to get out of the way."

"Bullshit!" said Duvall, his heart pounding. "Ain't nobody but Kohler gotta worry about nothin'." But he knew better. His insides were churning. He was worried plenty. Jerry Laker spat toward the bucket, gave him another friendly wink and pat, and shuffled off, whistling cheerfully.

In a panic, Duvall had shut down the restaurant and service area, trying to decide his next move. He felt Betty's eyes weighing on him from the kitchen doorway. The sudden arrival of the rental car convinced him. He ran out the back, scanning the sky for the dreaded Black Helicopters, the ones Crawford and them was always goin' on about. He was almost surprised there were none in sight. He raced for the dock and jumped aboard his old but sturdy skiff, which he kept ready for just such an occasion. He managed to get the Johnson outboard started on the third try, and sputtered out into the mist-shrouded river just as Bedrosian and Lowell ran around the side of the building from the parking lot.

Duvall silently fought back the tears at the injustice of it all as he roared upriver, around the bend and out of sight. Lowell stood on the bank, and watched him go.

Ten miles and ninety minutes later, Duvall reached the juncture of two streams. He turned hard to port, into the southern tributary. The cypress trees closed in above and on either side. On one side was Lejeune Farms property, the other side state forest preserve. That was the land that snooty Hunt Club was tryin' to take over, Jerry Laker had told him. He didn't care about that. Anybody brought more business into the area was fine with him, they'd be needing gas and beer. What he cared about was his freedom. It wasn't right that some government official should be able to take it away from him, for no good reason. That's what that bitch Marge had tried to do after he'd gone and been nice and even tried to show his feelings. Why couldn't she understand? And if that's what Officer Higgins had pulled on his friend Doug Kohler, fine, he wouldn't do that again no more. Kohler had done them both a favor. But what was that asshole Jerry tryin' to lay on him? That Kohler might just be inclined to get rid of any more witnesses? Like hell. No way he would want the real truth to come out, though. His heart sank at that, and felt near split in two. He felt the tears coming again, and the shame that came with them. At least this time no one could see him.

He couldn't understand how Laker knew so much. It had to be Kohler. He knew exactly where Kohler would be now: asking for money from Lejeune. And if there was any money to be got from that end, he was the one going to get it. That and get even at the same time. And maybe not just with Deputy Dawg Kohler. Maybe with every damn body who'd mistreated him, mocked him, underestimated him, and disrespected him all these years.

Duvall passed Donny Rossback's old skiff that was half sunk in the reeds; he'd just left it there, and not bothered to salvage, or pay rent for it, or anything. Maybe he'd come back somctime, drag it home. Get Billy to fix it. Billy. Damn mod dling ungrateful fool kid. Never was good for nothing. Tried so hard to teach him right, and now he couldn't even trust him to keep his mouth shut. Well, Billy boy, I brung you into this world. I can take you out, damn it all! But first thing first. Kohler. Kohler's gotta go.

Barbara Lewis, the bleached-blond miniskirted server, saw Lowell coming and reacted with all the properly rightful outrage of an abandoned lover, which was promptly compounded by a factor of ten when she saw the younger, fitter, and (in her mind) better-looking dark-haired woman with him.

"So," she greeted Lowell. "Back for another Cuban sandwich?" She pulled him aside and lowered her voice. "Don't you dare pretend you don't know me."

"Listen, Barbara, last night was great, and I would have stayed if I could. I'm sorry I had to bail like that but something bad happened, and I have to ask you something."

"Yeah? Like what?"

"I'll tell you the whole thing later, I promise. But I've gotta find that kid. Did he ever show up?"

"Billy?" she said grudgingly. "You haven't caught up to him yet?"

"He moves fast," said Lowell. "And I move slow."

"That's not how I remember it." Barbara looked sideways at Bedrosian, once more. "So who's your new friend?"

"This is my partner Lena, we work together," he said, by way of introduction.

"Yeah, right."

To Lowell's immense dismay, Lena responded by flashing her badge. "Detective Lieutenant Bedrosian, Manatee City Police Department," she announced. "We're looking for a William Patterson. I understand he frequents this establishment."

"You're a cop! Well, he's all yours, copper, right over there," she pointed, with finality, "and I hope he pukes on your grave!" With that she stalked off.

"I think she likes you," said Bedrosian, watching her go.

Billy was sitting alone in the back corner, drunk. When he saw Lowell, his dour look of despair changed to one of apprehension. He fiddled nervously with a small metallic device that lay on the table in front of him. "Go 'way," he muttered.

"Excessive sociability must run in the family," commented Bedrosian. Ignoring that, Lowell slid into the booth opposite the boy. Lena pulled up a chair.

A potbellied male bar server ambled over after a while. "Git you something?" he asked.

"Coffee," said Bedrosian.

"Who'da guessed," he said, looking her over. "And you, guy?" he asked Lowell.

" 'Nother beer," muttered Billy, fumbling for his wallet. It lay sprawled open on the table like a shot sparrow, empty.

"Make that three coffees," said Lowell, pushing Billy's wallet aside, along with his beer mug. The male server sniffed, and left in search of better prospects.

"That woman sure has it in for you, Lowell," Bedrosian commented, looking across the room. "What did you do to her, anyway? Never mind, I don't want to know." Lowell glanced quickly to where she was indicating. Where Barbara was pointedly flirting with five bikers wearing silver concha belts and the prerequisite black leather jackets.

"How can you tell?" he asked, puzzled.

"Call it a woman thing," she sniffed, turning her attention back to the business at hand. "So," she said, looking at Billy with a mixture of pity and scorn. "This is the prodigal son."

Billy's head was lolling, first to one side, then the other. His eyes were shut tight, his expression that of a yearning hound, listening for his master's vanished voice.

Bedrosian watched him for a moment, with a frown. "Lowell," she said, looking away, "whatever happened to that woman you were seeing up in Polk County? Bee, or something?"

"Bree," he said. "Nothing happened. She's still there." He didn't want to talk about Briana Cook Cahill, or the aftermath of her vicious marriage, just now. Let alone think about her. He gazed off into the smoky wilderness into which Barbara had once again vanished. Lowell suddenly wished he'd given at least a thought to AIDS, last night. Those guys she'd just been flirting with looked like they'd fuck an African warthog, given the chance. He only hoped Barbara had enough common sense to stay away from the likes of them. On the other hand, he wryly reflected, she hadn't had the common sense to stay away from the likes of him. He looked away, and saw Bedrosian glaring at him, accusingly.

"What's with you?" she demanded to know.

Billy's eyes fluttered open again, focused briefly on Lowell, ignored Bedrosian, then fixed a dark, blurry stare at the device lying in front of him on the beer-spattered tabletop. "They shot her," he suddenly muttered, in great, repressed rage. "They just fuckin' shot her." His voice cracked into a sob.

"Easy, there. Who shot who?" Lowell asked him, with a glance at Bedrosian. She was suddenly all business, notepad in hand.

"The mother," Billy moaned, his voice quivering with rage. "They must of. I found her tracker." He picked up the metal device, and tossed it down again. Lena quietly picked it up.

"What's this?" she asked.

Billy's eyes finally focused on Lena. "Who's she?" he asked, his voice slurred, his look hostile.

Ignoring Lowell's warning look, Bedrosian made a sound of disgust, and reached into her purse. "Police," she said, bluntly, flashing her badge. Billy gave Lowell a look of betrayal—the second such look in the last few minutes thrown his way. "I'd like to ask you a few questions, if you don't mind," she went on.

That sobered Billy right up. Sort of. "I'm outta here," he

mumbled, struggling to get up. He failed, caught between a sticky vinyl booth bench and a hard table. Lowell pulled him down again, not too forcefully.

"Easy, Billy. This is Lena Bedrosian," Lowell told him. "She's a police detective, like she says. She's also the cousin of Marge Pappas. It's probably best to cooperate with her."

Billy looked stricken, and risked a glance in Lena's direction. "Zat right?" he asked.

Lena nodded. "My associate here tells me you and Marge were friends, is that true?"

Billy seemed to shake his head and nod at the same time. "Yeah," he finally agreed. "We were friends." He looked to be on the verge of collapse, once again. The server brought the coffees and slammed them down. "That'll be three bucks." Lowell looked in his wallet—empty—then checked his pockets, sheepishly. Bedrosian glared at him and paid the bill.

"Billy," said Lowell, softly. "We're not gonna hurt you or anything. We just want to ask some questions."

"I found it in the swamp, it's gotta be hers."

Bedrosian gave Lowell a puzzled look. He nodded at the small device she was holding. "That's a radio tracking device. Enables the wildlife people to follow the movements of an animal it's implanted in. He's talking about a panther."

"Oh. Maybe it just fell off," she suggested.

Billy shook his head.

"Can I borrow this?" she asked, on a whim. Billy didn't respond, so she put it in her purse. "I'll run a check on it."

"We can talk to the ranger, Connors, about that," said Lowell. "He was Marge's supervisor."

Billy's face, still ravaged by his recent beating, suddenly broke up, and he fell forward onto the table, shaking with sobs. Lena hesitated, then finally reached out and touched him. "Hey," she said. Billy shook his head violently, and continued sobbing. Finally, he raised his head and looked at them, his eyes red, his expression one of anguish and despair.

"I didn't mean it!" he finally gasped.

Lena's jaw fell open, shocked. Lowell blinked. "Didn't mean what?" he asked.

"Billy Patterson!" Bedrosian's voice was caught between outrage and disbelief. "Did you kill Marge Pappas?"

He shook his head, once more. "No, no, no, no! I didn't kill anybody! I loved her!" He sobbed once again, his shoulders shaking. They listened, and the story came out, in blurts of pain and guilt. How Billy had had a huge boner for Marge Pappas, whom he had considered beautiful and exotic. How his father had flirted with her, acted like she was his own property, even though she couldn't stand the man. How he'd overheard his father talking with some friends of his one time at the Room, and how they'd goaded Duvall until he began to brag about how he could make her beg for it, anytime he felt like it. Billy had almost died with shame, and confronted his father about it, only to get whipped for his insolence.

"What friends?" Lowell interrupted him.

Billy's anguish shifted to fear. He looked at Bedrosian, and gulped. "They were deputies," he said, barely audible. "I don't know their names, but one was Spanish, the other, like a German guy—"

"We know who they are," said Lowell. "Go on."

"I'd went over to her campsite that night," Billy resumed, catching his breath. "Just to bring her some flowers. I didn't mean nothin'!" he pleaded, looking from one to the other. Lena, beginning to understand, now reached out once more, and stroked his shoulder a moment.

"It's all right," she encouraged him. "You just liked her, so you brought her flowers."

"Yeah," he resumed. "I got some hibiscus and roses from the nursery, 'cause she'd been all upset that day and worried about somethin', about this letter somebody had sent her. The one you showed me," he said, to Lowell.

"You didn't tell me your father was the one who wrote it, though," Lowell mentioned.

Billy stared. Then folded like a bad poker hand. "I told him to leave her alone," he sobbed. "I told him if Mom ever found out she'd kill him. And she would!"

Bedrosian frowned, at that. "Go on."

"I didn't know what to say to Marge so I just hung around on the road, trying to decide what to do. Then I heard somebody else coming, so I hid in the woods. It was—it was—" Again, he broke down.

"Your father?" Lowell prompted him.

"Y-y-yes." Billy wiped his nose on his sleeve, and continued. "D-dad didn't mean nothin', I don't think. I don't think he even knew what he was gonna do, maybe just prove somethin', or somethin'."

"Like, what a man he was?" Sarcasm, from Bedrosian.

Billy just nodded. "But she got away from him, and ran the other way, to her truck. She—she had a phone."

That caught Lowell and Bedrosian both, by surprise. "A cellular phone?"

"Yes. She c-called the cops."

"Oh, God," said Bedrosian. Lowell sensed what was coming, and felt sick.

"They got there in no time," Billy continued, after a time. "They must've been off duty or somethin'. Anyway they showed up, Dad's same two buddies, so they didn't do nothin'. So she got mad, and said some stuff—"

"What kind of stuff?" Bedrosian interrupted.

"I don't know. I couldn't hear it. They were just messin' around, showin' off, I think. Maybe tryin' to bug her or somethin', see what she'd do."

"So what did she do?" Lowell asked.

Billy shook his head, still pained by the memory. "They weren't gonna do nothin' about my old man, so she—she tried to throw them out. B-but—" he sobbed, "they wouldn't go!"

Lena shook her head, angrily. "So what did they do?"

"They laughed in her face. I wanted to crawl in a hole, they were all drunk and actin' jerky. Then one of them grabs her, the German guy I think, and she broke free. My dad tried to stop them, I think—"

"How?" asked Lowell.

Billy looked at him, quizzically. "I don't know. Just yelled at them. And I could've helped, maybe nothin' woulda happened then. But I didn't do nothin', I was too scared! I just hid in the woods like a damn"—he choked on his words now—"like a damn coward! While they—"

"Easy," said Lowell. "There were two of them with guns, and they were drunk. What else could you do?"

"I don't know, stop them somehow!"

"Go on," said Lena, trying to control her impatience. "Then what happened?"

Billy looked at her, reddened with shame. "They just acted nasty with her, at first, messin' around, reaching out, like, to pinch her—her boobs or something, and then it got worse."

"They raped her," said Lena, her voice flat.

Billy tried, and failed, to control his sobs, and succumbed once again. They waited, their coffee untouched.

"Bedrosian, maybe we should—"

"Don't!" she snapped, in warning. "Don't sugarcoat it, Lowell. I need to know exactly what happened to my cousin." She looked at Billy, his body wracked with anguish, and there was something in her look that was less than pity. "Billy," she ordered. "Tell us the rest."

He looked up, got himself under control once again, and finally continued: "It was like a game, to them. At first, but then it got violent. The Spanish guy raped her first, and then when she screamed, the other one started beating her. And my father"—this was the hardest part—"he just acted like he hated her, like she deserved it!"

"Then what happened?" Bedrosian prompted him. Lowell glared at her, but she ignored him. "How did she die?"

Billy sighed, and got control. "She broke away, and tried to run," he continued, his voice now icily calm. "Dad wouldn't let her. He hadn't had a—turn yet. He picked up this big rock and—and hit her with it, on the back of the head. It sounded like an egg breaking. She fell and didn't move. He must've killed her," he barely whispered.

Lowell heard an alarm go off in the back of his mind: a warning. "What do you mean 'must've'? Are you saying she might not have been dead yet?" he asked.

Billy covered his head with his hands, and began rocking back and forth. "I don't know. She must've been. She had to be!" He sounded as though he simply could not bear any other possibility.

"So you don't know?" exclaimed Bedrosian. "Somebody shot her, Billy. Who shot her?"

He just moaned, shaking his head. "I don't know," he wailed. "I ran. We all ran!"

"Your father and the deputies ran, too?" Lowell asked, startled.

"Y-yes. I think so. Everybody panicked. I don't know. They must've gone back and shot her later, to try and cover for the rock, made up the hunting accident story, and nobody questioned it. Then they must've dumped her out in the swamp, because there were hunters out that night. I was gone by then. I'd seen enough."

More than enough, thought Lowell, sadly. How could a young man ever recover from something like that? No wonder he'd turned into a drunk. He hoped Billy could find help somewhere. He sure as hell wouldn't find it here.

"So you kept quiet, all this time," said Bedrosian, ice in her voice.

"They would've killed me!" wailed Billy.

"Easy, Lena, what would you have done?" asked Lowell.

She dismissed that. "You're going to have to make a statement," she told Billy.

"Lena," Lowell reminded her. "You can't take him in."

"Why not?" she demanded, skewering him with her eyes.

"Because you're on administrative leave, remember?"

She stared at him and blinked a moment. She'd actually forgotten. "Maybe," she sighed, "I'd better call Arlen."

"You do that," said Lowell. "I'll keep an eye on Billy here. Drink up," he urged, pushing the coffee toward him. That's when Billy threw up.

"Damn! Not again!" he heard a familiar voice cry, from across the bar.

Lena went to the phone and came back a few minutes later, grim-faced. "I couldn't reach the captain," she said.

Lowell reached over to Billy, wiped his mouth with a corner of the paper tablecloth, and then shook him a little. "Billy," he said. "Where's your old man?"

Billy told them, just before he passed out. Over Lena's objections, Lowell carried him to the car, and loaded him into the backseat. "Let's go," he said.

It was total darkness by the time Lowell navigated Bedrosian's rental car to Devil's Garden and the entrance to Lejeune Farms. The gate was closed, but not locked. Bedrosian stopped long enough for Lowell to push it open, and check the roadbed. The tracks in the sandy clay were recent enough to still show tread marks. Lowell examined them closely with his penlight.

"Kohler's here. There's only one set of tracks, so he's still in there." He pointed along the road, which quickly vanished into the darkness ahead. The grove floodlights were not on tonight. Lena drove on, crossing a low bridge over what looked like a canal, and continuing again through what seemed like endless groves.

"Do I remember you saying something about a weapon?" Lena asked him, casually.

"That was for show," he said. "I'm not here to get into a shooting match." Lena switched off the lights and continued slowly forward, barely able to make out the road in the waning moonlight. The night closed in over the canopied forest road like a pillow over the face of a sleeping giant, smothering all sense of space, low mist closing in from all sides, trees so close together a ghost couldn't slip through. They drove on, the way illuminated only by the night sky. It was illumination enough.

The house suddenly appeared up ahead, its brilliant white lights slashing through the trees as the car came over the last sandy rise. Every light was switched on, along with banks of floodlights on all sides, starkly illuminating the bare grounds and barns, like a shriek of defiance against the all-enclosing night.

Lena coasted the last fifty feet with the engine off and parked the rental car behind a citrus truck. Leaving Billy to sleep it off in the backseat, Lowell and Bedrosian got out, as silently as possible. Bedrosian, still in city clothes, was impossibly dressed for the chill.

"It's a lot warmer than last night," Lowell reassured her, voice low.

"Oh, that's a relief. For a moment there I thought it was cold," snapped Bedrosian, beginning to shiver.

Rice Crawford couldn't believe it. After all he and Mr. Lejeune had done for these morons, some of them still wanted more. Like this second-rate sheriff's deputy, who had the gall to come into this house that was off-limits even to the help, except for himself, Maria and Rico Vega. And the cook. The guy just sat there in Mr. Lejeune's kitchen, his face hard and showing an attitude.

Quentin Lejeune sat in his bathrobe, a cup of cocoa cooling in front of him, Rice Crawford at his elbow. He looked at the man standing before him and motioned Crawford to lean forward. He whispered something to Crawford, a harsh metallic growl, and Crawford nodded.

"Make it quick, Deputy," snapped Crawford. "And you better have a damn good reason for barging in here like this."

Kohler ignored him and appealed directly to the rancher. "You gotta help me, Mr. Lejeune," he said, a note of whining entering his voice. "Somebody killed Mario, and now they're after me."

Lejeune frowned and looked at Crawford. Rice had respected Rico Vega's half brother, who'd maneuvered his way into the Collier Sheriff's Department. He'd heard only the scantest details about his demise earlier today. But this guy, his partner, he just plain detested him. He was almost as sleazy as the other one who ran with him: Patterson. That local self-styled denizen of demagoguery, archetypal backwoods Cracker, and all-around fuck-up. He looked at his boss, questioningly, and read the disgust in his eyes. Mr. Lejeune hated intrusions on his privacy above all. Kohler couldn't have made a worse decision, than to come here.

Kohler didn't seem to know it, yet. "You know how you say the militia serves people? Well I served in your damn militia, and I'm one of the people. And I got a right to—"

Crawford cut him off. "You ain't one of no people. You are a public employee. Moonlightin' for me. What rights y'all talkin' about?"

Again Kohler spoke to Lejeune. "I worked all night for you out there—"

Lejeune spoke up for the first time, his mechanical voice booming with surprising authority. "Like hell you did. I don't know where you were, Kohler, but you were not on my farm."

"I had a job to do," muttered Kohler, startled. "Anyways, me and the boys saved you what I hear is millions. Maybe you could at least come up with some cash—"

"Get out," said Lejeune, in disgust. "You are trespassing. And I've got a good mind to have you shot."

Kohler was the one with the gun. He pulled it with surprising speed. His hand was shaking. Lejeune looked at the gun, then at Crawford, and finally at Kohler, and his eyes were pale slits. "You pull a gun on me, in my own house?"

Crawford spoke up quickly, his eyes almost amused. "You must have a death wish, Deputy Kohler."

"I just want a couple thou, enough to get to the Bahamas, maybe Barbados. Then you won't have to worry about me no more."

"You didn't hear me tell you to get out?" Lejeune's mechanical voice had risen, just slightly. As though someone had twisted a knob.

"I know things about you, Lejeune. 'Bout your whole damn thievin' family. All the payoffs to INS for illegal migrants, all the political payoffs, the illegal pesticides. How you're tryin' to get the guv'mint to pay you for land they already own."

Quentin Lejeune paled slightly, but kept his eyes firmly fixed on the sweating deputy, so as not to give away the man who had just entered the kitchen from the direction of the garage, moving silently on sneakered feet.

"You're even a bigger fool than I thought, Deputy." he said.

Rico Vega looked at his boss, and understood. He knew what had happened to his brother already. And he knew that this guy had snitched on him. He would love the chance to kill him, but knew Mr. Lejeune would never allow it. He'd have to find another way to avenge the honor of Mario. Meanwhile he would do his job. He had to keep up his car payments on that almost-new pickup out there.

Deputy Kohler, an outsider who'd caused nothing but trouble, was on everybody's short list for removal in both Collier and Hondo Counties. Unfortunately, he was so self-absorbed with his resentments and troubles he didn't know it. He kept the gun trained on Lejeune, wondering why the man was so damn unconcerned. That must be how it is, when you own half of south Florida. And the bastard wouldn't even give him a couple thou to get out of his hair, after all he'd done for the man.

"You owe me, Lejeune!" he shouted in exasperation.

"I owe you?" Lejeune's eyes swiveled sideways, just a glance. It was all the signal Rico needed. He hit Kohler in the back of the head with a single blow from the bottle of Johnnie Walker Red he'd been bringing in for Crawford. Kohler collapsed to the floor with a groan, and Rico kicked him a couple of times for good measure.

"That's enough," said Lejeune. "Call the sheriff, and get him out of here."

Lejeune made a single motion with his head to Crawford, and left the room, carrying his cocoa with him.

"Now get Maria, and tie him up good," ordered Crawford. He heard a sound outside, and glanced out at the night, wondering what else was going to happen to ruin his evening.

Outside the window, Duvall Patterson looked in, already frightened half to death by his own audacity, wondering what to do now. His chest was pounding like the telltale heart in that story his daddy had told him once, just to scare the bejeezus out of him. He'd only thought enough to track Kohler here. He hadn't figured on something like this happening. Duvall had a vague plan in mind, of confronting Kohler and demanding a fair share of whatever he was going to extort from Lejeune, and make some kind of pact of silence with him. But now . . . he looked around in panic, looking for a way out. And saw one.

Lena and Lowell worked their way from the parking lot to the side of the house facing the barns. Lowell guessed that would be the service entrance. They stopped when they reached the house. Bedrosian drew her gun and nodded for Lowell to go around the front. She would take the rear. They split up, moving swiftly and silently among the shrubs alongside the house.

Lowell reached the front portico, listening at each window for any sound. He heard some thumping noises, followed by voices speaking in low, urgent tones. Probably coming from the back. He moved in that direction.

Bedrosian circled around the other way, ducking under the laundry room window where a woman was watching a small black-and-white TV, and moved behind a bush below what she guessed was the eating area. She strained to hear the voices inside, trying to locate them. She heard the movement behind her and turned ready to spring, but at that moment her foot slipped into a drainage hole and she lost her balance for just a moment: a moment too long. Instantly she felt the cold ring of blue steel shoved into her back.

"Don't even breathe," a raspy voice ordered her, barely a whisper.

She raised her hands slowly, automatically, like she'd been trained to do.

"Drop the gun," the voice demanded.

"You're making a mistake. I'm a police officer."

"I said drop it!" It wasn't a voice she knew, but then she was new around here. She could smell the fear. The man was reeking with it. Her years of training and experience had taught her one thing about fear. It was more deadly than a nest of rattlers, when combined with a lethal weapon and an unstable personality. This man sounded unstable as hell.

"Easy," she said. "I'm going to set it down so it doesn't go off. Okay?"

"Just move it, Goddamn it!"

She obeyed. He leaned down, and picked it up quickly. She looked at him and saw a small, wiry, frightened-looking man with ruddy skin and the signs of a life lived in his own personal hell. His hand was shaking—another bad sign.

"You must be Duvall Patterson," she said.

235

"Shut up," he muttered. "Move away from the house." He waved her toward the area behind the outbuildings—an open field leading to what she knew would be miles of orange groves. She thought of Billy's story. She didn't want to go into those groves with this man.

21

Patterson was already leering at her. She could feel his eyes exploring her body, that unattainable something he was craving with the aching yearning of the long-deprived, the growing realization that he had the power now. The control. To possess this prize, to have her for himself. Just as soon as he could summon up the nerve.

No way, she swore to herself. No possible way.

"Keep moving," he ordered her. They were already deep into the groves. The night was pitch-black and overcast. Clouds were scudding in from the Gulf. It was not as cold as it had been, but it was still cold. And Bedrosian, to her great chagrin, had not dressed for a long walk in the woods. She stumbled once and just caught herself before he did, cursing whoever invented dress shoes (these were low-heeled, but still . . .). He shoved her, petulantly. "Hurry up, damn it!"

"Don't do that," she warned him.

She knew him enough now to despise yet pity him with the deepest, most profound contempt. He was a weak, loathesome man. She would find her chance to fight him and make her stand. It was just a matter of time. He would get nothing, nothing, from her. Not while she was alive. She shuddered at the thought. Either way, she figured, he would rot in hell. She only hoped she'd have the chance to send him there.

Lowell was in deep trouble. He had walked straight into the unwelcoming arms of an angry committee of Lejeune henchmen who had just disposed of the previous visitor in a rather blunt fashion. By their demeanor he certainly didn't look to fare much better. They were actually laughing at him, there in the great kitchen: the ranch foreman Rice Crawford, and his sidekick Rico Vega.

"You Yankees are a whole new class of dumb, you are somethin' else! Walkin' unarmed into a man's house who believes in self-protection and just proved it," commented Crawford.

"For your information, I'm not a Yankee," Lowell informed him. "And because I'm unarmed is why you aren't just gonna shoot me." He looked down at Kohler, now awake and groaning, gagged and trussed on the floor like a bale of straw. His head was bleeding from a nasty scalp wound. "What happened to him?" he asked.

"Tresspassin'," said Vega. "Like you. But he's a cop, so he got special consideration. You aren't."

Crawford looked Lowell up and down. "Anyways, you ain't got no accent," he said.

"You should spend more time in the cities," Lowell suggested. "You'd get a broader view of things."

"I don't need no cities and never will."

"Sure you do," said Lowell. "That's who buys all your OJ."

Rico Vega laughed at that. "Hell, the government will pay for it whether anybody buys it or not."

"Cozy deal," said Lowell. "I guess you guys just can't lose."

"No, sir," said Crawford, aching to get at his Johnnie Walker

Red, which sat on the counter in front of him none the worse for having bludgeoned Kohler. "Mr. Quentin Lejeune was born a winner, and that's how he intends to go out." He sat down and poured himself a double shot. "Cheers," he said, and drank it down. He didn't offer Lowell any, and the younger Vega had disappeared.

Lowell hoped he would drink some more, maybe the whole bottle. It might make him talk. It might also make him even meaner than usual, but it would definitely take the edge off his response time and loosen him up, both physically and mentally. Lowell would take any edge he could get. Vega's sudden departure worried him, though. He hoped Lena was all right.

"So how did you get to be foreman for this operation?" he inquired, conversationally.

"Same way my daddy did, and his daddy before him," said Crawford, pouring himself another double. "Cheers."

Lowell glanced at his watch, his concern for Lena growing.

"And this militia of yours," he asked, "what inspired that?"

"Patrick Henry," said Crawford. "Him and Patrick Buchanan. Our kinda 'Murican." Bottoms up, once again. Lowell watched him with interest.

"So you're the Commandant around here. Congratulations. But I don't see any British coming," Lowell remarked, looking around.

"No, just guv'mint regulators and meddling environmental extremists, like you-all."

Lowell remembered he'd introduced himself yesterday, in such a guise. Oh well. He didn't bother to argue. Lowell sensed the danger—the beginnings of a mean drunk. And now he felt certain that something had happened to Lena. His heart sank. He was unarmed and on his own, in hostile territory. At least the second triggerman was indisposed at his very feet. But Duvall Patterson was still out there. And so was Bedrosian.

Rico Vega reentered, holding a squirming Billy Patterson by the scruff of the neck. "Look what I found, Rice."

Billy, sobering up rapidly, took one look at Kohler, who rather closely resembled the latest victim in a horror movie. "Arrrrgh!" he said, and threw up all over again.

Rico cuffed him on the head. "You idiot!" he shouted.

"Forget it," said Crawford. "What's one more fuckin' mess around heah!"

"Billy, have you seen Detective Bedrosian?" asked Lowell, urgently.

"What the hail is this, Miami Beach?" complained Crawford. "Who else is crawlin' around out theah? Get this trash outta here, Rico!"

"My dad's got her!" Billy blurted. "I seen it from the car, I was comin' to tell you!"

"What's he sayin'?" Crawford demanded, in exasperation.

Rico cuffed Billy a couple more times. "Shut up," he ordered.

"I came with Police Detective Lena Bedrosian, from Manatee City PD. If Duvall Patterson's got her, he's just kidnapped a police officer," Lowell announced.

"Sheeeit!" complained Rico.

"I don't know what the fuck you think ah'm supposed to do about it," snapped Crawford, all hopes of a quiet evening shattered, which improved his mood not one iota.

"Could be miles from here, by now," said Rico. "Duvall knows every inch of this country, every creek, every track. It's gonna take an army to find him out there."

There was a long pause. Lowell looked at Crawford. "Now isn't that a coincidence. And I'll bet you know just where to get one."

"Sheeeeit!!" Crawford slammed down his shot glass in disgust.

"Think about it. You could actually do a public service, like you keep talking about."

Rice Crawford thought about it. And the more he thought about it the more he had to admit to himself it sounded like a real good idea for public relations. If he could manage to roust the boys out again for the occasion, that is. They might just go for it. This time it would be like a real jungle-rescue mission.

Crawford looked at Billy, then at Lowell. His eyes grew watery with emotion at the thought of it. He looked at Rico, then back at Lowell. As though noticing him for the first time. "Rico," he finally said. "Better get Mr. Lejeune. Tell him we got a kidnapping situation out here, of a po-leece officer. Ask him if it's all right with him, I intend to call in the Hondo County Militia to assist in this manhunt. I assume the sheriff is already on his way."

"You got it," said Rico, and disappeared, leaving Billy standing alone with a bewildered look on his face.

Now Crawford offered Lowell a drink.

Lowell accepted. He needed one, just now.

"Me, too," demanded Billy.

"Shut up, kid," said Crawford. "You'll just puke agin."

Rico came back in, shaking his head, his face split with a grin. "The boss says go ahead, but no damn choppers, they make too much noise."

"All right, then. Let's move," ordered Crawford. "You tell the boys that I want Duvall Patterson brought in dead or alive."

"Tell them they damn well better bring in Detective Lieutenant Lena Bedrosian alive!" insisted Lowell. Rico shrugged and turned to go.

"Oh, and Rico," Crawford called after him. "Call the newspapers, and tell them what a great public service the Hondo County Militia is doin' out heah!"

"Yes, sir!"

Crawford hawked and spat in the sink, and lit a Cuban cigar.

"I'd like to start searching the groves from here, with your permission," said Lowell. "Billy can help, he knows his father better than anyone."

Billy had been standing there watching the proceedings, barely hanging on. "Wish I didn't," he muttered. "Weren't for him, she wouldn'a hadda go there."

Lowell looked at him sharply. "Who wouldn't? Go where?"

"Nothin'," said Billy, as though recovering from some lapse.

Crawford shook his head. "Better get goin', or they'll be long gone from these parts."

Lowell headed for the door, dragging Billy with him. Luckily, Lena had left the keys in the rental Buick. Lowell piled Billy into the front seat and jumped behind the wheel. He started the engine, backed around, and tore back out the service road. He was already wondering if he'd made a mistake by suggesting calling in the militia. Those guys were likely to shoot anything that moved. including Lena. He may have just made things a whole lot worse.

"Billy, I messed up," he said, urgently. "We have to find her before they do. They're likely to kill her, assuming your father doesn't."

Billy just hung his head out the window, and threw up some more. Lowell marveled at the boy's capacity for vomit.

As he headed for the exit road, Lowell glanced in the rearview mirror, and his pulse quickened. Someone was coming after them in a Dodge pickup. Lowell speeded up, but they caught up quickly, right on his rear bumper, with his brights on. Lowell decided it was just Crawford's way of urging them off the premises. But he was worried about the possibility of stranding Lena back there. For all he knew she could already have escaped, and be running desperately after them in the darkness. She could also be dead.

He slowed down, scanning the roadside and the trees and road ahead for some sign of Duvall or Bedrosian. He had a

sinking feeling in his stomach. He remembered the canal as
he saw the abutment up ahead. He slowed to stop, and the
pickup came right up on his bumper, flashing his brights,
blasting the night with a warning honk.

"What're you doing?" Billy asked, in panic.

Lowell just shook his head. "Lieutenant Bedrosian's out
there, somewhere. She may even be on the canal. Your father
had a boat, and he knows these waters, doesn't he?"

Billy's eyes widened.

The pickup stayed on his bumper, honking. Lowell swore
and gave up in frustration. He sped ahead to the main road,
and spun right, roaring north. Rico Vega slowed and stopped
at the entrance and turned left, with a good-bye wave. He was
in a hurry, was all. He had a militia to round up.

"I'll be damned," said Lowell.

Lowell sped back to the county road and turned left, toward
the state campground at Corkscrew Swamp, and Dave Connors's ranger station. Lowell knew Connors was his best hope
now.

Billy sat in numb silence, staring straight ahead into the
darkness. He would rather be anywhere than out there just
now. But he had to see it to its end. He had nowhere else to
go.

Superintendent Connors was waiting for them when they got
to ranger headquarters. "It's on all the radio bands," he
shouted, as they pulled up outside the building. The night was
shrill with sound: cicadas, tree frogs, great horned owls, an-
hingas, crickets, all competing with their warning cries and
mating calls, shrieks of death and pain amid screams of triumph. "They've started a manhunt! What the hell is going on
out there?"

"Duvall Patterson!" shouted Lowell, jumping out of the
car. "We're only minutes ahead of them. We've got to get to
them first."

"Get to who?"

"My dad got Lieutenant Bedrosian!" blurted Billy, before Lowell could reply.

"Aw hell," was all Connors could say.

"That radio tracker you had on the she-panther," Lowell shouted. "Billy found it in the swamp." He hesitated, then went on: "There's a new panther head in the Hunt Club lodge. If one is missing, I'm afraid—"

Connors shook his head, trying to cope with it all. "If they shot that panther, I'll—"

"Lena has the tracker beacon!" Lowell cut him off. "She took it, she was going to ask you about it. It's in her bag!"

"If she still has it," muttered Connors.

Lowell looked at him sharply. "Billy, where are they?"

"Dad grabbed her at Lejeune's place," Billy answered, his voice shaking. "He's gotta be headed into Big Cypress. Once he gets there ain't nobody'll find him, ever. Nobody!"

"I think he's going by water," said Lowell. "He took off this afternoon in a boat when we came to talk to him." He glanced at Billy. "Tell him," he said.

Billy gulped, his head swimming less now, his stomach no better, his heart like lead. "Dad was there with those two deputies when Marge got killed," he barely whispered.

Connors stared at him and let out a deep, despairing sigh. "Aw, hell," he said.

Connors had the radio tracking receivers for all the banded panthers in the ranger hut. He led the way in, and switched the main console on. "You sure it was her band?" he asked.

"N-no," said Billy. "I just assumed—"

"Then there's hope. I better check them all." He turned on a TV-size monitor similar to a radar screen, went down a row of switches, and turned them on one at a time. "There's the signals," he said, pointing to a scattering of blips on the screen. There were nine in all. "They're all working," he confirmed. He studied the screen. His face turned grim. "But if

244

one panther is down," he began, "how in hell do we know which one?" Connors turned and looked at Lowell, spreading his palms upward in a gesture of helplessness. "She could be carrying any of them. How in God's name are we gonna tell which one is her?"

Billy pursed his lips. Marge could tell, he wanted to blurt. Marge Pappas was the only one knew how to read those signals: interpret who was which by the patterns of movement, by the pacing, by the turf. Only Marge knew, and Marge was dead.

The forest outside the cabin suddenly fell silent, as though at a signal. They all rushed out to see what was happening. They could see flashing lights in the distance, hear the shouts, the roar of engines, the blare of horns. The low roar of an approaching army. The militia was gathering.

"Oh God," said Connors.

Then they heard a new sound. A chorus of challenge, a rising howl that spread terror into the forest: the braying of hounds.

Lowell looked at Billy, urgency in his eyes. "Billy," he asked. "If you were your father, where would you go now?"

22

Somewhere in the Big Cypress Swamp, Lena Bedrosian, sprawled unceremoniously in the bottom of a flat-bottom skiff, saw the distant lights of off-road vehicles and heard the horns, and at first her heart soared with new hope. She was already soaking wet, freezing cold, covered with mud and stings and cuts and bruises. Her clothes were long-since ruined, together with much—but not all—of her remaining confidence. She had read, had heard, how kidnapping can strip a person of his or her dignity. But the experience was excruciatingly beyond any prior comprehension or expectation. Her humiliation at having allowed this swamp rat to have surprised and over-powered her was bottomless. And she knew he could sense it, how it would give him strength, that would feed upon her fear if she allowed herself to feel, or show it.

He hadn't yet touched her, which surprised her. Instead, he was visibly weeping, as they moved deeper and deeper into the wilderness.

"What's wrong?" she'd finally asked him. To which he just shook his head, violently.

"Shut up!" was all he'd say, his voice cracked and broken. But his anguish gave her renewed determination to survive. And in spite of it all, she had to admire his navigational skill. He steered with impossible vision in the sheer blackness. Making his way resolutely, inevitably, toward what she knew was her doom.

She had to find a way to stop him. She had to. And now, knowing they were being followed, being tracked, she had the renewed confidence she needed.

"You better give up now, Patterson, before you get in any deeper," she told him. "They'll catch you for sure."

"Don't matter," he said weeping, "don't matter no more." He was a dark, trembling shadow lurking above her in the stern of the skiff, just a dark shape in the night. "They catch us they'll kill us both," he said. Something in his voice made her wonder who he meant by that.

"Duvall," she said, on a whim. "Who shot Marge Pappas?"

"Shut up!" he sobbed, and paddled harder.

"It wasn't you, was it?"

"I said shut up!" His voice echoed harshly across the water. "Either way," he snarled, "you are dead."

Lena believed him now. And for the first time in the ten years since her graduation from the police academy, she felt afraid.

Duvall had taken her gun, and had it in his belt. He had his rifle in his left hand, and was steering the boat with the right, navigating, as far as she could tell, by the stars. Or the treetops. Either way, he had to devote his attention to where he was going in order not to run aground or into the thick undergrowth that lined the banks of the stream they were following. What stream, or river, she had no idea. But she wanted to keep at least some kind of dialogue going.

"Where are you taking us?" she asked him.

He didn't answer. "You'll find out," is all he'd say.

Then they heard the hounds, and she knew that her time was running out. She wondered if this was how it had been for Marge. But there was a difference. Marge had been murdered as she tried to flee. Lena would stand her ground and fight to the end. Somehow. She need only the smallest opening, the slightest opportunity.

It came moments later. Two majestic oak trees spanned the river, their branches low across the water forming a natural tunnel decorated like an underground cavern, with heavy draperies of Spanish moss, like clinging curtains. It was in their hair, dragging across their faces, and that was when Lena saw her chance.

The three of them tore through the forest in Dave Connors's Cherokee, jouncing desperately along a little-used woodcutter's track, heading toward an intersection Billy knew: an abandoned road that had once crossed the southern branch of the river. The road was used by a few fishermen, and those rarely, because the undergrowth closing in was so dense that there was no place to turn around. Billy was convinced that if they could get to that road's long-since washed-out bridge, they might be able to head off his father. It was the only tributary, he assured them, that ran the whole way from Lejeune Farms to Caloosahatchee Bay. Duvall would have to come that way, and if they could get there quick enough, and before anyone else, they stood a chance.

That was the best Lowell could hope for now. A chance. "We'll worry about getting out later," he said, tersely. "Just get us there."

Billy was wide awake now. He directed Connors with quick, clear instructions, down the unmarked paved road, then off on an old two-track logging road, then another sandy track, into ever thickening forest. They could see glimpses of gleaming moonlit water on either side: Big Cypress Swamp.

"Hurry!" shouted Lowell, straining to see ahead in the darkness.

The crumbling, weather-ravaged old bridge abutment suddenly loomed ahead as the Cherokee rammed its way through yet another canopy of low branches and foliage into the narrow clearing at the river's edge. Connors slid to a stop, killed the lights and the engine, and they all leaped out of the car. They gathered at the overhanging edge of the concrete wall, and leaned out into the night. They could just make out faint glimmers of the current in the starlight, moving relentlessly toward upstream, away from the Gulf.

"Keep low," ordered Lowell.

"They'll be comin' from the left," whispered Billy. He lay down on his stomach, and reached down, dragging his fingertips in the water.

"Man, I wouldn't do that," muttered Connors. "Any way to tell if they've already gone by?"

"Nope," Billy replied. No one said anything. "Current is slow, tide's comin' in," Billy whispered. "Don't think they could have gotten this far yet. Not without the motor." Billy had told them Duvall would use the tides and currents to avoid detection. "That outboard would be a dead giveaway," he'd explained.

Lowell had agreed, but silently wished Billy would have made a different choice of words.

Connors had brought the portable radio tracking scanner, a bulky unit in a leather case, which he now switched on, set low. He had to scan each frequency separately, until he found the right one: the one that indicated something was coming their way.

They sat shivering and cursing softly as five minutes passed, then ten. At least it was too cold for mosquitoes. Then they heard the braying of the hounds coming toward them, ever so faint at first, across the swamp. The tracker unit began

250

to make a beeping sound. It grew louder, steadier.

"Something's coming!" Connors whispered.

"Turn it down, for chrissake!" Lowell commanded.

Even with the volume almost to off, they could hear, then feel, the growing tension. The dogs, too, seemed to sense something. They brayed anew, distinctly closer now.

Lowell waited, a dedicated but apprehensive state forest ranger hunkered down on one side of him, a terrified post-adolescent boy on the other. They heard a sound, just out of their range of vision. Not more than a hundred feet upriver, calculated Lowell. He nudged the others to silence. They heard another sound—a splash, closer, and then a strange scraping sound. Suddenly there was a startled yell, and a grunt, followed by a hoarse cry and a loud splash.

"That was him! That was my dad!" Billy hissed, urgently. Lowell could feel him beginning to tremble.

"Easy, kid," he whispered. "It's almost over."

They heard the cry again, cut off by another splash, then renewed, this time a cry of sheer terror. "Help!" they heard a shout, then louder, a louder splash, a gasp, and again: "Help!"

"No!" whimpered Billy.

"Shine a light!" muttered Connors. "I can't see!"

"Not yet," hissed Lowell.

The yell suddenly became an agonized scream, and they heard another shout: "Oh my god!" It was Lena.

"Bedrosian! Over here!" Lowell shouted. Another splash and scream, and the water erupted, some twenty feet into the river, in a tumult of cries, and a new sound, the hideous hiss and snarl of a predator that had seized its prey.

Connors, waiting no longer, switched on the powerful six-battery police light he'd brought.

They were frozen by the sight.

"Oh, God!" exclaimed Billy, in horror. "It's a gator! Help him! Help him!"

Lowell had to hold him back. In spite of everything, blood-

251

lines had sent out their cry, and Billy struggled to get free, to jump in, to save his father.

He could not. A shot rang out, then another, from the boat that now drifted into view: Lena stood, straddling the gunwales, firing Duvall Patterson's rifle into the dark churning water. Incredibly, she hit her mark. The gator dove, and took Duvall with it, still clenched in its jaws, now gnashing with pain. There was another, smaller splash, and a wake appeared in the current, rushing right past Lowell and the still-struggling boy, vanishing downstream into the night.

Billy screamed, and cried inconsolably, and Lowell held onto him. Connors managed to grab the line Lena threw them, and pulled the skiff to the side of the abutment. He helped her ashore, then Lowell held her.

The first dogs arrived moments later, followed quickly by Rice Crawford. The militia members traded blasts of light with Connors, then Lowell, into each others eyes and faces. Crawford joined them at the water's edge. He looked at the water and cringed.

"What the hell happened?" he asked.

They all were staring into the water, except Billy.

"Gator," said Lowell.

"It got my dad!" Billy sobbed.

"Gawdamn!" Rice Crawford muttered. The rest of the militia members straggled in out of the darkness to join them on the riverbank.

Crawford just nodded, hawked, spit into the rushing water, and said nothing. There was nothing more to say.

Patterson's Landing was shrouded in darkness when Lowell and Bedrosian returned there. The first light of dawn was creeping up over the forest to the east. It was going to be a fine day.

They'd convinced Connors to take Billy in for the night, and take him to the hospital in the morning for possible sedation. They needed to do what had to be done alone.

She was waiting for them. "The door's open," she called out. Lowell stepped through the double doors, Bedrosian right behind him. She had her weapon ready, just in case.

"Mrs. Patterson?" Lowell called out, into the dark room.

"I'm here," she replied. He could just make out her profile, as his eyes grew accustomed to the darkness.

"We have bad news about your husband, I'm afraid," said Bedrosian.

She sat in a chair, facing them, her pistol in her lap. She looked up at him, then at Bedrosian, and her mouth began to tremble, slightly.

"He's dead, ain't he?"

"Yes, ma'am," replied Bedrosian. "I'm sorry." Oddly enough, considering what she'd been through, she meant it. He hadn't been quite the monster he'd seemed, after all. Just a confused, frustrated, frightened, unhappy man. Lena had known a lot like him in her life.

Mrs. Patterson looked at them, accusingly. "Where's Billy?"

"He's with Mr. Connors, the ranger. He'll be all right."

"I don't think so," she said, her voice cracking. "He's seen too much. It wasn't right. He was a good boy." She looked at them again, and her face hardened. "What's gonna happen to him now?"

"Nothing. We'll try to get him some help," said Lowell.

She shook her head, sorrowfully. "Duvall done plenty, but he didn't shoot no hussy game warden."

That was when Lowell knew beyond doubt. He could see it in her eyes. He looked at Bedrosian and turned back to face her. "He treated you bad, didn't he, ma'am?"

She looked at him, and gripped the gun more tightly. "No worse than any man, I reckon."

He looked at the gun, and glanced at Bedrosian. He could tell she was thinking the same thing. One quick move to dis-

253

arm her, and it would be over. He nodded at Lena, ever so slightly.

"It was you, wasn't it," said Lowell, watching the gun. "You caught on to Duvall's obsession with Marge Pappas, didn't you?"

She didn't respond, but he knew he was right.

"You must have found out he was going to see her that night. And you decided enough was enough, and so you followed him," said Bedrosian.

"Them two pigs showed up," she spat. "Bad as he was. Worse, even. I'll see them in hell, God willing."

"So you were there when they raped her?"

"She shouldn't of led them on like she done," she muttered.

"So after they left her for dead you shot her just to make sure? Was that how it happened?"

"She was evil. God sent me to punish her. Someone had to, leadin' my man astray like that."

"Mrs. Patterson," said Lena, softly. "I think you'd better put the gun down, and come with us."

Her face crumpled like an empty cellophane bag. She shook her head one last time. "Tell my son I'm sorry. He shouldna never had to live with this, what his father done. And me. He's a good boy."

"Sure, ma'am, we'll tell him," began Bedrosian. "But please hand over the—"

"And that I love him," Betty Patterson added. And before they could react, with a quickness that caught both Lowell and Bedrosian off guard, she raised the gun to her sad, sagging mouth, and squeezed the trigger.

23

Eight hours north in Tallahassee, Senator Jack Kranhower, wearing his second-best gray worsted suit and an antique psychedelic purple paisley silk tie his wife gave him too long ago to remember, looked up in surprise as Representative Bob Hathcock entered his office. Hathcock wore his standard blue business suit with a thin black tie. Lobbyist Luann Perla was with him, in a two-piece charcoal number and silver earrings the size of cowbells. Both looked ready to do business.

"Hello, Senator," said Luann.

"How's the ticker?" asked Hathcock, solicitously.

"Still ticking, no thanks to your reception committee."

"I am sorry about that, really. It was those doggone Young Turks, all kinds of new money and feelin' their oats, but not one ounce of class. And that Lejeune fella was eggin' them on."

"I don't know about that. But I do know you were sure ready to hand him the rest of the damn county. As though he needed it."

Hathcock sighed. "You know how it is, Jack. Fund-raising gets tougher every year. The big contributors get fewer and fewer—"

"Which is why I don't deal with them."

"—and they ask for more and more. I'm an elected official, just like you. I'm only trying to do my job."

"Hear hear."

"What we're saying is," interjected Luann, "we've talked to the rest of the folks on the house committee, and if you're agreeable on the rest of the budget funding bill, we're willing to drop the amendment, no hard feelings."

"Then we can end this damn impasse," added Hathcock.

Kranhower leaned back in his chair, and twirled his antique Shaeffer fountain pen, thoughtfully. "How're you gonna face your constituents when you don't deliver the bacon, Bob? Or are you finally going to go down there and lecture them on ethics in government, and the importance of preserving our state's natural resources?"

Hathcock laughed, ruefully. "Touché. Fact is, the boys are sorry, and wanted me to tell you that. Anyway," and here he leaned forward with a sly wink, lowering his voice. "After his great escape from the deep freeze, Quentin Lejeune had a sudden conversion, sorta like."

"I'll bet."

Luann's eyes twinkled. "That's right, Senator. Mr. Lejeune has offered to donate the five thousand acres he was going to sell, to the state. As a preserve. All you have to do is initial an agreement that the Club get leasing rights." She nodded at Hathcock, who opened his leather pouch and pulled out a shiny new, very legal-looking document. He slid it onto the senator's desk.

"You boys work fast, Bob." Kranhower couldn't help a smile of admiration for Lejeune's new-found public-spiritedness. Hathcock and his lobbyist friends had probably burned the candle at both ends to pull this together, desperate for anything now. He was tempted to gloat a little. But his old ticker was tired, and his bones ached. He wanted to get out of here, and go sailing with his new friend, Tony Lowell.

"A couple of conditions, Bob," he said, ignoring the lobbyist. His eye showed a flash of that old cold steel that had bolstered his spine, all these years in politics.

"Go ahead," said Hathcock. Luann nodded, nervously.

"No more poaching. Period. They hunt during the season, like everybody else. They hunt only what's legal to hunt, and if I ever hear of another Cracker yahoo shooting a panther—I don't care if it's the mayor of Naples—I don't care if it was a Texas cougar and the runt of a litter of ten. I don't care if it turns up in his bathroom and bites his ass—then they are out of there for good, and this is all in writing. Got that?"

Hathcock practically fell all over himself with reassurances. "That one that got shot was a mistake, I swear it. Only an idiot would shoot a native panther, Jack."

"Yeah, that's what I'm worried about. There's a lot of idiots out there."

"Jack, the boys know they are an endangered species. They won't do it. You have my word on that."

"And no development."

Luann didn't like that one at all. Hathcock coughed, nervously.

"Tell you what," suggested Kranhower. "You have a guy that's a little bit nosy downstairs, that yes-man of yours—Buddy Burke I think his name is—"

Hathcock paled, slightly.

"I hafta tell you two, one thing I really hate is people eavesdroppin' on my conversations," Kranhower continued, smoothly. Hathcock coughed again.

"It'll be taken care of," promised Luann, giving Hathcock a steely look.

"All right. All right. No phone stuff. No development. No new roads except one—," Hathcock said quickly.

Kranhower was firm: "No new roads."

Hathcock threw up his hands. "Jack, you're killing me here. Okay, no new roads. They can use the existing fire road," he conceded, with a sigh, not looking at Luann. "So, Jack. Do we have a deal?"

Kranhower held up his hand. "What about that militia of theirs? They going to use this land?"

Hathcock hesitated. "Jack," he finally answered. "Between you and me, the Club doesn't want those yahoos anymore than you do, running around shooting up the place. But sometimes you just gotta give a little." He paused. "Y'know what I mean?"

Kranhower did know. He'd given a lot more than he ever wanted to, over the years. He sighed. "Yes, I know, Bob."

Luann nodded in emphasis. "They're just blowin' off steam, Senator. They aren't going to overthrow the government or anything."

"You have my word on that, too," pleaded Hathcock.

"Mr. Lejeune will keep the militia busy clearing trails, hauling deadfalls, that sort of thing, they'll be okay. They're hard workers," Luann added, flatly.

"So I hear," said Kranhower, wryly. "I got a complaint from human resources and the labor department about that."

"That won't happen again," Luann cut in. "That was a one-time emergency. And Mr. Lejeune has promised restitution and bonuses to all his workers."

"If they can be found," added Hathcock. "They kinda left in a hurry."

Kranhower sighed. "I see. Well, we try to do our best. Sometimes, we just hafta do what we can." They looked at him blankly. "So then. Let's get this government back to work, shall we? Where's my pen?"

Luann pointed at his breast pocket, where he'd absently tucked it away. Kranhower picked up the new bill, squinted at it, turned it sideways, flipped it over, studied it upside down, and tossed it back on the desk.

Hathcock looked alarmed. "What? Now what?"

"What is it?" exclaimed Luann, verging on panic.

Kranhower grinned, and leaned back in his leather chair, twirling his pen. "Just one more little ol' thing." He pressed the intercom button. "Amber!" he shouted. "Get in here and read this thing over for me, will you?" He twirled his pen some more, and gave Bob Hathcock a wink. "So tell me, Bob. You know anything about sailboats?"

Epilogue

SIX WEEKS LATER

Tony Lowell was putting the finishing touches on a wine rack for his galley-dining area, rubbing the blood-red rosewood trim with linseed oil until it shone like a ruby. Perry sat on the tool chest nearby, pondering the movement of the treetops among the tall pines bordering the mangroves. The sky was the usual azure, still-clean puffy clouds scudding by, racing toward Orlando. Perry had finally forgiven Lowell for leaving him out of the action, down in Big Cypress Swamp.

"You should thank me, we damn near froze to death, for one thing," Lowell had told him. "Anyway, you were in no condition for that kind of crap." Perry had not been appeased, but eventually let it drop.

"Gonna rain," he commented, thoughtfully.

"So what? It always rains. This isn't exactly the Sahara."

"This is dry season. Rains are rare in dry season."

The schooner was afloat, although still a long way from being seaworthy. Lowell would have to content himself with dreams of distant shores and billowing spinnakers another eon or two. Perry gave Lowell a look of dismissal, swung cleanly over the side, and was up among the stays before Lowell could even manage a protest. Perry climbed like a boy in a tree. He seemed to be good at pretty much anything physical, Lowell had long since observed. Not too bad intellectually, either, if one could forgive his tendency toward carelessness with the such trivial matters as facts. He was a lot of fun to boot.

"I can see for miles!" Perry shouted, from on top of the mast— a place Lowell carefully avoided ever since his infamous spin- naker dive over on the east coast a few years back. He'd never admitted to Bedrosian, who'd been there, how traumatized he'd actually been by that "act of lunacy," as she'd rightfully called it sometime later.

"Man! The view is great!" Perry shouted. "I can see that new mall going up over by Gulfbridge."

Lowell hated that mall—all malls—and said so. Perry re- joined him on the deck a few moments later, brimming with excitement. "Lowell," he shouted, breathlessly. "That mall gave me an idea."

Lowell braced himself. "Not again," he sighed. Perry was full of ideas. "Now what?"

"I wanna borrow your camera for a while, and I'll show you."

"What is it this time?" asked Lowell, alarmed.

"A photo essay. Maybe even like a coffee-table book thing. Billy can help, he's good at that sort of thing." Perry had taken young Billy Patterson under his wing, as sort of an unofficial Big Brother, pending legal adoption. Lowell had expressed surprise and skepticism, but Perry seemed sincere. He was teaching Billy Indian lore, astronomy, philosophy, and the history of rock and roll. Also some martial arts. "Nothin' too violent," he'd promised Lowell. Billy was doing well, considering, and Lowell had even taken him out sailing in the sloop once or twice.

"Coffee-table book? Perry, you don't even know how to load a roll of film, I've seen you. And you want to do a coffee-table book?"

"So? Like I said, Billy can do it. The idea is dynamite!"

"Anyway, I need that camera."

"C'mon, you never use it anymore. Listen, here's my idea. Me and Billy travel around the country in my truck, just taking photos, you know?"

"For *National Geographic*," suggested Lowell. "You could visit lonely farmer's wives. And daughters—"

"Just listen. We do only one theme: malls. We do malls in every city we come to. We could call it *The Book of Malls*."

"How about *The Malling of America?*"

"That's the whole thing! Every mall looks like every other mall. It's the same everywhere. So I got one page, shows McDonald's and JCPenney and Sears and the Gap or whatever, and that's, say Tampa. Then here's one, same thing, same McDonald's, same JCPenney, same Sears, and that's Orlando. Then there'll be Atlanta, and Dallas, and St. Louis, and Cleveland, and Boston, and Chicago, and Seattle, L.A., and they're all the same, man! You can't tell 'em apart! It's brilliant!"

"Why don't you just take ten shots of the Gulfbridge Mall and forget about it? No one would know. Like you said, they all look the same."

"Lowell, I am shocked."

Perry had something else to be enthusiastic about. He'd brought along an old LP record he'd found in his mother's attic. He wanted Lowell to play it for him. "This is really bodacious, man," he promised.

Lowell gave him a blank look, as he put away his polishing rags. "Bodacious? What is it?"

"It's really radical. Kind of long and windy, mind you, but

you know me, I like epic-type tunes, and this"—he was grop-
ing for words—"this is different. It doesn't keep a steady beat,
it really jumps around."

"Like a kangaroo mouse?"

Perry liked the analogy. "Yeah, kind of. It's moody, too, like
blues. It's really old, man."

Now Lowell was curious. He tried to look at the album
cover, but Perry pulled it back.

"Can I at least get a hint?"

"Okay," said Perry. "It's foreign." Feigning puzzlement, he
held the album cover before his eyes, and squinted at it.
"Somebody, by the name of—" He stopped, put the record on,
and played the opening bars, before finishing: "Brahms."

A smirking Perry ducked, his timing impeccable, as Lowell's empty beer can sailed past his head.

"Missed!" he hooted.

"Of course I missed. You're the one who taught me a beer
can was a deadly weapon!"

They spent the rest of the afternoon polishing wood, polishing off beers, and listening to Perry's new discovery: clas-
sical music. They went on from Brahms to Beethoven to
Schubert, and finished off the day with some eerily haunting
Berlioz.

As the springtime evening closed in, Lowell found himself
watching the bay, and the flower-splashed, still-forested woods
beyond. You could hike all the way to the Caloosahatchee
River without hitting a town. If you had hip boots, a machete,
and about two months. He wondered when Duvall Patterson's
remains would finally wash ashore. And where.